Little Souls

Little Souls

Sandra Dallas

St. Martin's Press ≈ New York

First published in the United States by St. Martin's Press, an imprint of St. Martin's Publishing Group

LITTLE SOULS. Copyright © 2022 by Sandra Dallas. All rights reserved. Printed in the United States of America. For information, address St. Martin's Publishing Group, 120 Broadway, New York, NY 10271.

www.stmartins.com

Designed by Meryl Sussman Levavi

Library of Congress Cataloging-in-Publication Data

Names: Dallas, Sandra, author.
Title: Little souls / Sandra Dallas.
Description: First edition. | New York : St. Martin's Press, 2022.
Identifiers: LCCN 2021047570 | ISBN 9781250277886 (hardcover) |
    ISBN 9781250277893 (ebook)
Subjects: CYAC: Influenza Epidemic, 1918-1919—Fiction. | LCGFT:
    Historical fiction. | Thrillers (Fiction). | Novels.
Classification: LCC PS3554.A434 L58 2022 | DDC 813/.54—dc23
LC record available at https://lccn.loc.gov/2021047570

Our books may be purchased in bulk for promotional, educational, or business use. Please contact your local bookseller or the Macmillan Corporate and Premium Sales Department at 1-800-221-7945, extension 5442, or by email at MacmillanSpecialMarkets@macmillan.com.

First Edition: 2022

10 9 8 7 6 5 4 3 2 1

For Kendal and Dana
Dream about clowns

Little Souls

One

The blue-black dusk had come on by the time I got off the streetcar and started down the sidewalk. It was cold, and there was the clammy feel of moisture in the air, as if rain were hovering over us. Dried leaves fell from the trees, rattling across the yards and into the gutter as the wind swept them up. I was in a hurry to reach home. It had been a long day, and I'd wanted to tell my sister about the parade. That was why I didn't pay attention to the handful of men gathered on the lawn at mid-block.

The streetcar clanged in the distance, its metal wheels screeching on the metal tracks, so I did not hear the murmuring. I tightened my coat around me. The first raindrops fell. After the overheated car, with all of us pressed together, I was suddenly chill. I hoped Helen had already gotten home. Perhaps she had started supper. The three of us could eat in front of the fire.

Then I saw him—the man lying on the ground—and I stopped. He might have been drunk. Bootleg whiskey could kill an iron dog. Although there was no national law on Prohibition, Colorado had passed one in 1916, two years ago. Bootleggers were in full swing in North Denver and in the old mining towns in the mountains. Or maybe the man had been hurt in an automobile accident. Perhaps the kid down the block who raced his auto at twenty miles an hour had finally hit someone. We'd said that sooner or later, he'd do just that. I didn't see his Model T, however. Perhaps the driver had not stopped.

"What happened?" I asked, pushing between two bystanders. "Is he hurt? My sister's a nurse. We live just down the street. I'll get her."

I stepped forward for a better look, but a man beside me held out his arm to keep me away. Then he removed it quickly, as if he shouldn't have touched me, and stepped back. "Better watch out," he said. I glanced at him, taking in the expensive gray suit, the kind we advertised at Neusteter's, the specialty store where I worked, as having "snap and style." I couldn't help but notice such things.

The streetlamp came on then, and I could see the man on the ground a little more clearly. A soldier. His brown jacket was buttoned up to his neck, and his boots were polished so that they gleamed in the faint light. His brown cap lay nearby, as if it had come off when he fell. Then I looked closer, at his face. Blood seeped out of his eyes and mouth, and he twisted in agony.

"Won't somebody help him?" I asked and started to kneel.

That was when the man grabbed my arm. "Watch out, lady. He's got the influenza."

The Spanish influenza. Of course. That was why nobody would come to his aid. They wouldn't even touch him. I held out my hand, but then I pulled it back. I wouldn't touch him either. I couldn't. I didn't dare. What if I brought the influenza home to Helen and Dorothy?

I had read the newspaper stories, pointing out the irony that this was 1918, the war was almost over, but soldiers who had survived it were dying of the influenza. They brought it back from Europe with them, and now everybody was afraid of getting it. I'd heard Helen's stories about it, too. For a month, she'd warned me every morning to be careful, told me to stay away from crowds, to take my lunch to work so that I didn't have to eat in a restaurant. We'd stopped going to the moving pictures, to the department stores, even to church, although that was no sacrifice, because we rarely attended church anyway. Maud, our tenant, had died of the influenza, and we'd taken in her ten-year-old daughter, Dorothy. There'd even been talk about canceling the Liberty Loan parade today. But it had been held, and I'd gone out onto the street to watch it, mingling with the crowd, heedless of Helen's warnings.

It came to me now that I could be that person on the ground, my arms and legs thrashing, my face dark blue. With the rest of the crowd, I stood silently, fascinated as well as repelled, as I watched the soldier stop jerking. He twitched a little and was still.

"He's dead," someone said.

I shivered. I was disgusted with myself for doing nothing. I should have knelt beside him, taken his hand. He should have died with a human touch. What if he had been Peter, my fiancé, who was fighting in France? If he were dying, I'd want someone to hold his hand for his last moments. But I was as frightened of catching the influenza as everyone else. I shuddered and stepped back, wondering if I'd been too close. Maybe someone in that handful of people staring at the body already had the influenza, and one of us would be dead by morning.

"We should call an ambulance," one of the bystanders muttered.

"There aren't any to spare," the man beside me said. "Besides, they don't send them for the dead."

"We can't just leave him there." I was surprised that I'd spoken up.

"Oh, they have the death wagons that go around every day. Or the Army will come for him," the well-dressed man said. "I have a telephone. I'll call Central when I get home. He shouldn't lie there too long. Dogs'll come around. Maybe kids." He tugged at his soft felt hat, pulling it lower on his forehead.

With a last look at the dead soldier, the men hurried off, shuffling through the brown leaves, thinking how they'd announce, "You won't believe what I saw today," embroidering the story so it would sound a little better. They'd make themselves look a little better, too, say they were about to help until they thought they might carry the sickness home. "If it wasn't for you, I'd have helped him," they'd say, shifting the blame to their wives.

I was the last to leave. Helen had seen dozens of dead people, but this was my first—my first outside of a funeral home, anyway, and there the dead had been prettied up until they looked like giant wax dolls instead of real people robbed of life. I didn't know the man lying on the ground in front of me. At least, I didn't think so. It was hard to tell with the blood and his dark face. Had he been walking to his girl's home or running to catch the streetcar? Maybe he lived in that house and had gone outdoors to die. Did he have a wife or a family who'd thought he was safe when he came home from the war? Maybe he'd promised to read a story to his daughter or play marbles with his son that evening. They would wonder where he was as they waited at the table, dinner getting cold. If they had a telephone, they'd call the hospitals to see if he'd been in an accident. At the backs of their minds, there'd be a tiny worry that it might be the influenza. But no. He'd survived the guns and disease and trenches of the Western Front. He wouldn't die of a little influenza.

I thought how awful it was to pass on as he had, outside in the cold, strangers gawking. I'd always thought of myself dying in bed when I was very old, my hair and nightdress white against the white linens of the bed, surrounded by people who loved me, weeping. And me peaceful, assuring everyone I wasn't afraid, but was ready for what lay ahead. That is to say, I hadn't thought much about dying, but now it came to me. I could be lying there on the ground, ugly, fouled, sending out the stench of death. People walking by with their handkerchiefs over their noses, staring at me with disgust. Dying wasn't my sanitized version. Helen knew that, I was sure. She'd never talked about death to me, but then, she'd always protected me, had tried to keep ugliness from me.

I took out my own handkerchief and held it over my nose, but I knew it wouldn't protect me. Some people wore masks made of gauze or cheesecloth, although the government didn't make any public statements about wearing them. Maybe President Wilson felt that too much emphasis on the influenza was bad for morale. After all, the war was still on, and people had to keep up their spirits. For a time you saw masks everywhere. They didn't always protect you from the influenza, however. Nurses like Helen wore them, but they still came down with it.

I would tell Helen about the dead soldier when I got home. Maybe I'd call the police, too, just in case the man who'd stood next to me forgot. We had a telephone, because Helen needed to stay in touch with the hospital. I could do that one little thing. It would make me feel better.

I was still holding the handkerchief over my nose when I reached home. By then the sky was black, and the street was lit by porch lights. I walked through fallen leaves that were wet from the rain. I picked up the evening paper, then pushed the front door open with my foot, surprised that it was not quite closed. Dorothy was fearful, and we always checked the windows and doors. Helen was like that, too. I was the one who was careless. The light on our porch was off, and when I went through the door, I switched it on. The living room was dark, too, and I thought that was odd, because Helen didn't like the dark. In fact, she slept with a light on. She and Dorothy must have been busy in the kitchen and had not paid attention to the failing light.

Dorothy had lived in our basement with her parents, Ronald and Maud Streeter. A few months earlier, Mr. Streeter had gone out and never come back. We were glad, because he frightened us. So did the people he brought to the house. We thought they might be bootleggers from North Denver or even Leadville, a silver-mining town where they made a potent whiskey called Sugar Moon. Maud and Dorothy had been frightened of him, too, because he hit them. Or at least that was what I concluded from Maud's black eye. I'd noticed bruises on her arms, too. Dorothy didn't have bruises, at least not ones I could see, but it was clear she didn't like her father. I'd seen her hide behind the bushes once when Mr. Streeter emerged from the basement. Other times, she would creep up the stairs when her father was yelling at Maud and huddle on our porch. Once, I went outside for the evening paper and found Dorothy asleep on the porch swing. She could have been there for hours.

Maud didn't tell me what happened to Mr. Streeter, only that he was gone. And I was glad, because Maud and Dorothy were happier in the weeks after he left. So were Helen and I.

Then Maud died of influenza, and there'd been no one to claim Dorothy. We could have advertised in the paper for her father, but Dorothy begged us not to. Besides, Helen didn't want him back. With all the children being orphaned by the influenza, the city wouldn't care. Dorothy was just one more child who wouldn't have to be placed in an orphan's home. She wanted to stay with us, and Helen had said we had to take her, that she was one of Peter's little souls. We would decide later what was best for her, but for now, anyway, she would be our sister.

"I'm home," I called. "I've had quite a day."

No one answered.

"Hello," I called, and I turned on a lamp in the living room. I stepped backward and almost tripped over a pillow that lay on the floor. When I looked around the room, I saw that a chair was overturned and another lamp was lying broken on the floor. "Helen?" I called.

I should have been frightened, but my mind was on the dead soldier. Still . . . "Dorothy? Where are you?"

I heard a sound in the kitchen. And then Helen's voice, high-pitched and almost strangled, called, "Lutie, we're in here."

I moved quickly to the kitchen. In the dark, I made out two figures, Helen and Dorothy. "What's going on? Turn on the—"

"No," Helen replied quickly. "Don't."

As my eyes adjusted to the darkness, I stared at Helen, who knelt on the floor, frozen, an ice pick in her hand. Beside her lay Mr. Streeter, and I knew he was dead.

That was the beginning of my long nightmare. A man lay dead on the ground down the street, another on our kitchen floor. In the dark days that followed, when death never seemed to leave us, I would learn that Helen had protected me from the world's evil. Until that day, I had taken my happy life for granted. But now I had come face-to-face with the randomness of death. I had always been safe. Helen had kept me safe, but in the days to come, I would know real fear—not just for me but for Helen and Dorothy, whom I would come to love as if she truly were my sister.

I came to know the power of love, and I learned that love lasts forever. Before that dreadful day, I had been a girl who loved gaiety and good times, laughter and nights on the town. I had given little thought to the sorrows of others. I think I knew the minute I saw Mr. Streeter lying on the linoleum floor of our kitchen that nothing would ever be the same.

Two

———

Helen was four years older than I. She was tall and had what was called a nice form. I was shorter and thinner. Helen's gold hair was curly and formed corkscrews under her nurse's cap, while mine was dark and straight as a nail. Her eyes were blue, mine gray—gray as a stormy night at sea, a boy once told me. I was flattered until I wondered where in the middle of Iowa he had ever seen an ocean. Helen was pretty, but people said I was beautiful, and I liked to think I was a vamp, like Theda Bara. I rouged my lips and cheeks and wore exotic clothes that I made myself. Of course, that was after I left Iowa and moved to Denver.

We had arrived in Denver in 1914, Helen, then twenty-two, with a nursing degree, and me, nineteen, with a two-year degree from the Welsh Design School in Cedar Rapids. We brought along a nice nest egg. Our mother had died two years before and our father not long after that, leaving us with money from his life insurance—a decent amount because he had been a life insurance agent—as well as a house without a mortgage.

I'd never thought about leaving Iowa. But one day, as we sorted through Dad's things, deciding what should be kept, what should go to relatives, what to the church charity drive,

Helen told me that she had applied for a position at Saint Joseph Hospital in Denver. "I did it before Dad got sick, and then I forgot about it. The offer came through this week. If I'd known Dad was in such bad shape, I wouldn't have sent the application. I'll tell them no."

"Why do you want to leave Cedar Rapids?" I asked. Helen had always liked our hometown, although when I thought about it, I realized that in the last couple of years she had been restless.

"I already know what the hospitals here are like. For the rest of my life, I'd be changing bedpans for old ladies waiting to die. I want something a little more exciting."

"Then you ought to take the job. I can manage here alone, hold on to the house in case you want to come home."

"I won't," Helen replied. Then she asked, "What if we both go?"

"Leave Cedar Rapids? What would I do in Denver?" I wasn't like Helen. I didn't plan ahead. I just sort of let things happen.

"We could sell the house and buy a place there, maybe something with rooms we could let. I'd work, and you could go to the art school at the university, a real art school, not some dinky place like the Welsh School. We could use part of the insurance money for your tuition." She paused. "We were born in Iowa, Lute. We Hites have been here for three generations. Cedar Rapids isn't a bad town, but do we really want to spend our entire lives here? I for one would like to see a little more of the world."

"Then why Denver? Why not Chicago or New York?"

"I don't want to see that much of the world," Helen said.

I removed our father's second-best suit from a hook in the closet—he had been buried in his best one—and laid it on the bed. Someday, if I stayed in Cedar Rapids, I might be doing the same thing with my husband's clothes, sorting through them after his death, maybe in that very room. The thought depressed me. "If we stayed here too long, we'd probably get married, and then we'd never leave."

"Ouch!" Helen said.

"I'm thinking that, too."

"We could always come back," Helen said, although she'd already told me she wouldn't.

"We could." The two of us looked at each other and laughed. If we left, I wouldn't return either.

So we sold the house that we had inherited and purchased one not far from downtown Denver, renting out the basement, first to a young couple and last year to Maud and Ronald Streeter and their daughter, Dorothy. We kept the rest of the house, with its front porch, for ourselves. Helen accepted the position at Saint Joseph Hospital, and I registered at the University of Denver to study for a degree in fine arts.

We loved Denver. From our house we could see the mountains, their peaks crusted with snow even in summer. The city had huge parks. Our favorite was Cheesman, which was built on Denver's first cemetery, called Jack O'Neill's Ranch. When there was a dusting of snow, we could see outlines of where graves had been. There were huge houses west of the park, where politicians and mining men and the owners of the *Denver Post*, the city's flamboyant newspaper, lived.

Farther west was the state capitol building, its gold-plated dome shining in the sun. The showy mansions near it on Grant Street were older—huge piles of stone and brick with turrets and towers. Inside were grand salons and ballrooms. We stared through leaded-glass windows speculating on the gold- and silver-rich families who lived there. One house had belonged to Colorado's "Silver King," who'd lost his money. My friend Florence pointed out his widow to me. She lived in a mine shack in the mountains but wandered the Denver streets. Once she had been noted for her beauty; now she was old and shriveled, dressed in rags, her hair hidden under a man's cap.

On Helen's day off, we shopped at the big stores on Sixteenth Street, stopping for lunch in the dining room at Daniels & Fisher, where the walls were papered with tropical scenes. We took the streetcar to Larimer Street, the site of Denver's first log cabins. We walked past saloons and gambling halls to the Manhattan Restaurant. Its steaks were so tender that the restaurant didn't furnish knives.

Once we took the train to Leadville, high in the Rocky Mountains. It had been a thriving mining town—Oscar Wilde had performed in the theater there—but silver had crashed in 1893, and the buildings were now dated and shabby. Our hotel had had silver dollars embedded in its lobby floor, but they had been long since been pried up. Helen bought a quart of Sugar Moon, but we'd never opened it. It was stored in the broom closet at home.

I graduated two years after we arrived in Denver and set up a studio in our spare bedroom. But since there was no market for paintings by an unknown artist, especially one who wasn't all that good, I'd gone to work at Neusteter's, a high-end specialty store, sketching clothing for advertisements. It was a wonderful job. I loved working with fashions. I would draw a dress or a skirt-and-blouse set, then go home and make it for myself from fabric I bought at the Denver Dry Goods.

By the time I was hired at Neusteter's, Helen had become a visiting nurse, making home visits to the poor and the elderly. She said the work challenged her more than hospital care. She liked being involved with her patients. It was why she'd become a nurse in the first place—to help others, she said.

She met her fiancé, Gilbert Rushton, at Saint Joseph's. They had been engaged for two years and were waiting to wed until Gil finished his internship. I thought Gil would have married earlier, but Helen held him off. I wondered if she worried she might get pregnant and he wouldn't be able to finish school. But as close as we were, we never talked about sex or pregnancy. The subjects seemed distasteful to her. When I asked Helen about sex once—after all, she was a nurse and knew about such things—she turned away. That was because of the work she did, I knew, helping poor women with too many children, women whose husbands beat them or insisted on their rights too soon after childbirth. With that knowledge, who wouldn't consider sex unpleasant?

Helen worried about me that way, afraid that I might let a boy go too far. If I lingered on the porch too long with a date, Helen turned on the living room light or pulled up the shade. But she needn't have worried. I didn't mind a boy kissing me good-night, but I wouldn't go beyond that. It wasn't that I was a prude. I had just never met a boy I cared that much about—until Peter. And then Peter was too moral to try anything. Perhaps that was just as well, because I was less principled. But that was an academic argument at the moment, since Peter was in France, fighting the Huns.

The war had been going on for three years when I met Peter, in 1917.

My friend Florence introduced us. Florence was a copywriter at Neusteter's, and her boyfriend was a fraternity brother of Peter's. I'd met him at a party Florence threw, and Peter had asked me out. He was a divinity student at the University of Denver's Iliff School of Theology.

"The Lord works in mysterious ways," I told Helen with a laugh.

"But a minister, Lute! Really," she replied, a touch of disgust in her voice. "Watch out for him. They think they're too damned good for everyday use."

In the past few years, Helen had developed a distaste for ministers. I didn't know where it came from. Perhaps she had gone out on a date with one who had been insufferable—or fresh.

"It's not like I'm going to marry him."

"Well, we can thank God for that. How awful to be married to a minister. They don't say poor as a church mouse for nothing."

It was hot for an early spring day, and we were sitting on the porch swing in front of the trumpet vine, which was just beginning to green out. Helen rolled down her white stockings, then took them off, along with her heavy nurse's shoes. She stretched her toes on the porch floor, which was gray and smooth because we had painted it last fall.

"I only accepted because I don't have anything else to do Saturday night."

"Then why go out with him at all?"

"I could tag along with you and Gil. Again."

The three of us often went to the movies together. In fact, Helen probably invited me more often than necessary, almost as if she didn't want to be alone with Gil. He was nice enough, and he would be a good doctor, although he was a little too serious for my taste. But then a minister was likely to be a serious fellow, too.

"Well, hell, maybe we'll tag along with you."

"Such language, Helen. You'll have to be careful what you say around this boy."

Helen took off the cap pinned to her head and set it on her lap. "What's his name?"

"Peter Howell." He was top-drawer society, I'd been told, and there was a number after his name, Peter Howell the third or the fourth or something. I hadn't paid attention.

"You didn't know him when you were at DU?"

"I saw him, but I never met him before this week. He's a splendid-looking boy." Peter was tall, with dark eyes and dark hair parted just off-center.

"Oh, well, that explains it," Helen said sarcastically. She gave me a sly look. "Do you think he'll make you kneel down in a restaurant to say grace?"

We looked at each other and burst out laughing. After all,

we were sisters. One of us could say a single word and the other would collapse in hysterics. We were that close. Our mother and father had been religious. Helen liked to say they were real Christians, people who helped the poor and downtrodden. They were generous and overlooked the sins of others. But they were praying people, and we had been raised with evening Bible reading and prayer, not to mention grace before breakfast that lasted so long I don't remember ever eating a hot morning meal. We'd kneel on the kitchen floor, cold as ice in the winter, while Dad thanked the Lord for the day, the weather, the crops, the animals, the family, and his insurance clients, and enumerated the people we knew who could use a little help. He didn't just list the names of those in need, but in case God didn't know, Dad told Him how each one could be aided and why He should intervene. Helen and I watched ants crawl across the floor and sometimes a mouse, careful not to catch each other's eye for fear we would giggle. That would unleash another flood of prayers asking God to forgive us for our irreverence. Eventually, Mother would say, "Dad . . . ," and he would finish. Then we'd bolt our cold breakfast and rush out the door to reach school before the final bell rang.

"Maybe this boy can take you to Baur's for a soda, and you can kneel there," Helen said.

"Oh, stop. You're becoming tiresome. I imagine he's heard all the jokes. We're just going to a movie. It's only for laughs."

"With a minister?" She stretched a stocking over her hand to inspect a snag.

Perhaps my sister was right. Maybe I should have turned him down.

"Well, I'm sure he's thrilled you're going out with him," she said.

"Of course he is. Who wouldn't be?" I replied.

We swung slowly. With my foot, I nudged a faded leaf off the porch floor into the flower bed below. When I raised my head, I could smell the soapy scent of laundry hanging on the line next door. I rocked back and forth in the swing, thinking about the young man I'd met the night before.

Suddenly, Mr. Streeter appeared, startling us. He tugged at his cap and grinned, and I felt Helen stiffen. "Evening to you, ladies," he said.

"Mr. Streeter," Helen replied.

"How's the job search going?" I asked. He hadn't paid the rent that month because he was unemployed.

He shook his head and gave us a mournful look. "Not so good, Miss Hite. There's not much call for an honest, hard-working man."

"With the war on, I thought there would be work even for men who aren't honest and hardworking," Helen said with an edge.

"That's a good one," he told her, although both he and I knew Helen wasn't joking. "I'll catch up on the rent when I get a job of work," he said.

"See that you do," Helen told him.

We watched him go around to the back of the house and duck under our clothesline, shoving aside the clothespin bag so savagely that some of the pins fell onto the ground. He left them there. "If it weren't for Maud and Dorothy, I'd get rid of him. I don't like him," Helen whispered, as if he could still hear her. "I don't like the men who come here looking for him."

"He scares me, too," I said.

Helen fanned herself with her cap, complaining of the heat.

"Do you wish you'd been an army nurse?" I asked, putting aside thoughts of Mr. Streeter.

"Sometimes."

"You still could be, you know. I read in the paper they're desperate for nurses. If you went to France, I could take care of the house until you got back."

"It's not that I haven't thought about it," Helen said. "I've always wanted to see Paris. But not that way. I just don't know if I could handle it."

"You could. You moved to Denver with hardly a moment's thought."

"I speak the language here."

I laughed at that. "So how hard would it be to learn to ask 'Where does it hurt?' in French?"

"Oh, that doesn't matter. In war, it's pretty obvious where it hurts. It's where your leg gets blown off or your intestines are falling out. You can tell a soldier's been gassed because he sounds like he's being strangled. And he is. Language isn't the problem. It's that I'm not sure I'm fit for the work. A nurse I met who just came back from the front told me it's ghastly. She quit. She couldn't take it."

"You could."

"I don't know, Lute. I used to think I could take anything, but I can't." She looked off to the west, to the mountains. "I left the hospital because I wanted to work with women and children who really need me. Women who, you know ... I do want to make a difference, to help people who might die without me. So sometimes I think maybe I could work over there. But something happened today that makes me wonder. I changed the dressing on a little girl's legs, or what was left after a train ran over them. The poor kid couldn't have been more than eight or nine. She was picking up coal by the railroad tracks because her family couldn't afford to buy it. What's the future for her? When I left and got on the streetcar, I sat in the last row and cried. If I get all torn up over a tragedy like that, how am I going to handle boys who get their faces blown off or lose both arms? Sometimes I want to be compassionate, and other times I want to cut myself off from feeling anything. And where's the humanity in that?"

"Peter said something like that. He said to really help those in need, you have to feel their sorrow."

"Who?"

"Peter, the minister you think I'm going to marry."

Helen shrugged. "How would he know?" She fanned her face with her cap again. The day was humid, and where Helen's hair had escaped from the knot on the back of her head, it curled around her face.

"Besides, I don't think Gil wants me to go," Helen added.

"Well, that's the real reason, isn't it?" I said, although I wasn't sure.

"He doesn't like the idea of me going overseas. I think he'd wait for me, though."

"He could get drafted. They need doctors."

"He could." Helen turned to me. "Do ministers get drafted?"

"How would I know?"

"Ask him."

I smiled. "My sister doesn't care what your intentions are, Mr. Howell. She just wants to know if you're going to war."

The two of us laughed. Helen said, "I love you, Lutie. You always make me laugh."

I loved her, too, and I thought how lucky I was to have her as a sister.

I was pleased at Helen's surprise when Peter showed up at the door. He was tall and slender, his straight hair neatly brushed, and he wore a suit so smart it might have come from Neusteter's. He looked like a model for Arrow shirts. I think Helen had expected a fish-face dressed in something from the charity box.

"At least he isn't wearing a turned-around collar," Helen whispered. We went to her bedroom to pin on our hats. I was mad about hats and had tried on several that evening. I'd wanted to wear my newest one, a fifteen-inch-wide fancy-weave straw that I'd trimmed with a grosgrain ribbon, but we were going to a moving picture show, and it would block the view of the whole row behind us. So I decided on a patent Milan straw with a satin bow. It went nicely with my black suit, its skirt so short that I wondered if it would shock Peter. I hoped so entirely.

We'd left him in the living room with Gil while we completed our outfits, and when we returned, the men were talking about the war. "The killing's not the way people think it is, getting shot in the heart and dying a clean death," Gil said.

"I know doctors who've been there. They say the soldiers suffer first from foot rot and gassing and rat bites . . ." He stopped when we entered the room. "Sorry, ladies, this isn't a fit subject for you."

"I'm a nurse, remember?" Helen said. "I know what it's like. I know that more people die from the side effects of war than from direct attacks. War's always been like that, I think."

"Only now we have more and better ways of killing. We didn't have gas before. Or some of the other weapons," Peter said.

"Why don't you join up, Peter?" Helen asked.

I sent my sister a stern look, hoping Helen wouldn't spoil things right off, but she ignored it.

"Good question. I've thought about it. Maybe I will. But I want to wait until I have my degree. I might be of more use then."

"As a minister?" Helen snorted. "Of course, as a minister, you'd be perfectly safe."

"Why don't you join?" Peter asked. "You're a nurse."

Helen looked startled, and I poked her in the ribs. "*Touché*, Helen."

"*Touché*? What does that mean?" Helen asked.

"It means 'got you.'"

Helen was a good sport, and she laughed.

Then Peter said, "We're going to a moving picture show. Do you two want to come along?"

"Oh, I don't—" Helen began, but Gil interrupted her.

"What one?" he asked.

"There's a William S. Hart picture. I've always liked him.

But my choice would be *Tarzan of the Apes*. That is, if Lutie would like to see it." He turned to me.

"Sure," I said, and almost laughed. At least Tarzan didn't part the Red Sea.

"That sounds swell. Don't you think so, Helen?" Gil asked.

Helen gave me a disdainful look and said without much enthusiasm, "Right. Swell."

The four of us went out onto the street, where Peter pointed to a neat little Buick roadster. He said it had room for only two, so they'd have to take Gil's automobile.

"I don't have one," Gil said.

"Then it's the trolley or shank's mare. It's a bit of a hike, but I say we walk," Peter said, taking my arm.

"All the way to the theater?" I protested.

"I'm game, aren't you, Helen?" Gil asked. "Walking's good for you."

"In these shoes?" she asked.

Peter glanced at Helen's slippers, which had pointed toes and tiny slender heels. "I don't know why women wear those things, why they buy all that useless stuff and get trussed up like a turkey at Thanksgiving. It's because of the stores. The ads that people like your friend Florence write. Women get snookered into thinking they'll look as glamorous as the models in the illustrations. Advertising's a racket."

I let go of Peter's arm and put my hands on my hips. "What did you say?" Maybe Helen was right: maybe he was too damned good for everyday use.

"Uh-oh," Gil said.

Peter looked confused. "I'm not talking about you," he said finally. "I'm talking about women who buy into those ridiculous advertisements, the kind Florence works on."

"Those ridiculous advertisements put bread on the table for one of us here," Gil told him. I liked that Gil stood up for me.

Peter frowned at Helen. "I thought you were a nurse."

"I am."

He turned to me. "You said you're an artist."

"I am. Do you think those ads draw themselves? I guess you didn't realize I work with Florence."

Peter looked flustered. "Gee . . ." he stuttered.

"Yes, gee," I repeated. "Maybe we should call it a night. You wouldn't want to go out with someone dumb enough to—"

Peter put up his hand to stop my catnip fit and said, "I guess I'm a real horse's neck for spouting off like that. Don't be peeved. If you forgive me, I'll spring for the movies and ice cream for all of us. I'd go for cocktails if they were legal."

"I'll buy that," Gil said.

"You'd drink? I thought you were a minister." Helen said.

"Not yet."

Peter smiled. He was so beautiful that of course I forgave him. But not before I defended my work. "Those fashions you're so disdainful of provide jobs, not just for me but for clerks and people who work in mills and factories, for farmers who grow cotton and raise sheep. Without advertisements, there wouldn't be any newspapers." I stopped, feeling foolish. Since when had I ever cared about all that? Since when had I ever even thought about it?

"I didn't know America's economy revolved around advertising. You've certainly set me straight," Peter said. "I'm sorry. I got off on the wrong foot."

"It's all right," I told Peter. "Hey, I'd like to be a fine artist painting pictures that make people see the injustice in the world, that cause them to protest discrimination, pictures that cure the sick and uplift the weary. All that. Heck, I'd be happy if I could paint something that helps America give all women the vote. But the truth is I'm lucky to have this job. There aren't many positions out there for girl artists. Besides, I like it."

Peter grinned. "Maybe we can start over. As I was saying, who's for walking and who's for taking the trolley?"

In the end, we took the streetcar to the Isis Theatre, where we saw Elmo Lincoln as Tarzan of the Apes, swinging through trees like the ones I'd drawn in first grade.

"Maybe not the best choice," Peter apologized afterward as we walked down Curtis Street. It was Denver's theater district, called Denver's Great White Way, and there were thousands, maybe millions, of lights on the movie palaces. "He's a little hefty to be flying through the air. In fact, I was rooting for the dirt. I was hoping he'd land in it once or twice."

"Well, I liked it. It's not every day you look at a half-naked man," I said, glancing at Peter to see if I'd offended him. I might have overstepped.

"That's because you're not a nurse," Helen told me. "They don't look so good lying flat on their backs." She took Gil's arm and started down the street.

Peter and I walked behind them, and he said, "You were a good sport about the movie. It was pretty awful, wasn't it?"

"Not so bad. I've known a boy or two I thought was raised by apes."

Peter grinned, and I smiled back. We had dropped behind Helen and Gil. "I like them," Peter said. "But your sister doesn't think much of me, does she?"

"She doesn't like ministers."

"Why's that?"

"I couldn't say."

"I admit some ministers are pretty awful—self-righteous, long-winded, insufferable bores."

"Are you one of them?"

"Not around you."

Peter took my arm, and we caught up with Helen and Gil. "What say we stop at Baur's for ice cream?" Peter asked. "Would you like that?"

"You bet we would. You serious about buying?" Gil was struggling to put himself through medical school, dropping out from time to time to earn enough money to pay the next semester's tuition. He had little spare cash.

Perhaps Peter sensed that, because he said, "Sure thing. I gave my word, didn't I?"

He steered the four of us to the pink-and-white marble soda fountain counter, and we watched the soda jerk mix up concoctions with ice cream and chocolate, cherry syrup and whipped cream. Then he said, "I'm sorry it's not a cocktail."

"I thought ministers didn't drink," Helen said again.

"Jesus made wine out of water, didn't He?" Peter smiled and added, "But of course, He wouldn't do it now because it's illegal in Colorado. I'm not one of those uptight chaps who believes God's sitting up there with a notebook writing down every sin for Judgment Day." As if to prove his point, he took out a package of Lucky Strikes and offered them around. We each took one, and Helen and I let Peter light them for us.

Helen blew smoke from the side of her mouth. Then she smiled at Peter for the first time. The men began talking about baseball, and Helen whispered to me, "I guess he's not so bad."

"Not so bad at all," I whispered back. "I think he's all mustard."

Three

After that first date, Peter and I spent most of our free time together. We attended concerts and moving pictures and patriotic rallies. We listened to Negro musicians play in the Five Points joints and attended the plays at Elitch's, an amusement park with acres of gardens. Or we just walked along Sixteenth Street, looking into the store windows so that I could study the fashions.

We spent Saturday afternoons together, too, since I worked only a half day. Peter would meet me in front of the store, and we'd have lunch at the counter of the five-and-dime, then wander about the store looking for treasures. We roamed City Park, walking around the lake or looking at the animals in the zoo. They weren't exotic, just deer and elk and a brown bear, animals that lived in the mountains, but I'd never seen them up close. A few times Peter drove us west in his roadster, to where the mountains began. We'd go into little cafés and drink coffee that was thick and bitter, and listen to old men talk about the mining days that were long gone.

Peter often brought books and studied in our living room or in the backyard, stopping from time to time to play with Dorothy. She was an odd little thing, barely ten years old, and looked even younger. She seemed afraid of men, but Peter drew her out. He gave her a storybook once, but Mr. Streeter said the book wasn't fit for a child and threw it in the ash pit. Gil rescued it, and I kept it in the house, and one of us would read it to her when she came upstairs.

At other times, Peter talked about what he'd learned in school, and I tried to be enthusiastic when he expounded on religion, although the truth was I didn't care much. I had my own interests. I drew designs for hats or for fabrics. Or I sewed. Working at Neusteter's had piqued my interest in fabrics. I was enchanted with the crepe de chine and cut velvet, the Egyptian cotton and fine Scottish woolens used in the clothing we sold at the store. I was intrigued with patterns that required pieces to be cut on the bias, with gussets and interfacings and trims, and all the intricacies of the stitching. I convinced the seamstresses in the alterations department to set aside scraps of material, the bits of ribbons and trim they snipped from clothing altered to fit Neusteter patrons (as we'd been instructed to call customers), and give them to me. I used them to trim hats and to make patchwork scarves. I also bought exotic fabrics at the Denver Dry Goods next door and combined them with the salvaged scraps to piece together throws. Sometimes I quilted them. These quilts were bolder and more sophisticated than the dowdy, old-fashioned calico ones Helen and I had slept under as children.

When Peter didn't have to study, we scoured the thrift stores to find antique shawls and old beadwork and lace, which I incorporated into my creations.

"Why don't you make dresses and sell them? Wouldn't that

pay better than being a department store artist?" Peter asked me one day when we were rummaging through a bin of worn clothing. "I think you'd be first-rate at it," he added. I pulled out a velvet dress so old it had been worn with a hoop. The bodice was shredded and would have to be discarded, but the skirt, a deep claret color, might be salvaged. I rubbed the velvet against my cheek, feeling its silky smoothness on my skin, and told Peter it was "swellegant." I'd picked up that word, like most of my slang, from my friend Florence. I wondered who had worn the dress so many years before, whether it had been made for a ball or a Christmas party. Sometimes the old clothing had bits of paper pinned to it, identifying the dress or the wearer: "Mary's wedding gown" and "My mourning dress" and "Worn to the Grand Duke Alexis ball, January 17, 1872." I bought that one just because of the note. Once, I found a white satin ball gown trimmed in ostrich feathers with the name "Tabor" embroidered inside and thought it might have belonged to the wife of the Silver King. But usually the clothing was anonymous, and I was left to make up stories about the women who had worn such lovely creations.

"I don't want to be a dressmaker. It's too much of an undertaking," I said. I set the dress aside and picked up a soiled bodice with intricate turquoise trim. I could use the beads on an evening dress I was stitching. "I'd have to spend a fortune on stocking fabrics, and I'd have to find a studio. Then where would I get customers? It's not as if the sales clerks in the better dress department at Neusteter's would turn over their patrons to me. I'd have to be half sales clerk, too, and I'm no good at that. I find it awfully hard to flatter people." I didn't add that I really did not care to design things for other women, prefer-ring to design only for myself.

"You could make hats. You're quite good at it, you know. I think you could be a wow. Mother spends a fortune on hats."

"I don't really *make* them. I just trim them," I told him. "I don't know anything about blocking straw or felt."

"You could learn, couldn't you?"

"If I wanted to, I suppose, but I'm not sure I do." In fact, I'd never had any great desire to go into business on my own. I'd all but deserted my easel and was happy to get a weekly paycheck from Neusteter's. I had a feeling I might not be all that good at anything. Painting had just seemed like the thing to do with my degree, and of course I hadn't been successful at it. What I liked best was design, but at school we didn't sit around talking about becoming designers—or illustrators, which was what I was now. We said it was *commerce* and was beneath us. It would be as if Peter got his theology degree and then became a Bible salesman.

"Well, I think you have style. So does Father."

I had met Peter's father because he had invited us to the the Brown Palace Hotel for dinner. He was a prominent judge and there had been talk about him running for governor, although Peter said that wasn't likely. I hadn't yet met Peter's mother. She was spending the summer in Kansas City with one of Peter's sisters, who was ill. The Howells lived in a mansion on Capitol Hill. Peter had driven me by it once, and I recognized it. Helen and I had walked past it when we first explored Denver. When his mother returned, he said, she would invite me for dinner.

Would she? Judge Howell was nice enough but rather

stern, and I wondered if the Howells thought I wasn't good enough for Peter. Or maybe they believed I was interested in his money, because it was clear they had plenty. Judge Howell's father had made a fortune selling hardware in the mining towns. But I wasn't after Peter's money. I wasn't even sure I was after Peter. I was after a good time.

It was Helen who made me think about whether I wanted to be married to a minister. "He'll propose soon enough. You know that," Helen said one blustery evening as we sat by the grate in the living room, she knitting and me mending.

"Oh, I don't know any such thing," I replied as I inserted a darning egg into a stocking and inspected the tear.

"You do know he's crazy about you. It's obvious. Even Gil sees it."

I didn't reply.

"He's a nice enough fellow. I'll admit that. Gil thinks he's almost good enough for you. But do you really want to marry a minister?"

I didn't want to answer her and held up my mending. "Honestly, this stocking is new! I don't know how I could have ripped it."

"Face it, honey. He will ask. You have to decide what you'll answer when he does."

I put down my darning then and looked at her. "I haven't thought about it. Besides, I'm not as sure as you are that he will."

"Oh, fudge!" Helen snorted. "Of course you've thought about it."

I went to the grate and held my hands over the fire. Although it was still summer, the day was cold, and the house was drafty, so we'd built a fire to take off the chill. In winter, the wind swept down from the mountains across the prairie and under our door. "Did you order coal for the furnace? I would hate to run out in the middle of winter. It'll be bad enough having to practice heatless Mondays." President Wilson had asked Americans to honor not only heatless Mondays but meatless Tuesdays and wheatless Wednesdays for the war effort.

"Lute!"

I turned around and almost shouted. "I don't know, Helen. I adore Peter. He's the best man I've ever met. I'm crazy about him. But I don't know if I can be a minister's wife. I don't care about helping the downtrodden. I don't even knit stockings for the soldiers like you do." Helen was working on a stocking now. They were ugly, the color of coal, but they would keep some doughboy's feet warm.

"You don't know how to knit," Helen interjected.

I ignored that. "I've never even read the Bible all the way through. And I think I prayed enough in Iowa to last my lifetime."

"And you'd have to wear those depressing out-of-fashion clothes." Helen knew how to make me laugh.

My mood lightened. "There's that."

"You'd have to give up working at Neusteter's, too. Did you ever know a minister's wife who held a job?"

"I never knew any wife who had a job. What about you, Helen? Will you stop working when you marry Gil?"

"Nursing's different. It's a calling, not a job."

"Oh." I wondered if she caught the annoyance in my voice.

"At least you wouldn't have to live on a minister's salary." Helen knew that Peter's father was wealthy.

"No, perhaps not." But I wasn't sure Peter would accept his family's money.

"Maybe he'll be a missionary and you'll go to darkest Africa."

"I doubt it." I was tired of Helen's jazz, as Florence would say. "I really don't know what I'll do if he asks. I'm not sure I'm up to being married to a minister. I'm really not a good person like Peter."

Now Helen set down her knitting and leaned forward in her chair. "Don't you ever think that, Lute. You say that because you're an artist and you like clothes and good times, so you think you're flighty. Maybe there are others who think that, too. But I'm your sister. I know you better."

Helen always gave me more credit than I deserved.

I sighed. The truth was I actually had begun thinking about whether I should marry Peter if he asked me. I loved him, of course. I'd realized it not long after we started going out. I had been sitting in the yard when Peter came up behind me and dropped a rose from his mother's garden into my lap.

"It's almost as pretty as you are," he told me.

That had been a mawkish thing to say, and I had almost told him so. But I'd held my tongue, and when Peter picked up the flower and held it next to my face and repeated, "Almost as pretty," I treasured the silly words.

I'd always assumed I'd marry one day, of course. Girls did. One of the reasons I'd studied art was it was something I could pursue as a wife. At least I had planned that far ahead. I could paint portraits of my family, perhaps paint flowers or landscapes that I'd enter in art shows. I'd never had grand plans for a career, didn't want one, in fact. I'd work only until I married, then be a good wife, giving nice little dinner parties and going to tea with the wives of my husband's associates. Maybe I'd be considered a little bohemian because I'd once held a job, but not enough that I'd embarrass my husband.

I'd always believed I'd marry a man who sold insurance, like my father, or a banker or a lawyer, or perhaps someone who ran a store or a lumberyard. But a minister?

I started to tell Helen I was tired of talking about Peter when we heard a noise below us, in the basement, and Helen shook her head in disgust. "Mr. Streeter's drunk again, drinking with our rent money."

"At least we don't have a mortgage payment." Because we'd sold our parents' home in Cedar Rapids, we'd had the money to buy the house in Denver outright—a good thing, because it was unlikely a bank would have given a loan to two women. And since we were both employed, we could cover the taxes and utilities bills without the Streeters' rent money. It wasn't the first time Mr. Streeter had lost his job and Maud had begged Helen and me not to evict them.

"When he drinks, he's vicious," Helen said. "Remember the time Maud's face was bruised and she said she'd run into a door?"

I remembered. Maud had had a black eye.

"As a nurse, I've seen too many women like that. I know what men can do when they get angry."

"I'd leave any man who hit me."

Helen scoffed and put her knitting on the table, then stood and went to the window. It had drizzled all day, and now rain was coming down hard. "Yes, I suppose you would. You could get a job and support yourself. But how could Maud get on? She's too frail to work as a domestic, and she's not attractive enough to find a job in a shop. If she left him, she'd be on charity."

I'd never considered that, and I stared at my sister for a long time. "He's probably difficult only when he's drunk. They seem to get along pretty well when he's sober. He always buys her little presents afterward."

"With more of our rent money."

"I doubt that he hits her often. She probably says things that set him off."

"No woman deserves to be blamed for a man hitting her."

Helen looked so dejected that I stood and put my arms around her. "I shouldn't have said that. I'm so sorry, dear."

Helen was silent for a moment. Then she said, "Maybe if you're a minister's wife, you can help women who've been . . . mistreated, help children like Dorothy."

"Me?"

"Why not? Why don't you talk to Peter about it?"

"You mean I should say, 'Peter, in case you're going to ask me to marry you, would you mind awfully if I help women whose husbands smack them around?'"

I laughed, but Helen didn't. "Don't you think it's more important than selling clothes to women who already have too many?"

"That's not fair, Helen."

She looked away. "No, of course it isn't. It's just that I get so knotted up over the women I take care of. Sometimes I want to pick up a coal shovel and whack their husbands on the head."

"I know you do, and I wish you would." Just the week before, Helen had told me about a woman with four daughters who'd given birth to a stillborn boy. Her husband had beaten her, claiming she was responsible for the boy not having lived. Then he'd locked her out of the house, and she'd had to sleep in the chicken coop. The woman actually believed she deserved the punishment, and she begged Helen not to tell anyone what had happened. She was too ashamed.

We were silent for a time, busying ourselves with our work. At last, Helen put aside the half-finished stocking and said, "I've really put a cloud over our day, haven't I?"

"No, of course not. You care too much. You care about me, and you care about the soldiers and the women you help and all those little souls you encounter."

"Little souls?"

"Oh, it's something I heard Judge Howell say. Peter says it, too. It comes from some Roman emperor. It means the poor, the hopeless, the common people nobody ever notices. In truth, it applies to all of us. We're all lost little souls in our way—you and me and maybe even Peter." I smiled at my sister and added, "It certainly includes those who are unlucky enough to be married to ministers."

Helen laughed, and her mood lifted. "I do get gloomy sometimes, don't I?"

Before I could reply, we heard a knock on the door and exchanged glances. "Maud?" I mouthed. Helen put aside her knitting, and we hurried to the door. Dorothy stood there, her dress soaked, her wet hair hanging limp around her face.

"Mama said I should stay outside until Papa goes to sleep. But it's cold, and I'm all wet from the rain. Can I come in?" she asked.

"Of course. You can stay with us," I told her.

"Papa's sick again," she repeated. "I don't like it when he's that way." She went to stand before the fire, shivering, her arms wrapped around herself, while Helen fetched a blanket.

I wondered if Mr. Streeter hit the little girl when he was drunk. "I know. I'll fix you cocoa, and then we'll pop corn. Would you like to do that, Dorothy?" I asked as Helen wrapped the blanket around her. We took her into the kitchen.

"When your mother comes to get you, we'll have a party," I said, getting out the popcorn popper.

Dorothy looked at me solemnly. "All right. Can we give Mama some popcorn? We didn't have any supper."

"Sure," I said, then turned to Helen and mouthed, "But not Papa."

Helen didn't notice me. Instead, she stared at Dorothy with tears in her eyes. "Gil said he would say something to Mr. Streeter," she whispered to me.

"About Maud?" I asked.

"About Dorothy."

I didn't understand.

Four

Peter and I were alone on a bench in City Park. The rally was over, and the women in the big hats who sold Liberty Bonds had gone home. The crowd that had cheered so loudly a few minutes earlier had scattered, leaving behind streamers and soiled newspapers that had been wrapped around ham sandwiches and fried chicken. Even the vendors with their hot sausages and boxes of fudge had packed up. The area was deserted except for a man dressed in a work jumper who was taking down the bunting that decorated the stage and folding it up. Peter and I were too comfortable to leave. He sprawled on the bench, one arm stretched along the top rail behind me, and I snuggled beside him.

"You were a good sport to buy a bond," I told him.

"There's nothing sporting about it. I don't understand why you hold off."

"It's the principle of the thing. I support the war, of course, but I don't think it's right for the store to pressure me to buy a bond." Neusteter's was pushing its employees to purchase war bonds. It wanted 100 percent participation. Many of the clerks and stockroom workers who couldn't afford to buy the bonds had caved in under pressure, but Florence and I had held out. My boss, Mr. Neil, had called me into his office to say he was disappointed in me. He had suggested I was un-American.

"The employers don't have a choice," Peter told me. "President Wilson's pressured them to push the bonds. He needs the money to win the war."

"I voted for him to keep us out of the war." Women in Colorado had had the vote since 1893.

"Me, too," Peter said.

We had talked about the war often enough. Peter didn't want the war. I hadn't believed in it, not at the beginning, but after reading so many stories in the newspapers about the Germans and their cruelty, the way they garroted children and mutilated women, I'd changed my mind. I might even have bought a war bond if Neusteter's hadn't pushed me so hard.

"Why did you buy a bond if you're against the war?" I asked. I picked up a small flag that had blown against the bench, then folded it and set it beside me. I could make something out of the streamers and tiny discarded flags. I reached for a banner that lay on the ground.

"There isn't much choice. I thought the war wouldn't last long. Remember the line from the Shakespeare play we saw: 'If it were done, when 'tis done, then 'twere well it were done quickly.' But the war didn't end quickly, and we joined the fighting, and we're in it to win. So buying a Liberty Bond is an act of patriotism. It's a way of supporting our country."

"Even if you're a pacifist?"

"That's taking it too far. I never said I was a pacifist. I just don't believe in war."

"There's a difference?"

Peter thought a moment, then reached for a flag on the bench in front of us and handed it to me. "What are you doing with all these?"

"I'm not sure. Maybe making a quilt. My grandmother Eliza made one for her husband during the Civil War."

"Her husband? You mean your grandfather?"

"Her first husband. It's a long story."

Peter stood and picked up another flag from the bench in front of us. Then we wandered back and forth through the rows of deserted benches, gathering flags and banners. Perhaps instead of keeping them, we should have given them to the worker who had dismantled the decorations on the platform. He had limped a little, and I wondered if he had been injured in the war. But the man had gone away.

We sat down again, and I began folding the red, white, and blue cloth. "The material's awfully flimsy. I don't know if it will hold up." I paused, then said to Peter, "You didn't answer my question."

He didn't say anything for a while. Instead, he took out a package of Lucky Strikes. He offered me one, but I was busy with the flags. He lit a cigarette for himself and sat smoking, leaning forward on the bench with his forearms on his knees. He stared across the grass that the people had trampled at the rally. Then he said, "It was easy to be against the war when the Europeans were the only ones involved. But then America joined, and that made things different. Since we're in it, I want us to win." He paused a moment. "I've been thinking of joining up."

I turned to look at him. "You're a student—a *divinity* student. You don't have to go."

"That's beside the point. It's a question of what's the right thing."

"But we know how awful the war is now. At first, it was all about slogans and uniforms and 'Over There' and all the other songs. It's not glamorous anymore."

Peter turned to me. "Lutie, it never was."

"No, I suppose not." Ducks rose from the lake and flew over us, their quacks as loud as an aeroplane. Then it was silent again.

"Besides, something happened last week." He had finished his cigarette and threw the butt onto the grass. He looked far off, at the mountains. "Something rotten." He stopped, and I heard the anguish in his voice.

I had been looking at the natural history museum in the distance. I turned and stared at him and saw he was biting his lip. "What?"

Peter turned away from me as if he were ashamed. "A woman gave me a white feather."

"What! She had no right!" Women gave white feathers to able-bodied men to shame them for not being in the war. The feathers were a sign that they were too chicken to fight. It wasn't fair, because the women didn't know the reason a man hadn't joined up. When our neighbor was presented with a white feather, he pulled up his pants leg to show he had an artificial leg. The woman fell all over herself apologizing, then called him a war hero. He didn't tell her he'd lost his leg in an auto accident.

"She called me a slacker."

"How awful."

"Maybe she was right."

"You're not a slacker." I was incensed.

"Aren't I?"

"You have a reason not to join. It's perfectly legitimate."

"But does that make it right? I think maybe it's time I do my part. I've thought for a long time that it's not fair that boys I know are fighting and dying in France, while I'm sitting here on a bench with the girl I love."

Peter had never before said he loved me, and I felt myself flush. I wondered if he was about to make some sort of declaration.

But Peter seemed oblivious to the words he had just said. "It's not a question of what I have to do. It's a question of what I *should* do, of acting honorably."

"Oh, honor. That's what President Wilson talks about, peace with honor. But what does that mean? You could be killed. What's honorable about that?"

Peter took my hand. "I could not love thee, dear, so much, loved I not honor more."

I frowned. "That sounds like something you read. Are you quoting?"

"Richard Lovelace. The poem's called 'To Lucasta, Going to the Wars.' Maybe it ought to be called 'To Lucretia.'"

Peter knew that my real name was Lucretia, of course. I hated it. Mother had read it someplace just before I was born and thought it romantic. She didn't learn about Lucrezia Borgia until later, but by then everybody called me Lute or Lutie.

I shrugged off that last comment and said, "I still don't see what honor has to do with it. I don't get it."

Peter turned to me suddenly. He took the banner away

from me and set it on the bench. "Well, do you get this . . ." He swallowed, then took my hands. "We've known each other only a few months, but I love you. I think you're the grandest girl I've ever met. I'd like to marry you when all this war business is over."

I stared at him. Had Peter just asked me to marry him? I opened my mouth, but I didn't know what to say. I could only look at him, and my eyes must have been as big as silver dollars. Finally, when Peter said nothing more, I stuttered, "What?"

"It wasn't a very eloquent proposal, I'll grant you, but I think I just asked you to marry me."

"I think you did."

"And you're supposed to answer. You're supposed to say yes. At least I hope you will."

"But there's so much we have to talk about."

"You mean about me being a minister?"

I nodded. "It's not that I don't love you, Peter. Of course I do. I'm crazy about you. But I don't know if I . . ." I was embarrassed to say how much I dreaded being a minister's wife. What's more, I knew Helen would be unhappy if I married a minister, and I cared what she thought. I turned away and stared out at the lawn. I felt foolish. What other girl would turn down a proposal from a man she loved as much as I did Peter because she didn't like his profession.

Peter understood, however. "You don't know if you want a preacher for a husband. That's it, isn't it?"

I took a deep breath and gave a slight nod.

"I've always known that about you." He laughed and drew me

close to him. "Just because I'm studying theology doesn't mean I have to be a minister. For a long time, I thought it did. And you know what? I wasn't sure I'd be any good at it. But there's lots I can do with a divinity degree besides preaching. I've been thinking about it lately. I could write or be a teacher, maybe run a charity. I could take over my grandfather's hardware business or even go into politics, where, Lord knows, there's a mighty need for somebody who's trying to be a Christian. I don't know just what it is I'll do, but I believe we could figure it out together, don't you think?"

"Would you mind awfully?"

Peter shook his head. "The truth is, I'm relieved. It's the theology that interests me, not standing in a pulpit pontificating. Does that make a difference in your answer? You can think about it, of course. I've been awfully abrupt. Still, I hope you won't leave a fellow hanging forever."

My doubts had disappeared, and all I felt was a surge of joy and excitement at the idea that I would be engaged to a soldier going off to war. I took one of my hands from his and touched his cheek and looked up at him. "I won't keep you waiting at all. It's a grand proposal. I'd be glad to marry you, Peter."

Peter put his arm around me and held me tight, and we both looked out over the park, to the lake where children fed stale bread to the ducks. I thought about our life together, with children like those—like Dorothy—for years stretching out forever.

"I want to make you happy," he said. "Love seeketh not its own."

"That one sounds like the Bible."

"First Corinthians. It refers to charity, but I believe it refers to love, too. I interpret it to mean love is not what you receive but what you give."

"It's a swell verse."

"We should wait until the war's over to marry," Peter said. "If something happens to me, I don't want to leave you a widow."

"Then you are going to join up? I'd really rather you wouldn't." A little doubt crept into a day that had been almost perfect.

"I wish to serve." He paused while he thought something over. "It sounds awfully egotistical to say this, but I'm wondering if I could, you know, maybe help some of the soldiers with their faith. A lot of them lose it in wartime. Maybe I could talk to them—not preach exactly, but just tell them about God, explain that men, not God, make bad things happen." He gave an embarrassed laugh. "I do sound self-important, don't I? It's just that I believe so strongly . . ." He shrugged.

"I'm sure you could help. Do you think God chose you to go?" I asked.

Peter thought that over. "God makes choices every day, but sometimes He leaves the choices up to us. We have to make them, difficult ones, in His name. And I believe He is with us, even when the decision is wrong."

"The war is such a dirty mess. I'd be very afraid if you were over there."

Peter grinned at me. "I'll take care of myself. I have good reason to now." He held me against him. His lips brushed my hair and he said, "Oh, Lute," in a strangled voice. And then he asked, "Would you mind very much if I went? It won't be for long. The war will be over soon."

I knew then that he'd made up his mind and if I opposed him, he would resent me for it. Maybe he could indeed help some poor soldier. "Of course I mind. But it's not up to me. As you said, you have to choose what's right for you. And God will take care of you." I was startled to hear myself say that.

We sat for a long time without speaking. We should have spoken, because there were so many things to say—about the army, about the wedding, about our future together. The wind came up and scattered the little clouds, and the dandelions sparkled in the sun. And still we stayed. We were very like an old married couple who could talk to each other without saying words.

Peter went away just as the trumpet vine on the porch was blooming. I would always associate him with the bright orange-yellow flowers.

We told a few people about our engagement. Helen, of course. Florence, my friend at Neusteter's, who let it slip to my boss, Mr. Neil. And Peter's father. Peter sent a telegram to his mother, who wired back that she was pleased and eager to meet me. I received wires from both of his sisters, too, but they sounded perfunctory. Peter told me they approved, but I wasn't so sure.

Because of the war and people dying overseas—as well as his mother's absence—we decided it wasn't right to have an engagement party. But Peter gave me a ring that had belonged to his grandmother. It was Victorian, with a design of garnets and diamonds surrounding a very large diamond, and he said he knew it wasn't my style. But his mother had written that she wanted me to have it. We'd pick out a wedding ring that suited me after he returned from France. I liked the ring just fine, however. I would look at it and rub my fingers over the stones and feel a connection to Peter, wherever he was.

Peter's father was more concerned with his joining the army than with our engagement, which was to be expected. Everybody knew enough about the fighting over there to be worried. Helen and Gil cared for men who had come home, their feet amputated because of the rot, their arms and legs and faces shot off, men who had gone crazy from the suffering and the fear and the omnipresence of death. Peter told us the fighting had changed from the way it was at the beginning of the war, that artillery and aeroplanes were important now, and that fewer men fought from trenches. But that just gave me a new set of worries.

I'd heard the story about the Christmas Eve truce along the Western Front in 1914. Soldiers on both sides sang Christmas carols. The Germans even sang "God Save the King." The men called "Merry Christmas." On Christmas day, they climbed out of their trenches and exchanged cigars and bottles of brandy, cigarettes and cake. They even helped to bury the enemy dead. There was no shooting that day. But when Christmas was over, they began killing one another again. There hadn't been any Christmas truces since then. But maybe the war would be over before next Christmas.

On the day Peter left, I hurried to the station to say goodbye. I'd skipped my lunch so that I'd have time to see him off. The depot was jammed with soldiers, many in brand-new uniforms, some of them just boys who'd barely begun to shave. Peter looked old beside them. There were men in wheelchairs and others who walked slowly with empty coat sleeves carefully folded and tucked into pockets. A one-legged man in uniform propelled himself along on crutches, the tapping reverberating in that big barn of a depot. Other soldiers sat on the huge benches and looked as weary as death. Their eyes were empty and their faces drawn. I tried not to look at them, but Peter was smart and courageous. He wouldn't falter.

In the days before he left, he tried to reassure me. "The war's almost over. Why, I probably won't even get there before the fighting's done with. I'll be spending my time in Paris. I'll make a list of all the places to see, and someday we'll go there together."

But he didn't fool me. He didn't fool his folks, either. We all knew he was scared. At the station, I saw him watch a soldier with a scarf wrapped around his face that covered his eyes. The boy was blind, and an old couple led him through the station, the father's face filled with despair, the mother crying silently into her coat collar so her son couldn't hear. I refused to think that Peter might come home like that. So I turned away and forced myself to find a soldier who looked strong and healthy and happy, one who had come through the war all right. And when I did, I wondered if that soldier had been to war at all.

Although Peter's mother had planned to stay in Kansas City through the summer, she returned to Denver the night before Peter left. I was introduced to her at the station only minutes before Peter boarded his train. She looked like Peter, handsome, with dark hair that was turning gray, and she greeted me with more warmth than I'd expected. "I hope we shall become great friends," she said, but she gave me only a brief look before turning her eyes to Peter.

We walked Peter to the train, his mother and father on either side of him, me behind, trying not to dirty my new gray shoes. I had worn a white starched shirtwaist and a gray suit that Peter had helped me pick out, with a mauve hat that I had trimmed with an ostrich pompon. I know it was silly of me to care about how I looked, but I wanted Peter to remember me as stylish.

Mrs. Howell was trying not to cry, and Judge Howell kept clearing his throat. The train was already packed with dough-boys. Mrs. Howell put her arms around Peter. Judge Howell shook his son's hand and said, "You'll make a first-rate soldier" and "God help the Germans now!" and "Give hell, boy!" and other things that sounded hollow. He took out his pocket watch, opened it, stared at it a moment, then clicked it shut.

Peter replied, "You bet I will, Father."

Then Peter's parents stood aside and let me say good-bye. I didn't want Peter to kiss me in front of them. It would have seemed tasteless, and maybe he thought so, too, because he didn't. Instead, he hugged me and said, "Be a good girl." And he told his parents, "Take care of her. She's mighty sweet."

Then the conductor, a small man in a blue uniform with a gold watch chain across his chest, called, "All aboard," drawing out each syllable. Peter climbed the metal steps onto the train, and we followed him, walking alongside as he went through the coaches until he found a seat. Peter's seat was on the aisle, and he reached across the soldier next to him and grasped my hand through the window, which felt far more intimate than a kiss. He held my hand until the train began to move, shuddering at first as if in protest. Then he called out, "So long!" We walked beside the car, trying to keep up with it, but after a while the train began moving too fast and we had to stop. Peter waved, but so many soldiers were waving that I wasn't sure which hand was his.

We stood beside the tracks until the train disappeared. Then Judge Howell suggested we all go to the Brown Palace for lunch. Denver's finest hotel, it was a big sandstone triangular building not far from Neusteter's. But by then I'd taken more than an hour away from work and had to get back. Mr. Neil would be furious that I had been away for so long. And perhaps the Howells would be relieved I wasn't going. They might want to be alone.

"You must come for dinner so that we can get to know each other," Mrs. Howell said as we parted outside the station. And then, as if she had held back the tears so that Peter wouldn't see them, she broke down and put her face against her husband's chest. He looked as if he, too, would cry. She reached out a hand to me and included me in their despair. I loved her for that.

Five

One night in the fall after Peter had gone, Helen and I went for a walk. The sky was stormy, but Helen needed fresh air and I thought maybe she needed to talk about her day, about who had been stricken by or died from the influenza, which had gotten very bad. But she was silent as we went along the dark streets past the bungalows with their wide porches and the square two-story houses that were being built all over Denver. The wind had come up. I shoved my hands deep into my pockets and was glad when Helen turned to go home.

The wind blew dead leaves in front of us as we hurried up the walk to the porch. I watched them swirl into the air and nearly tripped over the dark bulk curled up in front of the door.

"It's Dorothy," Helen said, and knelt beside her. "What is it, sweetie?" she asked.

Dorothy looked up at us, tears streaking her face.

"What is it?" Helen repeated in a soft voice as she sat down on the porch floor and put Dorothy's head in her lap. "What's wrong?"

"Oh, Miss Helen," the little girl moaned.

"Is it your father? Did he . . ." Helen's voice trailed off. She cleared her throat and asked in a firmer voice, "Did he come back?"

Dorothy didn't answer. She was shivering, and Helen said she might be in shock.

I wanted to ask Helen what was going on. But my questions could wait. We needed to take care of Dorothy first. The two of us led her into the house and settled her on the davenport. Helen took off her cape and spread it over Dorothy.

I went into the kitchen to make tea. After I had gotten the tea canister and mother's silver pot, cream and sugar, and the cups with the roses on them, I returned to the living room. Helen was sitting on the davenport beside Dorothy, stroking her hair. There were tear lines through the dirt on Dorothy's cheeks, so I went to the bathroom and fetched a wet washcloth. Helen took it from me and gently wiped Dorothy's face, then her hands.

"What is it, dear? You can tell me," Helen said. "Did your father . . . hurt you again? It's not your fault. Don't be ashamed. You can tell me."

So Mr. Streeter really had beaten his daughter, I thought.

"No," Dorothy muttered. "Papa hasn't come home."

Helen seemed not to want to push the girl. I returned to the kitchen and brewed the tea, then set the cups on a tray and carried it into the living room.

"Why look, Dorothy, Miss Lutie has made us tea. Wouldn't you like sugar in yours? It's ever so much nicer with sugar, don't you think?" Helen picked up the sugar bowl and one of the spoons on the tray. When Dorothy nodded, Helen said, "See how prettily the tea tray is arranged. Miss Lutie is an artist. She always makes things nice. Shall I add the sugar for you?"

Dorothy sat up and stared at the tray, but she didn't comment, only nodded again. After Helen handed her a cup, Dorothy gulped down the tea.

Helen said to me, "I imagine she hasn't eaten."

She turned back to Dorothy. "Would you like toast and jam? Then you can tell us what is wrong."

"Yes, please," the girl whispered.

I went back to the kitchen and took a sack of bread out of the bread box. I put two slices into the toaster, and when they were done, I spread the toast with butter. It was soft, since with the influenza the iceman was not making regular deliveries and the icebox was no longer cold, but the butter had not turned rancid, so I used it, along with the plum jam Helen and Gil and I had made in the summer. It was very good, and Gil had suggested we send a jar of it to Peter. I hoped the jam had made its way to him and had reminded him of sitting beneath the plum tree in our yard.

When I returned to the living room with the plate of toast, Helen said to Dorothy, "Do you think you can eat it as you tell us what's wrong?"

"Yes, ma'am," Dorothy said. She gobbled the toast. "It's Mama," she said at last, and Helen looked at me sharply. We should have realized immediately that something was wrong with Maud since she rarely left Dorothy alone. Maud must have gone out on an errand and left Dorothy by herself, and the girl had become frightened.

"Did your father come around?" Helen asked, but Dorothy shook her head.

"I haven't seen him. Mama's sick." And then, as if a dam

had broken, she said, "We were at the grocer's and Mama threw up, and the store man told her to get out before she made everybody sick. And we went outside, and Mama lay down on the sidewalk for a minute. Then a big white truck came along, and two men, they picked her up, and they took her away."

"The influenza?" I asked Helen.

"Most likely," she replied.

She turned to Dorothy. "Didn't they let you go with your mother?"

Dorothy shook her head. "They didn't know I was with her. Mama didn't tell them. She was too sick. I begged them to let me go with her, but they said no, and they drove away. So I came here."

"That was a wise decision to return home," I said.

"Won't you find out where they took her so I can see her?" Dorothy asked. "Do you think she's all right?"

Helen and I exchanged a glance.

"Maybe Gil would know," I suggested. "We could telephone him."

"Yes, please," Dorothy said. "Dr. Gil could make her well."

"If we could reach him," Helen said. "Who knows where he is."

"Shall I go and try to find Maud?" I asked Helen.

"No," Helen said. She knew the hospitals and the emergency medical facilities better than I did, and the doctors were more likely to talk to her since she was a nurse. "You stay here with Dorothy." She sighed. I knew she was tired and did not want to go out. "Maybe it's not the influenza at all but an upset stomach. Lots of things are being misdiagnosed as the influenza."

We both knew it was not an upset stomach, and I said, "All right, but I hate to see you have to go."

"It can't be helped. It's Maud."

Helen put on her cape and took an umbrella and left, and Dorothy and I went into the kitchen, where I rummaged around in the icebox for something that hadn't gone bad. Finally, I fried an egg for her and made another piece of toast, and she ate at the table.

When Dorothy finished, I asked her if she wanted a bath with lovely soap that smelled like roses that I had bought at Neusteter's. The basement apartment had only a shower and large laundry tubs where Dorothy bathed. I ran the taps and got out towels, then asked if she would be all right if I went downstairs to get clean clothes for her, and she said yes. I left her to undress and climb into the tub by herself.

As I went down the basement steps, I remembered how each year, Helen and I had made a May basket for Dorothy and left it on the doorknob. We'd gather violets and daffodils from our yard and add sprigs of myrtle and put them in a paper basket with a note saying the fairies had left it for her, although this year we suspected that, at ten, Dorothy recognized the flowers from our yard and no longer believed in fairies.

I unlocked the basement door and went into the apartment, then into the little room where Dorothy slept, taking out socks and a dress from the bureau. Dorothy had few enough clothes, and those that she had were seedy. Helen and I should buy some for her, I thought. Shoes, too, and boots for the winter and perhaps a coat. Then I spotted the Whitman's candy box in which Dorothy kept her treasures. She had never shown me the contents and I was curious, so I opened it. Inside were bits of ribbon and lace, the cards from her May baskets, a rock with flecks of mica, two jacks, and a golden button. Dorothy liked to sit in the yard and go through her treasures. I took the box with me because I thought it might take her mind off her mother.

In the bathroom, Dorothy was leaning against the white porcelain tub, moving her legs back and forth, forcing the water over and under them, so that they looked like logs in a flowing stream. Her eyes were closed, and she didn't hear me come into the bathroom. When she saw me, she leaned forward and covered herself with her hands.

I thought she was being modest. "Shall I soap you?" I asked.

"No. I can do it."

I sat on the edge of the tub and unwrapped the soap, then sniffed it. "Smell," I said, holding it in front of Dorothy's face. "Isn't the scent heavenly? Just like summer. I saved it for a special time, and what's more special than you?"

Dorothy smelled it without moving her hands away. I bustled around, straightening the things in the medicine cabinet and checking the temperature of the water in the tub. When she saw I was not looking at her, Dorothy moved her hands and took the soap from where I'd placed it in the little wire soap holder attached to the porcelain rim and began washing herself. I thought I might sit on the stool beside the tub and talk to her, comfort her, because I knew she was afraid for her mother. When I turned to her, however, I saw the bruises on her chest. I could tell they were old because they had turned yellow.

"Good God! What happened to you?" I demanded, then bit my tongue because I had alarmed her. How foolish of me to have cried out like that. Dorothy had been hiding the bruises. I wished that Helen had stayed; she would have known the right questions to ask.

"I fell," Dorothy said, raising her head as if to challenge me.

Fell, my eye! Thank God Mr. Streeter was gone, because I was mad enough to choke him. "Do you like the soap?" I asked.

"It smells like my May basket," she said.

"That's a rose scent. There weren't any roses in your May basket."

"How do you know?" she asked slyly, and for the first time that night, she gave a glimmer of a smile.

"Because roses aren't in bloom on the first of May."

"They are in fairyland."

She was too old for fairies, but maybe she did believe in them. Perhaps when her father was drunk, she escaped into a sort of fairyland. Helen had told me about such things.

"Do the fairies bring you a May basket every year?" I asked.

"Not until we moved here. I think fairies live upstairs."

We smiled at each other, and I reached for the bath towel and held it up, held it above my eyes so that Dorothy would not be self-conscious when she stood up. She dried herself, then wrapped herself in the towel.

"I forgot to fetch your nightgown," I said.

"Oh, I don't have one."

"Then you shall wear one of mine." Dorothy wasn't a whole lot smaller than I. I got out a warm gown that smelled of lavender from the sachet I kept in the drawer with my gloves and underwear and silk stockings, and I held it over Dorothy's head. Then I found sheets and a blanket and made a bed for Dorothy on the cot in my studio.

"When is Miss Helen coming back?" she asked, and suddenly she was very serious and looked frightened again.

"When she finds your mother."

"Is Mama going to die?" Dorothy sat on the cot. Her eyes filled with tears.

"Certainly not," I said, which was foolish. How did I know?

"I hope Dr. Gil finds her. He'll make her well," she said again.

"Do you want to say your prayers and go to bed?" I asked.

"I don't say prayers."

Everyone I had known when I was a girl said prayers. I still did—prayers to keep Peter safe. I didn't know if I believed they would help, but they couldn't hurt. "Let's kneel down and ask God to"—I started to say—"to keep your mother safe." But what if Maud was already dead? So instead, we prayed, "Now I lay me down to sleep . . . ," the prayer I had said as a child.

Dorothy lay down, and I told her she was my good girl and covered her with the blanket and stroked her hair. Then I said, "Dream about clowns." It was what Helen and I had said to each other as children. Father had taken us to the circus, and we had laughed so hard at the clowns that we had almost choked.

I was ready to go to bed, too, but it didn't seem right that Helen should be out searching for Maud while I slept. Rain was coming down hard, and there was so much moisture on the window that I couldn't see outside. I opened the front door and went out onto the porch. The cold felt good after the warmth of the house, which had begun to seem oppressive. I stood there a long time, peering into the darkness in hopes of seeing Helen coming down the street. But there was only the rain and the yellow light from the streetlamp at either end of the block. A big touring car drove slowly down the street, and for a moment I wondered if it might be the Howells' auto, but it went on past, splashing water on the parking, and disappeared into the black. The only sound was the rain and the tinny strains of "Red Wing" on a Victrola far away. The song ended, and the night was silent again. And then I heard our ring on the telephone, two long and one short, and I went inside and took down the receiver, standing on tiptoe to talk into the speaker, because it was mounted high on the wall.

I was sure the caller would be Helen, but it was Gil asking for Helen. "She's gone off," I said. "They took Maud somewhere, and Helen is trying to find her."

"Well, she's here," he said.

"Helen?"

"Maud."

"Where?"

"South High School. In the gymnasium."

"You spoke to her?"

"No, but I'm sure it's Maud. That's why I called. I recognized the coat. It used to be Helen's. Helen told me she gave it to Maud because she didn't need a coat when she had her cape. Then I looked closer and realized it really was Maud."

I remembered the red coat. Helen had bought it when she graduated from nursing school, before she realized she would have to wear a cape. It was warm, and she'd worn it when she was not on duty. But after she saw Maud shivering under an old-fashioned shawl, Helen gave her the coat.

"Is Maud all right?" I asked.

"Of course, everything is George," Gil said acidly, then added, "She wouldn't be here if she were."

"No, of course not."

He apologized. "Sorry to take it out on you, Lute. I'm run ragged. Sometimes I think I'll go off the deep end."

"I understand entirely. I hardly know how you and Helen cope."

"I can't tell how Maud is. She's asleep. Like I said, she's still in her coat, so I don't know if anyone has even examined her. It's chaos. I wonder how she got here."

I explained what had happened and said we hadn't known where she'd been taken. That was why Helen was searching.

"It's a pity Maud's not home. Any place is better than this. A hospital is the easiest place to die, and a high school gymnasium is even worse. This place is like a war zone. But the cab drivers won't pick up influenza victims, and the ambulances take them to wherever's closest."

"I could come, but I don't want to leave Dorothy alone," I said. "Helen should be back before long."

"No, don't come. And don't let Helen come. There's nothing either of you can do. Not tonight, anyway. I'll be here. Moving Maud would only make things worse. I'll keep an eye on her."

We were about to hang up when the front door opened, letting in the smell of rain. "Wait, I think Helen's home," I said and let the receiver dangle and went into the living room.

Helen was soaked, despite the umbrella. She shook her head to tell me she hadn't located Maud.

"Gil is on the telephone," I told her. "He found Maud at South High. He'll look after her tonight. We can go there in the morning and fetch her home some way."

Helen nodded solemnly. "If she's still alive."

"If," I agreed.

Helen went into the hall and spoke to Gil a moment. "Sleep!" she said. "Maybe three and a half hours . . . It can't be helped . . . You be careful, too." She hung up the receiver, went into the kitchen, and poured herself a glass of water.

"Go to bed," I said.

"I will, but it won't do any good." She drank the glass dry and refilled it and stared at the water. "I think I would sell my soul for a night's sleep, but when I lie down, I keep thinking about all those people with the influenza, some of them like Maud, hauled in like firewood and dumped on cots or even on the floor. Nobody knows who they are. They're—what did Peter call them?—little souls. They work hard all their lives, marry, have children, go to work, pay their bills, say their prayers, and where do they end up? Lying in their own filth, calling out in agony, without a single person to hold their hand or wipe their brow. And then they're gone, and the nurses are too busy even to notice they've died. And when they do notice, why, they're glad for another bed, because there are so many other victims waiting. I don't think I shall ever get over it."

I took Helen's hand, and after a moment she looked at me and smiled. "I think Dorothy will be all right alone here for an hour or so in the morning, don't you?" she asked. "She won't mind being by herself if she knows we've gone to see her mother."

"Hasn't Maud anyone who can take care of Dorothy?"

"There's no one. Maud told me she was raised in an orphan asylum. And I doubt very much that Mr. Streeter kept up with family. Maud knew nothing about his background. It's odd, isn't it, marrying a man you know so little about. She told me that when they met, he was so charming and full of life that she couldn't help but fall in love with him."

"Maud never leaves Dorothy alone," I said.

"That's because of Mr. Streeter."

I remembered the bruises and told Helen about them.

She nodded and opened her mouth to say something but stopped. "We'll talk about it tomorrow after we've seen Maud," she said.

Helen did fall asleep, and she slept so late that I had to wake her up. I wouldn't have done so except that I was anxious about Maud. While Helen dressed, I explained to Dorothy that we had to leave her alone for an hour or two, that it wouldn't be wise to take her to the high school, where there were so many influenza victims. "Besides, someone has to make up my studio for your mother. If she's better, we'll bring her home. It would be ever so helpful if you would put fresh sheets and pillowcases on the cot in there. And I think she would feel better if there were pictures she could look at when she got here. Won't you make some for her?" The little girl had been apprehensive about staying alone, and after what Helen had told me the night before, I understood why. If anyone came to the door, I said, she was not to answer it.

Helen and I walked to the trolley stop and stood in the damp, waiting. When the streetcar came along, we climbed on board and sat in the back with the window open, since the newspapers said fresh air was a good way to prevent getting the influenza. Near us a little girl recited in a singsong voice:

"I had a little bird.

"Its name was Enza.

"I opened the window

"And in-flu-enza."

She recited it over and over again until I wanted to put my hands over my ears.

We went into South High and looked at the rows of people lying on cots. Some were moaning, others crying out, and still others not moving at all. "How will we ever find Maud?" I asked.

"We'll find Gil," Helen replied, and we went into a school-room that had been set aside for the doctors and nurses. They slept there when they were too tired to go home. Gil was sitting on a cot and looked exhausted.

Helen asked how he was, and he smiled and said, "Oh, I'm up to the mustard, I suppose. But, God, Helen, do you think we'll ever get a full night's sleep again?"

"The odds are stacked against us now, but the influenza will run its course. Epidemics always do."

He smiled again and said, "You're darb."

Helen asked how Maud was doing. Gil said he had been sleeping and didn't know. He'd told the nurse that Maud was a friend and to be sure to sponge her off when she got hot, which was most of the time. He'd explained that there wasn't much he could do for her except make sure she got plenty of water. "We're trying everything—Dover's powder, Vicks VapoRub, Pierce's Pleasant Purgative Pellets. Some doctors are ordering icy sheets, and others want us to bathe the victims in scalding water. But nothing works. Nothing prevents you from catching it either. One woman told me she got it from listening in on the party line."

We followed him to the gymnasium and down an aisle between two rows of cots. Some of the influenza victims called out to Gil and to Helen, who had on her uniform and cape, and asked for water or medicine. Others simply raised an arm, perhaps to show that they were still alive.

"She's second to the last, on the right," Gil said. I looked at each face and wondered who would live and who would die. When we reached the end of the row, we saw a man lying on the cot Gil had indicated. Gil frowned and said perhaps he'd been confused, that Maud must be in the next row or maybe she'd been moved nearer to the nurses. "The woman in that bed," Gil said to a nurse who was cleaning up a patient covered in vomit. "Where is she?"

The nurse turned around. "Who?"

"The woman who was here last night. She had on a red coat."

"Oh, her." The nurse straightened her mask and said brusquely, "She died this morning."

Helen made arrangements to have Maud buried. There wouldn't be a funeral. The city wouldn't allow them. Then we went home to give Dorothy the awful news.

She was sitting at the dining room table and looked up and smiled when we opened the door. She held up a picture she had drawn of her mother. She saw our somber looks, and her smile faded.

"I'm so sorry, Dorothy," Helen said, taking her hands. "Dr. Gil tried to save her, but she's gone."

Dorothy looked at the picture. "But I drew it for her. See. She looks fine."

"I know," Helen said. "She would have loved it."

"Maybe she's looking down at it now," I said, then thought my words were silly. I sat down next to Dorothy and put my arms around her. Tears ran down her face, and I began to cry, too. We sat there for a long time, the three of us, crying. Helen explained there was nothing Dorothy could have done. Or Gil. Or anybody. It was just a terrible, terrible thing.

At last, Dorothy wiped her face with her dress. "Who will love me now?" she asked in a forlorn voice.

"We will," Helen said, and I knew at that moment that Helen had made the decision to take Dorothy in, to raise her. I agreed entirely. After all, there was no one else, and neither of us could bear sending her to an orphanage.

"You belong with us now," I said, nodding my approval.

It was odd how a decision made in just a fraction of a second would surely change our lives. We would be a family. Perhaps Helen and Gil would take Dorothy when they married. Or Peter and I. We would decide that later. But right now, she belonged to both of us.

Helen took one of Dorothy's hands, and I took the other. Three sisters.

Six

I would remember the details of that day in October forever. It started with the flags—hundreds, thousands, maybe millions of them. They flew from the buildings along Sixteenth Street, big ones hanging from the tops of department stores and office buildings and dime stores, flags displayed in store windows, flags pinned to lapels and worn on hats. Red, white, and blue bunting was strung across doorways and wrapped around light poles. The mannequins in display windows were dressed in patriotic colors. The sky was blue with white clouds hovering over red roofs far off across the city.

I left my drawing board to watch the Liberty Loan parade with the others in the advertising department of Neusteter's. We leaned out the window over the crowd lining Sixteenth Street, which was a sea of patriotic color, the hand-held flags moving back and forth in rhythm. Our cheers blended with those of the crowd below and formed a cacophony with the marching bands that passed beneath the windows. We sang along to the music of flutes and trumpets—"It's a Long Way to Tipperary" and "There's a Long, Long Trail." I thought of the parade as a personal tribute to Peter, who was fighting "Over There." He had been sent off to France not long after he enlisted, and he wrote me long letters from trenches and pockmarked roads. The carnage was awful, he told me, but he had seen God's face in the humanity of some of the soldiers. He hoped he could be their equal.

Florence grabbed my arm and pointed to the governor, who was riding in an open touring car. He passed the Denver Dry Goods next door, and as he reached us the cheers became so deafening, even four stories up, that I put my hands over my ears. A man in front of Gano-Downs Clothing across the street ran up to the governor and handed him a flag, and the governor laughed and tucked it into his hatband. Then he looked up at Florence and me and waved. We waved back.

A dog dashed out in front of the Fort Logan band, and a woman in a blue shirtwaist and red-and-white skirt ran after it, clapping her hands and calling the animal while the band members slowed and fell out of step. She caught the dog, turned, and ducked her head in embarrassment, and I saw that her blue hat had white stars on it.

I said suddenly, "Let's go out."

"We can't just leave. We'll get fired."

"We can take our lunch break." I glanced at Mr. Neil, whose head was partway out the window. "May we go out, sir? We'll skip lunch."

He frowned and gave us an imperious look. "You're not getting any work done hanging out the window. You may go, but you'll have to stay late. Miss Grace is out sick, you know." He leaned forward and said in a low voice, "She was foolish enough to eat Spanish food on Monday. That's why she has the influenza."

Florence and I exchanged looks, and she said, "Oh, the influenza. The papers told us not to worry about it. The mayor said everybody in Denver should go to the parade, and the influenza be damned."

She looked away as our boss frowned at the swear word and said, "Miss Florence, please."

Florence didn't apologize. "I think everybody in the city is watching the parade," she said. Then, after Mr. Neil left, she whispered to me, "The *Rocky Mountain News* said we wouldn't need to be afraid of the influenza if we voted Republican."

"Aw, shucks, I'm a Democrat," I said, laughing. "But I do stay away from Spanish food." For a moment, I thought of Maud and the influenza victims on cots lined up in the South High gymnasium and wondered if I had been foolish to go. Still, I pinned on my hat and pulled on my gloves, and Florence and I went to the elevator in the back of the store. The front elevators were reserved for patrons. The first floor was all but deserted of shoppers, and the clerks were gathered in the doorway watching the parade. We made our way through them and out onto the street. A man in a banner identifying himself as a veteran of the Spanish-American War handed us each a flag, and we waved them as we pressed into the crowd.

"I guess if the influenza's going around, everybody in Denver will get it," Florence said.

"Helen told me not to go out. She said it's too risky." I shrugged. "She claims the government doesn't want people to know how serious the influenza is, because it might be bad for morale. That's silly, because the war is almost over."

"Oh, she's a nurse," Florence said dismissively. "They're

always dour. Besides, the *Post* says the influenza's bypassing Denver."

I wasn't so sure. Just the day before, as Helen and I were sitting on the porch swing, I'd told Helen I thought the influenza wouldn't be as bad as predicted.

"Don't be dull, Lute," Helen told me. "You saw what it was like when we found Maud. It's a terrible thing, and nothing protects you. Older people don't seem to get it much. Most of the victims are young, just our age." She began to shiver and put her arms around herself.

I looked at Helen. Her eyes were deep-set and dark, and she had lost weight in the past week or two. I hadn't seen much of her and knew she'd been overworked caring for her patients.

"Oh, Lute." She turned to me, her eyes filled with tears. "I took care of three children with influenza, one of them a boy who was not right in the head. He was ten years old, but he couldn't talk, and he wore diapers. His mother had to be with him almost every minute." Helen stood and looked out at the dead stalks of hollyhocks that we had failed to trim. "Two of her children died."

"How awful," I said and gave an involuntary shudder. "Was one that poor boy?"

"He was the one who lived."

"Of all of them, he should have gone," I said.

Helen shook her head. "Here's the irony of it. The mother was grateful he lived. She told me that God had spared the child who needed her most." She sat down on the swing and put her head on my shoulder. "You know, Lute, they're saying the influenza could kill as many people as the war."

Still, I decided I wasn't going to worry that day. I wasn't going to worry about Peter either. After all, the parade was a way to honor our doughboys. I hadn't felt so carefree since he went away.

We pushed through the viewers until we stood on the curb, where we cheered with everyone else as a group of women bearing Allied flags marched by, followed by the Olinger Highlander Boys Band. An open car with three wounded soldiers, their heads and arms bandaged, passed us. A man followed them carrying a banner that read "Buy Liberty Bonds." He shouted, "Think of boys like these with their hands cut off. If you don't buy bonds, you're helping the Huns."

Florence elbowed me. "Did you buy one?"

"No, did you?"

She looked sheepish. "I gave in. Mr. Neil said it was unpatriotic not to. After all, the Neusteters themselves bought a hundred-dollar bond."

"They can afford it. They make a hundred times what we do."

"You're still holding out, then?"

"I don't know."

Mr. Neil had called me in just that morning and told me it was time to stop dithering. "You of all people ought to give," he said. "You have a fiancé over there." He paused a moment. "Your fiancé has made a sacrifice, and so must you. Don't you want to end this war, Miss Lucretia?"

Mr. Neil had a son who'd gotten a deferment, and I said, "Please don't tell me about sacrifice, Mr. Neil."

He stared at me until I said, "I'll consider it."

"Well, don't consider it too long. You have until the end of the day. What would our patrons think if they knew our employees were un-American?"

Now, as I stood with Florence, I said, "Mr. Neil threatened to fire me if I didn't buy a Liberty Bond."

"And he means it," she replied.

"It's the principle of the thing."

"Oh, principle. Forget that. It's about money, and you won't have any if you lose your job." Her words were drowned out by the El Jebel Shriners band playing "The Washington Post March." Behind it came a group of Colorado & Southern Railroad employees dressed in grimy overalls and carrying a banner declaring that C&S was "Over the Top" in the bond drive.

"I can't be the only one keeping Neusteter's from going over the top," I said.

Four men carrying a giant stuffed eagle with the banner "Fight or Buy" paused in front of us, and I sighed. Florence was right, of course. I did have a responsibility to purchase a Liberty Bond. I could cut out cigarettes and bring my lunch from home. Shoot, I could afford to buy one even if I didn't sacrifice.

A group of Red Cross volunteers followed Carl Sandel, the seven-foot doorman from Daniels & Fisher, the fancy department store down the street with a tower copied after one in Venice. They carried a white quilt with red crosses stitched on it stretched out in front of them. Maud had volunteered for the Red Cross, and I remembered she had made a square for the quilt. I searched for it, but the women went by too quickly.

Someone threw out red, white, and blue whistles and I

caught one to give to Dorothy, but a boy beside me, dressed in shabby clothes, gave me a hangdog look, so I handed it to him. "Thanks, lady," he said and darted off.

"You're such a jellyfish," Florence said.

We stood arm in arm watching the veterans' fife-and-drum corps, followed by marchers with a dummy of the Kaiser hanging from a stick. An old man with a peg leg hobbled by carrying a poster of a Hun baby-killer with "Treat 'Em Rough" written across it. Finally came the Sells Floto Circus calliope, and at the very end were the White Wings with their push brooms and carts, sweeping up the confetti and flags and streamers and horse droppings, the remnants of the parade.

In minutes, the streets and sidewalks were almost back to normal, except that they were covered with newspapers and taffy wrappers and small flags that had come loose from their sticks. They were trampled by hundreds of feet into red-white-and-blue rubbish.

We made our way back into the store, which was now crowded with patrons. A smartly dressed woman I recognized from the society pages sniffed the perfumes at the cosmetics counter. Another, dressed in furs with a little glass-eyed animal head hanging over her shoulder, although it was too hot to wear fur, rubbed cream on her hands, careful not to smear it onto her diamonds.

A front elevator stood open, and Florence walked into it as boldly as if she'd been a patron. The operator recognized her but only shrugged as he closed the gate, then turned the lever to take us up. "We don't have time to wait for the back elevator. It's so slow," Florence told him. He nodded, as if the three of us were joined in some sort of conspiracy.

"Did you see the parade?" she asked.

"Heard it," he replied. "Couldn't leave."

"Did you buy a Liberty Bond?" I asked.

The man looked startled. "What, you think I'm not a one-hundred-percent American? I'd join up, but I have the arthritis. They won't take me." He stopped the elevator expertly, lining up the cage with the floor so he didn't have to jockey the elevator back and forth. "Fifth floor. China, silver, wedding gifts, and corporate offices," he said, as if we were patrons.

I hurried to my drawing board and opened up the swipe file. This was where we kept advertisements from out-of-town newspapers that we could copy for our own ads. We didn't have time to design each ad from scratch, so we traced the ones that ran in the New York and Chicago newspapers for the layouts. Then Grace, the other artist, and I sketched the figures and clothing we were advertising.

I took out an advertisement of six women in suits. The figures were arranged down the sides and across the bottom of the ad. Once the layout was finished, I would sketch the figures in various poses, thin and tall in hobble skirts, two of them holding muffs. One would stand coyly looking over her shoulder to show the back of her suit. They'd all wear hats, of course. I loved drawing the hats. I'd checked the ones in the millinery department that morning.

Florence came over and peered down at my drawing board. "I love those suits. They cost thirty-five dollars."

"Would you pay that?" I asked.

"Of course not. But our patrons would think thirty-five dollars was cheap." She paused. "Let's say this is an opportunity for remarkable economy." She thought a minute. "We'll call it a Vigorous Underpriced Sale of Our Finer Suits. How could they not get sucked in with that?"

"Only three weeks' salary. That rings the bell," I said, and we giggled until Florence stopped suddenly and I realized Mr. Neil was standing behind us.

"Is something funny?" he asked.

"No, sir," Florence answered.

He nodded, dismissing Florence, who hurried back to her desk. "Miss Lucretia, have you thought about our conversation this morning?"

I glanced at Florence, who mouthed, "Miss *Lucretia*."

The other two women in the room stared at their desks. They worked on promotions and special events, and one of them modeled clothes. Of course, they were listening. It was silent in the room now. No cheers or bands outside, just autos going up and down the street and the creak of wagon wheels and the clop-clop of horses' hooves.

"Yes, sir."

He waited, his arms folded. Finally, he removed his pince-nez and polished the lenses with a white handkerchief that he took from his breast pocket. Without the spectacles, his eyes looked small and watery. He carefully folded the handkerchief and returned it to the pocket of his suit—a seventy-five-dollar suit from Neusteter's men's department. Not a remarkable economy. "And?"

"I suppose I'll buy one."

"That will be fine" was all he said.

I felt foolish then. Peter and thousands of other boys were risking their lives for our country, and I had had some mistaken notion that I was standing up for principle, when in fact I had been nothing more than self-righteous.

I had to work late that afternoon because, as Mr. Neil had pointed out, Grace was out—and because, I thought, he was punishing me for spending so much time at the parade. The streetcars were crowded and I'd had to stand, and then some oaf stomped on my foot. A man stood up to give me his seat, but before I could sit down another woman slipped onto it, grinning at me. She was old and dressed in the uniform of a domestic, and I figured she deserved it more than I did, although she was wearing sensible shoes and I had on fashionable slippers that made my feet hurt.

The streetcar creaked to a stop at every street, waiting while passengers got off and on. The air was stiff with sweating bodies and cigarette smoke, and we were pressed together. I heard a woman mutter "Masher" as she pushed through the passengers, sending an angry glance backward, but I couldn't tell the identity of the masher or whether he had touched her on purpose or had been thrown against her when the streetcar jerked.

I was glad when the streetcar reached my stop. As I climbed down, the man in front of me stared openly at my legs as my hobble skirt hiked up. I stepped in front of him and walked quickly down the street. That was when I saw the soldier writhing on the ground. And when I got home, I found Helen standing over Mr. Streeter's body with an ice pick in her hand.

Seven

A lamp in the living room was on, casting a glow of light in the kitchen. My eyes had adjusted to the dimness, and I could see better now. Helen stood frozen with the ice pick in her upraised hand. Dorothy crouched on the floor, her head turned away. Mr. Streeter lay on his side.

"Helen," I said.

She flinched at her name.

"Is he dead?" There was no blood on the floor.

Helen nodded. She seemed unable to move, so I took the ice pick from her and turned on the faucet in the sink, letting the water wash away the blood. Then I put the pick on the drainboard, where a huge chunk of ice rested. Helen must have been chipping away at it when Mr. Streeter came in.

She knelt beside Dorothy then and cradled her, and I sat on the floor beside them, putting my arms around both of my sisters. I stroked Dorothy's hair, something she liked, but now she was as unresponsive as the linoleum floor.

"It's Mr. Streeter, isn't it?" The man was lying on his side, and I realized I hadn't seen his face.

"He came back. I didn't think he would."

"I thought he was dead."

"He is now," Helen replied with a grim laugh. "I left Dorothy for only a minute, Lute. I thought she'd be fine. She was reading a book. She said it was all right. All I did was go to the drugstore. I had to pick up a prescription for one of my patients. I locked the door." Helen shifted so that she was seated on the floor. "I should have known better. Dorothy said this morning that she'd thought her father was looking in the window last night, but I told her it was only a dream. I think she believed me. That's why she didn't object when I said I had to go out." Helen said again, "I should have known better."

"How could you have known?"

Helen looked up at me, her eyes moist. "I just should have. I know men like that don't stop. Why didn't we think to change the locks?" The basement-door key unlocked the upstairs door, too.

"He must have been waiting for me to leave." Helen put Dorothy's head in her lap.

I hadn't looked closely at Dorothy until then. Now I saw that her dress was torn and her face bruised. "That awful, awful man. She must have been terrified," I said.

"He was . . . well, he was attacking her."

"Oh, Helen, I'm so sorry," I said. "I can't imagine anything more horrible than a man beating his own daughter."

Helen brushed Dorothy's hair from her face. The girl's eyes were open, and she was staring into space. She wasn't listening to us.

"Oh, there is something worse. He wasn't just beating her.

He . . ." She stopped and added, "There was no reason for you to know."

I stared at Helen. "Know what?" I asked.

Helen glanced at Dorothy, who wasn't paying attention. "He . . . well, he treated Dorothy like a wife."

I frowned, not understanding at first. Then slowly I did, and my jaw dropped. "You mean . . . oh my God, Helen . . ." I couldn't put it into words.

Helen nodded.

"That's unspeakable. Are you sure?"

"Maud told me. You remember several weeks ago when Dorothy was sick?"

I remembered.

"Maud was afraid it was a venereal disease. She asked me to examine Dorothy. I asked how that could be, and she admitted what had been going on."

"She knew, and she didn't stop him?"

"She was terrified of him. He'd threatened to kill her if she told or if she tried to take Dorothy and leave. She believed him. With good reason."

"And then he just disappeared?"

"You could say that." Helen thought a minute. "I told him to get out, that if he ever came back, I would turn him over to the police."

"He could have killed you."

Helen shrugged. "I said Maud had put it all down in a letter that I'd stored in our safety deposit box. I said if anything happened to Maud or me, Gil would give it to the police."

"We don't have a safety deposit box," I said.

Helen shrugged again.

Dorothy stirred then. Helen said, "We have to take care of Dorothy first. Then we'll decide what to do with Mr. Streeter."

"Shouldn't we call the police?"

"I'm not sure that's a good idea." She helped Dorothy stand and said, "Let's get you out of your clothes, and Lutie will run you a nice bath."

I went into the bathroom and turned on the taps in the tub, then took out a bar of scented soap and set a fresh towel on the stool. "Helen can help you," I said when Dorothy came into the bathroom dressed only in her underwear. She did not want to take off her clothes in front of me. "Since she's a nurse, Helen's used to bathing people."

I went into the living room and waited until Helen came out of the bathroom, telling me Dorothy would be more comfortable by herself. Dorothy was embarrassed to have anyone look at her, even Helen. I understood. Helen was like that, too.

"Tell me what happened," I said.

She picked up a pillow and plucked at it, then threw it across the room. "The vile man tried to rape her. Here. In our house. The poor thing was putting up an awful fight. If I hadn't walked in, he would have done it. Then he would have taken her away."

"So you stabbed him?"

Helen stared at me a long time. Finally, she asked, "Is it that obvious?"

"I don't think he fell on the ice pick," I replied, then bit my lip. It sounded as if I were trying to make light of death.

"No, of course he didn't. I'd been chipping ice, and the ice pick was lying on the drainboard. I'd left it there when I went to the drugstore. I picked it up and stabbed him. I didn't even think about it. I just did it."

"Well, thank God you did. It's what I would have done, what anyone would have done." Then I added, "Even Peter."

"Yes, anyone would have done it. Gil, too," Helen said. She put her head on my shoulder and cried. She didn't make a sound, but I knew she was crying because I could feel her head shake and the dampness of her tears on my neck.

"Don't you think we should call the police now?" I asked.

There was a look of horror on Helen's face when she raised her head. "Oh no, Lute. We can't."

"You saved Dorothy from being attacked."

"You don't understand," Helen said.

"Understand what?"

Helen swallowed a couple of times and looked away. I thought she would explain. Instead, she went to help Dorothy get ready for bed.

"Would you like Lutie to read to you?" Helen asked Dorothy when I came to check on them. "Her voice is ever so much nicer than mine." I had read to Dorothy almost every night since she'd been with us.

"Yes," she said. Her face lit up with a smile, and I did not understand how she could look so angelic after the awful things that had been done to her.

"Reading will make you sleepy," Helen said, picking up *Black Beauty* from the nightstand and handing it to me.

I couldn't understand why Helen was stalling. We should contact the police right away. Still, she always knew best. So

I sat down on the edge of the bed and began to read, while Dorothy reached under the bed and took out the Whitman's candy box where she kept her treasures. A beau had bought the chocolates for me, and I'd given the box to Dorothy. She loved the picture on the top of the girl with long blond hair with stars in it. I glanced over and saw that her mother's wedding ring was in the box along with Maud's blue bead necklace. After a time, she shut the box and set it on the table beside her, then closed her eyes.

A few pages later, Helen said, "She's asleep." I pulled the covers over Dorothy and kissed her good-night. Then Helen leaned over her and whispered, "Dream about clowns."

"Helen, we have to call the police," I said after we closed the door to Dorothy's room. "We can't just leave a dead body on the kitchen floor."

"I know that," Helen responded. She went into the kitchen and pulled the shades. Then she turned on the overhead light, and I winced. The body was still crumpled up on the floor, of course, but it was no longer just a dark shape. It was a man I knew. I saw his face, unshaven, and a scar on his nose from a knife fight Maud had told us about. There was white in his hair that I'd never noticed. His hands were curled into fists, and I thought he had made them to hit Helen. Or Dorothy. His clothes were old and dirty, as if he'd been sleeping in them. He'd always been clean when he lived in the basement. Maud did their laundry with ours each week.

"We have to call the police," I said again.

"We can't. Think what it would do to Dorothy if she had

to tell in court what her father did to her. She's what we call traumatized. She may even have blocked it out of her mind."

"But *you* could tell the police what happened."

"What if they didn't believe me? The police would think I killed him so that we could keep Dorothy. After all, he had a right to her. And do you think any court would let us adopt her after they learned I killed her father? She'd be sent to some orphan asylum or put to work in a sweatshop. She deserves better."

"She deserves us," I said.

"The police might charge me with murder," Helen said.

"Murder? Oh, Helen, they wouldn't. Anybody who knows you knows you'd never hurt anyone."

"Wouldn't I? Didn't you just now say I did?"

"Then what do we do with him?"

"I guess we bury him someplace."

"My goodness, Helen." I almost laughed. "Where, in the backyard? Or do we put him in an auto and drive out to the prairie and dig a hole? Two girls digging a grave. It would take days. And we don't even own a car."

"I suppose we could dump him somewhere. In the park, maybe."

I thought for a moment, then nodded. "That's exactly what we'll do," I said. "It's a perfectly fine idea. On the way home, I saw a soldier die just down the street. I was going to tell you, but I forgot all about it when I saw Mr. Streeter. People said the soldier had the influenza, and they just left his body there. Someone said the death wagon would pick him up."

Helen thought that over, then nodded her approval. "It's

a fine idea, Lute. We'll put a sign on him that says 'influenza victim.' We'll take his body to that vacant lot down the street."

Then I considered how Mr. Streeter had died. "Won't somebody see the wound from the ice pick?"

"Maybe not. They don't examine the victims very carefully. There isn't much blood. We can clean it off and button his coat."

"We'll put him in the wheelbarrow. Do you think the two of us could move him?"

"We don't have any choice, do we?"

Helen and I knelt beside Mr. Streeter, who gave off a foul odor. I wondered if it was his own smell or the smell of death. I couldn't bring myself to touch him, so Helen took over and cleaned the little bit of blood off his chest. She was buttoning his coat when we heard a knock on the front door.

"The police," I said. "They know."

"Of course they don't." But she wasn't so sure. "Turn out the light. If it is the police, we'll have to tell them what really happened. Maybe they know about him and they'll be glad to be rid of him."

"What if it's one of Mr. Streeter's friends?" I went to the front window and moved the curtains aside so that I could peer out. An automobile I had noticed on my way home was still there, and a man stood on the porch. He was tall, and he had a blue muffler around his neck. I breathed a sigh of relief and opened the door. "Hello, Gil."

From the kitchen, Helen said, "Thank God."

"Helen up? I wouldn't have stopped, but I saw the lights on. I hope I didn't wake you."

"No, I'm glad you're here. We need help. Something terrible has happened."

"Helen doesn't have the influenza?"

"Oh, no," I said quickly. "It's Mr. Streeter, and he's dead. He tried to attack Dorothy." I swallowed, wondering if I should tell Gil what happened. But he was sure to find out. "Helen killed him."

"She what?"

"To save Dorothy. She was very brave."

"Not so brave," Helen said from the doorway. "Just frightened."

Gil went past us into the kitchen and knelt down beside Mr. Streeter's body, putting his ear to the man's chest, then taking his pulse. "He's dead all right. Have you called the police?"

Helen and I exchanged glances. "We're not going to," I said. "We're going to take him down the street and leave him in a vacant lot. Whoever finds him will think he died of the influenza. Don't you think it's a swell idea?"

Gil looked shocked. "That's against the law, and there would be consequences if you were caught." He thought a moment. "But it might be best for Dorothy. I don't think she would bear up under police questioning."

"You know about Mr. Streeter and Dorothy?" I asked.

He glanced at Helen, who said, "I had to tell him."

"You told him and not me?"

Helen put her hand on my arm. "I had to. Mr. Streeter just laughed when I threatened him. Gil's a man and a doctor, so Mr. Streeter was wary of him. I told Gil what was going on, and Gil threatened Mr. Streeter, saying he knew about the incest and would tell the police if he didn't get out. Gil was the one who said the proof was in our safety deposit box. I didn't tell you, Lutie, because, well, why should you know about such things?"

We wrapped Mr. Streeter's body in an old tarp and carried him to the front door. We'd wait until it was very dark and the porch lights on the street were out before we moved him. I fixed us tea, but there was no place to sit. We didn't want to be in the living room with the dead body, nor in the kitchen, where there were a few blood spatters. So we put on our coats and went out the front door and sat on the stoop. We sat there for a long time, listening to dogs barking and cars driving down the street. We smoked cigarettes, and Gil said he wished he had a flask. It got quiet and the porch lights went out one by one. Someone started the automobile and drove off. Gil held up his watch so that he could read the hour in the moonlight. "Nearly midnight. I think that's time enough. Let's go."

Helen agreed to stay with Dorothy. So Gil and I loaded the body into the wheelbarrow and took it across the street and down to the vacant lot. We left it near the sidewalk, where someone would see it. I pinned the slip of paper saying "influenza victim" to Mr. Streeter's coat.

"They don't look very closely at the bodies," Gil said to reassure me. "Nobody wants to touch them for fear of catching the influenza. Sometimes they just pile the bodies up like cordwood—the ones they can't identify, at any rate."

We walked back to the house, looking up and down the street, but there were no pedestrians, no cars. To our surprise,

Helen was sitting in the living room with Dorothy on her lap. "She couldn't sleep," Helen explained. "Nightmares."

Dorothy said in a quiet voice, "Helen told me you took my father away."

"He'll never hurt you again," I said.

"You won't tell, will you? What happened to him. You won't tell?"

"Never."

"Me neither."

"If anyone asks, we'll say we haven't seen him since before your mother died."

Dorothy nodded solemnly.

Eight

I slept poorly that night. I dozed off, then awoke at every sound and stared at the clock until I slept for a few minutes again. Once, I got up to check on Dorothy. She was restless, moaning. Helen was awake, however. The light was on in her room, but then, it always was. Neither she nor Dorothy could sleep in the dark. I heard her in the kitchen and went there and found her in her nightdress scrubbing the floor.

"There was blood," she said, although I had wiped it up the night before. "I had to get it out." She had scrubbed the linoleum so hard that it was scratched and faded where Mr. Streeter's body had lain.

"There's no blood now," I told her, taking the scrub brush out of her hand and helping her stand. I took the bucket of dirty water and poured it down the sink, then ran a flour sack towel over the floor to mop up the water Helen had spilled. "You ought to try to sleep, Helen. You won't be any good to your patients if you're dead on your feet." I instantly regretted saying the word "dead," but Helen didn't seem to catch it.

"I know, but I can't sleep, Lutie. I can't get Mr. Streeter out of my mind."

"I know how horrid it is for you. Taking a life, it goes against everything you believe. No wonder you're distraught."

She stared at me a moment, letting my words sink in. "It's not just Mr. Streeter's death," she replied, wringing out the edge of her nightdress, which had gotten wet. "I keep seeing him attacking Dorothy. I see it over and over again. I can't get rid of the image of what he did to that poor, poor girl."

"He was beastly. I'm glad he's dead. You were so brave you ought to get a medal."

Helen began to shake, and I put my arms around her. "You couldn't have done anything else." I eased Helen away from the kitchen, into the living room.

"It's just that it brings everything back," she said.

"What?"

Helen considered her words. "Oh, everything I've seen and heard as a nurse. It makes me think how wretched men can be."

"Of course they can be. But there are good ones, too. Look at Gil—and Peter." Gil was indeed a fine man, as fine as Peter. He was strong and thoughtful and loving. He adored my sister, although she seemed in no hurry to marry. I thought that was because she cared so much about her career and was afraid she would have to give it up.

Helen nodded. She sat down on the davenport. "Go back to bed, Lute. I'm going to sit here a minute."

I went to the linen closet and took out a throw I had made from velvet scraps. They were soft and silky, and the fabric would feel warm against Helen's skin. I lifted Helen's feet and put them on the couch, then spread the throw over her. "Try to sleep, dear," I said, then added, "Dream about clowns."

"You, too," she said and smiled at me.

I went into my room and closed the door to keep out the light from the other rooms and thought about Helen. Ever since we were little girls, she had looked out for me. Now perhaps it was my turn to look out for her. And for Dorothy. I hated Mr. Streeter then, not just for what he'd done to Dorothy but for making Helen stab him. She was sweet and sensitive, and she would always bear the sorrow of taking a man's life.

I woke in the morning realizing how much I wanted Peter. I wished I could tell him what had happened. I hadn't considered until he went away how strong he was, how reassuring, how full of goodness. Peter would make me feel better. But of course, I couldn't put into a letter that my sister had killed Mr. Streeter. I'd tell him when he came home. Or maybe I wouldn't.

There had been a little rain during the night, and I awoke to the morning sun shining in my room. When I went to the window, I saw the light glinting off raindrops scattered on yellow and crimson leaves. How could there be such a beautiful day after the wretched night?

I turned on the bedroom light, and there on my bureau was a letter from Peter. Helen must have left it there the previous day and I hadn't noticed it. I slid my fingernail under the flap of the envelope and took out the letter, which was written on a scrap of cheap newsprint—so different from the thick writing paper on which Peter had written notes that accompanied the corsages or boxes of chocolates he gave me. I suppose he was lucky to get even that.

I held the paper to my nose, hoping it contained Peter's smell, but it had no smell at all. The letter was written in pencil and was dirty and wrinkled. I smoothed it with my hand before I began to read.

Dearest Lute,

The latrine rumor is that we will move out within the hour, so I have only minutes to write. I suppose I should try to catch a few winks instead, but thinking you might be sitting on the porch on one of Denver's beautiful fall days reading this calms me. I picture you in the gray suit you wore to the station and how it picked up the gray in your eyes. I wish you would send me a photograph of you in that suit. Even a snapshot would do. Thinking of you that way makes it easy for me to share my thoughts with you. But then, I have always been able to tell you what I am thinking and hoping. I am so blessed. I've always known that, but it is even clearer to me now. There are men here with no girls, no families, who receive no letters, who have no one to come home to. I try to tell them that what came before this war doesn't matter, that they can go home and find a girl, start a family, and have children they will love as no one has loved them. Most think I am simple. But last week, a young soldier who had grown up in an orphanage told me he had thought over what I said. "I guess it matters where I go from here," he told me. And then he added, "I ain't never had nobody that cared about me except you." He turned away to hide his embarrassment. Yesterday, I saw him shove another soldier out of the path of a bullet. He might have been killed, but both were all right, and later they were sharing a bottle of wine. When he saw me, he held up the bottle and invited me to join them.

It's a little thing, Lute, and what I said to him may have played no part at all in his bravery. I certainly do not claim credit. If there is credit, it belongs to God for bringing me here. You see, I believe that things happen for a reason. Even bad things. Especially bad things. God challenges us to rise above them. Nothing happens without a purpose, and nothing happens that we cannot overcome. God loves us so that we can love others.

Well, now, I sound like those preachers your sister doesn't like. And maybe one of those preachers you don't care to marry. But I want to say that if something happens to me, you will know there was a reason I lived. Of course, I don't plan to let anything happen. Someday when we are old, we will read these letters together and find them silly.

I hear the guns far away. My best love to you, dearest Lute. From your soldier boy

I stared at the letter for a long time, thinking there was something eerie in its message, arriving as it did when I needed Peter and his support. I wished again I could write and tell him what had happened the night before and how he had comforted me, but of course I couldn't. Only Helen and Gil, Dorothy and I could know.

I placed the letter in the shoe box where I kept every letter and note that Peter had ever written to me. Then, quietly, so I wouldn't wake Helen or Dorothy, I opened my bedroom door. To my surprise, I saw Dorothy sitting at the dining room table, drawing a picture.

She looked up at me, her eyes shining. "You can't see it till it's finished," she said. "Almost done."

"What are you drawing?" My box of pencils was on the table, the pad of paper in front of it. We had turned my studio into Dorothy's bedroom, and she must have found the art supplies in the closet there.

"I'm not telling." She put her arm around the picture so that I couldn't see it. "Go away. I'll tell you when it's done."

The door to Helen's room was ajar, and I slipped inside. Helen was still weary, her face gray, but she was dressed in her uniform.

"Did you sleep?" I asked.

"A little."

That meant most likely not. "Did you check the vacant lot?"

Helen shook her head. "I haven't been out. And Gil said it's best we don't go anywhere near the lot. He'll walk by later. If the body isn't picked up today, I'll call from a pay telephone."

"Did you know that Dorothy's up? She's downstairs drawing a picture. She's as happy as a clam. I don't get it. Doesn't she remember last night?"

"Maybe she doesn't."

"Of course she does. How could she not?"

Helen went to the mirror and pinned on her cap. "The mind plays tricks on you, Lute. Some people actually don't remember the terrible things that happen to them. Others, it's as if they're two persons—one tormented, the other as happy as Dorothy is right now. They can't deal with what's happened, so they develop the ability to lock the bad thing away in some corner of their minds. I think it must be the body's way of protecting you against things you can't handle. Maybe Dorothy is like that. You saw how she was last night. She'll curl up and go almost catatonic. It's as if things are so bad she's gone off into another world. She's done that other times. You remember the night she came upstairs to hide from her father and curled up on the floor? I think when her father did . . . well, you know . . . her mind simply left her body. That must be what happened after her father's attack last night."

"You mean she doesn't remember it at all?"

"My guess is she does, but she keeps herself from thinking about it. Doctors are just beginning to understand how the mind works. I've read about it, and I've even had patients who seem to fit whatever category this is. But I'm only guessing." She adjusted her cap in the mirror and turned back to me. "The thing is, it comes and goes. You heard her last night, crying out in her sleep. One minute a person can be normal, and the next they're caught in an overwhelming depression."

"Then do we deny what she saw in the kitchen?"

"No, that would only make it worse for her. I believe we should let Dorothy take the lead. If she wants to talk about it, then we do. But we let her bring it up. And in the meantime, we try to carry on as if everything were normal." Helen closed her eyes a minute. "At least, I think that's what we do. I wish I knew more about it. Maybe Gil does. I'll ask him."

"Finished!" Dorothy called.

When Helen and I went to the dining room, Dorothy stood in front of the table, the back of the picture pressed against her chest.

"Surprise!" she said, and turned the picture around.

In the center of the picture was a girl with bright yellow hair. Two women were on either side of her, one with curly yellow hair and the other whose hair was straight and black.

"Why, Dorothy, it's the three of us," Helen said.

I looked at the picture critically. All three were smiling. Dorothy clearly had artistic talent, because the figures stood close together and there was a sense of affection, of connection. At the bottom of the page Dorothy had written "My family."

Helen and I each put an arm around Dorothy until we were very like the figures in the picture.

Both Helen and I had to go to work that day. I thought about calling in sick, telling Mr. Neil that I was afraid I'd caught the influenza. But Dorothy wanted to go to school and said she didn't mind coming home to an empty house. Helen shrugged. Dorothy had been doing this since her mother died, and if she was all right with it, so were we.

"I work only a half day tomorrow because it's Saturday," I said to Dorothy. "So you can take the streetcar downtown at noon and meet me after work. We'll have lunch and go shopping for a coat. You'll need one for winter."

Helen frowned, and I thought she was afraid we might expose ourselves to the influenza. Maybe we would, but it was important that Dorothy get away from the house and have a good time.

On Saturday, Dorothy met me in front of Neusteter's. Then we went to the dime store and sat at the lunch counter, Dorothy swiveling back and forth on her stool as she read the menu posted on the wall. We both ordered hot dogs. Afterward we walked up the street, Dorothy lagging behind a little to stare into store windows the way I once had with Peter. Remembering our days together made me a little sad, and I took Dorothy's hand. She might have been sad, too, because she and her mother used to take walks through downtown as well. At Neusteter's, we stopped to study a woman's ensemble in the window. I thought how I would sketch it so that the skirt was a little longer and the jacket more slimming. A wide-brimmed hat with a feather would look better than the cloche the mannequin wore in the window.

We took the elevator to the girls' department at the Denver Dry Goods, where Dorothy tried on half-a-dozen coats.

"Which one does your daughter like best?" a clerk asked me.

"She's not my daughter," I said, and Dorothy glanced up at me, a look of disappointment on her face. "She's my sister," I added quickly.

Dorothy smiled, then pointed to an orange coat.

"Orange?" I asked. "Like the davenport."

She nodded. "You told me once it's your favorite color. I like it, too. It makes me feel warm. And safe."

I paid the clerk, and she started to wrap up the coat in brown paper.

"Can't I wear it?" Dorothy asked.

"Of course," I told her and helped her take off the old one. It was shabby, and my finger poked a hole in the thin fabric. "Perhaps somebody can use it," I said, handing it to the clerk. Then I saw a tiny muff made of white rabbit fur and asked, "Would you like that?"

Dorothy's eyes were wide. "Really, Lutie?"

"We'll take that, too," I said, thinking how soft and warm it would feel against Dorothy's cheek.

The clerk handed it to Dorothy, who clutched it in both hands.

She would need other clothes, and I thought about taking her to the fabric department, where we could pick out material and patterns, but then decided I'd save that for another Saturday.

I should have taken Dorothy home then. I wished later that I had. There were signs on the street warning about the influenza, and the stores were all but deserted. It was foolish of me, but I thought that with so few people around, we were safe. It had been a wonderful afternoon, and I wanted to top it off by going to Baur's. So we walked down Sixteenth Street to the old ice cream parlor.

"Peter took me here on our first date," I told her.

"Mama brought me here when I was little," Dorothy said.

"Your father, too?" I asked, knowing I shouldn't bring him up. But I was curious.

"Oh, yes. Sometimes he was nice."

"When did he change?" I asked.

"Change what?" she asked, and I knew he had slipped out of her mind and I should not question her further.

We sat down at the marble counter, which was the color of strawberry ice cream, and I asked Dorothy what she wanted.

"What do they have?"

"Ice cream, sodas, sundaes with any kind of topping you want."

Dorothy watched the soda jerk make a concoction with ice cream and fudge sauce, whipped cream, and a cherry on top and pointed to it. "That," she said.

The boy told her to choose the flavor of ice cream and asked if she wanted fudge or chocolate sauce. Dorothy watched him wide-eyed, and when he was done, she whispered to me, "Do you think I could have two cherries?"

The soda jerk heard her and added a second cherry. Then a third. With a flourish, he set the sundae in front of her, and I told her to go ahead and eat it before the ice cream melted. While the boy made my soda, I glanced at the women reflected in the mirror in front of us, appraising their clothes, wondering whether the dresses had come from Neusteter's. Dorothy ate her ice cream, carefully circling the cherries, saving them for last.

She watched as the boy made my soda. She glanced in the mirror, which ran the length of the soda fountain and reflected most of restaurant and its painted beams and plaster cherubs. She smiled at me in the mirror, then rose up so she could see her new coat and smiled at herself. She read out loud the signs pasted on the mirror—"Coca-Cola, five cents" and "Baur's, the Original Ice Cream Soda, ten cents"—then turned her head so she could see the back of the restaurant. Suddenly her smile faded and she froze, dropping her spoon, which clattered to the floor.

"What is it?" I asked as the soda jerk set down a clean spoon in front of Dorothy.

"That man," she whispered, clutching my arm.

I didn't turn around but looked in the mirror and spotted a

black-haired man with broad shoulders and a checkered coat. He looked a little like Mr. Streeter and seemed to be staring at Dorothy. He glanced at me, then at Dorothy.

"Everything's all right, Dorothy. That's not your father. You can finish your ice cream. You haven't eaten the cherries." I put a straw into my soda and took a sip.

Dorothy turned and stared at the man, then began shaking so hard that I had to put my arm around her. "I don't want any more. Can we go?" she asked. "Right now, please?"

"Of course," I said. I threw money onto the counter and the two of us hurried outside. Dorothy clutched her muff, her knuckles white.

"That wasn't your father," I told her again.

"I know." Suddenly she leaned over the gutter and vomited. I held her until she was finished, then wiped her mouth with a handkerchief. I wondered how long it would be before images of her father would stop making Dorothy sick. Maybe never.

She went slack against me and I had to hold her up. Then she began to cry. "You won't leave me like Mama did, will you?" she asked. "Please, you won't go away? You won't let anybody have me?"

"Of course not," I told her. I would kill to protect Dorothy. So would Helen. In fact, she already had.

When we reached home, Helen was waiting for us. She admired Dorothy's new coat and muff, but I could tell she was anxious about something. When Dorothy went to the closet to hang up her coat, Helen whispered, "Gil telephoned. He had to be careful what he said, of course, in case the operator or someone on the party line was listening, but I knew what he meant. Mr. Streeter's body is gone."

"Then it's over," I said.

Helen shook her head. "It will never be over, not for Dorothy." She added, "And not for me, either."

Nine

One Sunday afternoon, Dorothy and I went to tea at the Howell mansion. Helen had been invited, too, but with the epidemic, she could not take time off for something so frivolous.

"I don't know if it's wise for you to take Dorothy on the streetcar again. The influenza has gotten so awful. We shouldn't expose her," Helen told me. "And the men on the streetcar might frighten her."

"But she knows her father is dead. I don't understand why she's so afraid of men."

"Wouldn't you be if your father had done to you what Mr. Streeter did?"

"I can't even imagine it." Then I told her that Mrs. Howell was sending the chauffeur to pick us up.

Later that day, I gave Dorothy a dress I had made for her from fabric in my stash. Then I helped her into her new orange coat and handed her the fur muff. We waited on the steps until a black touring car stopped in front of our house.

The Howells' Grant Street mansion had been a showplace when it was built forty years before. Its neighborhood, Capitol Hill, had been Denver's most prestigious back then, and it was almost as desirable now. When we had first moved to Denver,

Helen and I had walked up and down the streets, speculating on who lived in the houses. And now I was engaged to a man who had grown up in one. The house had been built by a judge and his wife who were later involved in a scandal. The wife had been sent off to an asylum, and the husband had wanted to be rid of the mansion. The Howells had not planned to live in such an elegant house, but they bought it for a good price. At least, that's what Peter had told me.

It was as fine a house as I had ever visited, more elegant and less gaudy than the showy mansions around it. Dorothy stopped and gazed at it in awe. "It's as big as a hotel. Did Mr. Howell live here all by himself?" she asked. I had told Dorothy that she should call Peter by his first name, since he would be her brother-in-law one day. But she kept forgetting, just as she sometimes forgot and called Helen and me Miss Helen and Miss Lutie.

"He lived here with his parents, and he has two sisters who grew up here, too."

"It's swell," she said, then "It's swellegant," imitating me.

"It is that, all right." Since Peter left, I had been invited here several times for dinner. "Wait till you see inside." When we reached the door, George, the butler, was waiting for us.

"Good day, Miss Hite." He turned to Dorothy. "I have not had the pleasure of meeting this young lady."

"This is Miss Dorothy Streeter . . . or rather, Dorothy Hite. She's my new sister. That is, she will be before long."

"Welcome, Miss Dorothy," he said formally.

Dorothy took a step backward and looked at me uneasily. She didn't like it when men paid attention to her.

"Judge and Mrs. Howell are waiting for you in the library."

George helped me off with my coat, while Dorothy slipped out of hers by herself. George took the coats and reached for Dorothy's muff, but she held it back and whispered to me, "He won't keep it, will he?"

"You can trust him. He always gives me back my purse." Then I said to George, "Guard it with your life."

"A sacred trust," he intoned.

He handed the wraps to a maid, then announced us to the Howells. Judge Howell rose and stood by the fireplace. The room was dark, gloomy even, with its dark paneled walls and leatherbound books. Still, it was cozy, with a fire just dying down and yellow light coming through the parchment shades of lamps. The wooden shutters were partially open, and there were slanted streaks of sunlight on the walls.

Mrs. Howell stepped forward, a hand outstretched to each of us. "Lucretia, dear, what a blessing you are to us. And you must be Dorothy." She clasped our hands. "I have been anxious to meet you ever since Lucretia told me you had come to live with her." She glanced at her husband. "The judge must go to the courthouse, but he waited to greet you."

Judge Howell walked toward me and inclined his head. Now that I knew him a bit better, I liked him very much.

"This is her ward, Dorothy." Mrs. Howell leaned down and whispered to Dorothy, "Judge Howell is not nearly as fierce as he looks. In fact, you must think of him as a pussycat."

"Now, Anne," he said, amused. "It would never do for the people who come through my courtroom to hear you say that."

Dorothy edged toward me. "He's Peter's father," I whispered to put her at ease. "He's all right."

Mrs. Howell seemed to notice Dorothy's reticence. "Well, perhaps an alley cat then. He can get very tough with bad people, Dorothy."

Dorothy was startled.

"He's a judge," Mrs. Howell explained. "He puts people in jail."

"People who kill people?" Dorothy asked.

"Yes," Mrs. Howell replied. "But you needn't worry. He loves little girls. We have two of our own, you see, but they're all grown up. That is why I am very glad you will be part of our family when Lucretia marries Peter. We have missed having a little girl around."

"I must be going," Judge Howell said, taking his gold watch from his vest pocket and flicking it open. The watch was attached to his vest by a heavy gold chain. "You would think that crime would drop off with the influenza, that pickpockets and mashers and other assorted lowlifes would stay home, but it is as rampant as ever. In fact, the influenza has spawned its own wave of crime. You would not believe what people blame on it. There was a case just this week in which two men in influenza masks held up a grocery store. They took the money and walked brazenly down the street, their masks covering their identities."

"How were they caught?" Mrs. Howell asked.

"They stopped at a speakeasy, one of those saloons that closed because of Prohibition and reopened the next day as a 'candy store.' Of course, the men had to take off their masks to drink. The grocery store owner came in for a toddy himself and saw them." The judge chuckled. "Next somebody will blame the influenza for murder. In fact, I am told that a man was murdered this week and someone put a sign on him that read 'influenza victim.'" He laughed, but I swallowed hard and felt Dorothy tighten against me. "Never worry, dear. That one did not get by the police. There was a bullet hole through his temple. Half of his head had been shot off."

I gasped, and Mrs. Howell said, "You must not frighten Lucretia with such things."

"It's all right." I glanced at Dorothy, who was staring at the floor.

The judge bade us good-day, and as he left the room, he squeezed his wife's arm and kissed her cheek. I wondered if Peter would treat me with such affection after so many years of marriage.

When her husband was gone, Mrs. Howell led us into a small parlor that was bright with sunlight. "The library is a perfectly nice room, but this is so much more pleasant, and it doesn't smell of cigars," she said.

The furniture in the room was old, and it was very fine, covered with damask that was expensive but a little worn. Yellow satin draperies hung from gilt cornices. A large fern was set on a stand in the window, and hothouse flowers were arranged in a blue bowl on a table that was covered by an orange silk shawl.

"Orange is my favorite color," Mrs. Howell said.

"Mine and Lutie's, too," Dorothy told her, and I had a feeling Mrs. Howell had glimpsed Dorothy's orange coat through the window.

Dorothy looked around the room. Above the carved marble mantel was a painting of a little girl in white dress with a blue sash kneeling in a garden. I thought it trite, but Dorothy went to the fireplace and stared at it.

"Won't she get her dress dirty?" she asked, and Mrs. Howell laughed.

"I suppose she would at that. Do you think a bouquet of flowers is worth a dirty dress?"

"Maybe." Dorothy stared at the painting until George came into the room with a tea tray.

Mrs. Howell poured tea, then handed a cup to each of us and told Dorothy she could have as many cakes as she liked. Dorothy reached for the most elaborate one, a tiny square confection with a flower made of icing on top, and plopped it whole into her mouth. Then she picked up her teacup, but the handle was small and delicate, and the cup tipped, spilling the tea on her dress. She looked horrified.

Mrs. Howell said, "Those silly cups. The girls were always spilling their tea. I can barely hold on to one myself." She rang a bell, and when George entered the room, she asked him to send Molly, one of the maids, to help Dorothy clean her dress. Molly came in, and Mrs. Howell told her to find a dress that Evelyn, one of Peter's sisters, had worn as a girl—Evelyn's dresses were in a trunk in the attic, she said. When Dorothy had changed, Molly could wash off the tea stain.

After Dorothy was gone and the door closed, Mrs. Howell said, "I am very glad that we have a moment alone." She studied me for a few seconds. "It's quite all right if you want to smoke, dear. I know young women do so today."

"You won't mind?" I asked, reaching into my purse for my cigarette case. It was gold and ivory with my initials on it. I had bought it with my employee discount at Neusteter's.

Mrs. Howell opened a drawer in the table beside her and took out a thin porcelain ashtray shaped like a seashell, so small it would hold only one or two cigarette butts. Then she asked me, "Have you an extra I might have?"

I looked at her in surprise. "An extra cigarette?"

"Yes, dear. Does it shock you? It does not seem so depraved to smoke in front of family, and you are family."

I was pleased with the acknowledgment and held out my open cigarette case. Then I lighted her cigarette and my own. She held the cigarette between two fingers and placed it in the center of her mouth. She puffed the way people do when they first start smoking and did not inhale.

We watched the smoke curl in front of us for a minute, then Mrs. Howell said, "So you and your sister are serious about taking on the girl yourselves."

Did she disapprove? I said rather starchily, "Yes."

"That is admirable. An orphanage is a frightening place for such a sweet child."

I told her that Dorothy did not yet understand what it meant to be our sister. She had offered to do the laundry—she had helped her mother with it before—to pay for rent. She had even mentioned quitting school, an idea we had quickly rebuffed.

"Does she have no family?" Mrs. Howell asked.

"She has a father."

"I thought so. I recall Peter saying something about her parents. Does her father not want her, then?"

"We don't know where he is. And if we did, we wouldn't let him take her. He is . . ." I thought for a moment. I could not tell Mrs. Howell what Mr. Streeter had done. She would be even more shocked to learn about such things than I was. She probably wouldn't believe it. "He's gummy." And then in case she did not understand the slang, I added, "Disgusting."

"Did he beat her?"

"Yes." I did not go on.

"Then of course you must not let him have her. I know more about the evil of men than you might expect. The judge tells me about his cases. He is very shrewd, and he sees right through criminals. You would be surprised at how many people confess their crimes when they stand before him. I have heard a number of stories myself, because I was one of the founders of the Presbyterian orphan's home."

But not a story like Dorothy's, I thought.

"Have you had the legal work done?"

"We haven't started. In fact, we haven't even thought about it."

"You must begin at once. If her father returns, he could cause trouble. After all, he does have the right to her. And there could be relatives who would want her. Shall I speak to Judge Howell about it? He will know the best attorney to engage."

I couldn't very well tell her that Mr. Streeter wouldn't be coming around anymore. Remembering him made me feel a little sick. What would Judge Howell think if he knew Helen was a murderer? She could end up standing in front of him in a courtroom. And what would Mrs. Howell think if she knew her future daughter-in-law had helped dispose of the dead man? "That is a very good idea. I would be grateful," I said.

Mrs. Howell coughed a little and waved away the smoke in front of her. Then she stubbed out the half-smoked cigarette. It was sweet of her to try smoking just to make me feel comfortable. Without looking at me, for I think she was a little embarrassed at her smoking failure, she picked up her tea, holding the cup gracefully. She had clearly never spilled her tea. Mrs. Howell had been bred to fine manners.

"Are you quite certain this is what you want to do?" Mrs. Howell asked. "I hope you are not acting out of some emotion—sympathy or guilt for surviving when her mother did not. If you were to change your mind later and Dorothy were to go to an orphanage, it would be ever so much harder for her. She would be twice lost."

"No, it's what Helen and I want." I paused. "And do you know what, Mrs. Howell? I think Peter will approve of it, too. She's one of his little souls."

"Ah, the little souls. You may know that is one of Judge Howell's phrases, from Emperor Hadrian, I believe, although I have no idea what the context is. He applies it not only to the downtrodden and forgotten but to anyone in despair. Peter always liked it."

Then I asked, "Are orphanages really so bad? I've never been inside one."

Mrs. Howell picked up the heavy silver teapot. Her hands shook a little, and she had to use both of them to lift it. I declined, but she filled her own cup. Then she indicated the silver tray of cakes. "Have one, won't you," she said, and I chose one to be polite.

"Many orphan's homes are not so bad, I suppose," she said.

"They feed and clothe the children and keep them safe. I am quite proud of the way the Presbyterian orphan's home is run. It is one of the best. Still, young children need love and affection, and there is never enough of that in an institution. They may form bonds with their little friends, but there is no mother to nurture them. I must say, any such place is better than the alternative, which is no orphanage at all."

Helen had told me of the children who lived on the streets, who slept in doorways and abandoned buildings and scrounged through garbage pails for food. The boys turned to theft, and the girls, if they were pretty enough—and even if they weren't— became prostitutes. That world was a long way away from the mansions on Grant Street.

As if she knew what I was thinking, Mrs. Howell smiled, deepening the lines around her eyes. "Perhaps Peter never told you that I was not born to wealth. Nor to a good family." She paused as if considering whether to continue. Or perhaps thinking of Peter had made her wistful. "My father was a silver miner in Leadville, in the mountains. There was never enough money, and when my mother developed tuberculosis, most of what we had went to pay the doctor. After she died, my father drank away the rest, and then he disappeared. I do not know what happened to him. Maybe he died, or perhaps he just didn't want us."

She smiled at the surprise on my face. "Yes, that is all true. I had a younger brother . . ." She stood and went to the window, then drew back the lace panel and stared out at the lawn. The yard was brown and bare. "My brother . . . well . . . he died . . ." She shook her head, as if she did not want to think about him.

Mrs. Howell was quiet for a moment as she picked dead leaves off the fern, crumbled them in her hand, and threw them into the fireplace. She turned and sat down again. "I was taken in by a baker and his wife. I was allowed to attend school, although I had to rise at three in the morning to begin the day's baking." She looked at me and smiled. "I was lucky. I had a place to sleep and enough to eat. If they hadn't cared for me, I might have frozen to death. The winters in Leadville are very cold. It could have been much worse."

I was stunned. Mrs. Howell was gracious and well-spoken, with fine manners, and nothing about her suggested the story she had told me. "Was there no orphanage you could go to?" I asked.

"None that would take older children. I was twelve."

"Good God!" I said. I had finished my cigarette and wanted a second but did not think the small ashtray would hold another butt. And I would hardly be so boorish as to throw it into the fireplace. "That's only two years older than Dorothy."

"And just like Dorothy in finding you and your sister, I was extraordinarily fortunate. Many fashionable ladies came into the bakery, and I learned how to speak and act properly from them. I knew I did not want to bake bread all my life." Mrs. Howell gave a short laugh. "In fact, I believe sometimes I am stuffier than they are." She picked up her teacup and drank. "I learned something from the prostitutes, too. Some were fine women."

I laughed and was mortified when I realized Mrs. Howell was not joking. She studied me for a moment. "As I said, I was fortunate, because among the men who frequented the bakery was Judge Howell. He had come to Leadville to open an extension of his father's Denver hardware store. That was before he decided he'd rather nail criminals than sell nails." She smiled. The wordplay seemed to please her. "He visited each morning to purchase a bun. He told me later that he always waited until the crowd was gone so he could engage me in conversation."

And she hooked him. It was not a very nice thought, but still, if I were working in a bakeshop with no opportunities, I would set my cap for a rich man.

As if she sensed what I was thinking, Mrs. Howell said, "I suppose there are some who believe I married him for his money, and indeed, he was a fine catch. But it truly was a love match on both of our parts."

"Peter never told me how you met," I said.

"It's no secret, although it seems to embarrass my children, even Peter. You see, Denver society is so new that most of our prominent families like to forget the past and hide their common origins. Fortunately, Judge Howell and his parents did not care that I was a poor orphan girl. In fact, the judge tells the story, and at the most inopportune times. I rather like that about him."

"Then you didn't care that Peter was engaged to a career girl? Before I met you, I was afraid you might try to put an end to it."

Mrs. Howell leaned forward and took my hand. "Put an end to it? My dear, I was delighted. I was so afraid he would choose one of those bloodless young things in the smart set. I knew they would never understand his passion for helping others."

Like Mrs. Howell, I hadn't set my cap for a rich man. I did

love Peter, although I wasn't sure I cared about helping others the way he did.

Mrs. Howell obviously thought better of me, because she said, "That is the real reason I wanted you to come to tea. I am worried about him."

"Of course you are—"

Mrs. Howell held up her hand. "Yes, we both worry about the battles, but this is something else. I very much believe Peter is in danger. I think we may hold his life in our hands."

Ten

I leaned forward in my chair. "What is it?" I asked.

"I believe Peter is in danger of losing his faith."

Is that all? I wanted to respond.

As if she knew I did not take her seriously, Mrs. Howell said, "His faith means so much to him. It is the mainstay of his life. Without it, he would be lost, and I believe he could grow careless. You see, he believes God sent him to France for a purpose, that nothing good or bad happens without a reason. That purpose is helping others. He has told you, so I suspect."

I nodded. I was ashamed that I had thought to dismiss Mrs. Howell's concern about Peter's faith. "What happened?" I asked.

Mrs. Howell turned toward a Bible sitting on the orange cloth, and I wondered if she was going to read a passage. Instead, she took an envelope from its pages. "This came a few days ago. I have not shown it to Judge Howell." She removed a sheet of cheap paper from the envelope and handed it to me.

I unfolded the paper and smoothed it on my lap, then looked up at her.

"Read it," she said.

Peter's writing was precise, but the handwriting was sprawl-

ing, as if it had not been written against a hard surface. For a
moment, I wondered if he wanted to break off our engagement
and had asked his mother to tell me. I glanced at Mrs. Howell
again, and she smiled at me. I turned the paper a little to catch
the light and read.

Dearest Mother,

*You know better than anyone that one of the reasons for
my going off to be a soldier-boy was to help men who were
shell-shocked, who'd lost their faith. I believed I could lead
them back to God again. Wasn't that arrogant of me? One
man called me a holy Joe and told me to go to hell. Well, I have
been in hell, and now who will help me find God? Mother, I
believe I can turn to you in this crisis, for you have always been
the one who answered my questions about faith. Now I have to
ask you, where is God? How can this slaughter be the work of
a loving God? I want nothing to do with a deity who burdens
us with this torture.*

*Yesterday, I ran into Wilson Thode. You remember him. He
was the pitcher for the East High School team when I was the
first baseman, and he went on to play for the Denver team.
He was sitting in an ambulance, waiting to be taken to a hospital,
and when I passed by he called my name. Of course I knew he
was hurt or he wouldn't have been there. But I tried to be hearty,
and before I could think I said, "Hello there, Wilson. How's the
throwing arm?" He held it up, and I could see that his hand had
been shot off. What could I say after that? "Oh, sorry, fellow, God
knows best." I started to cry, and Wilson said, "That's all right,
old man. I've got another," and he held up his left hand. Mother,*

he was the one who'd been maimed, and he was comforting me. What possible use could I be to him or to God or to any-one else?

I am sitting here in a trench—no, trench warfare is not done with—next to the body of a new soldier who was foolish enough to raise his head to look out at the German line and got a bul-let through his eye. I'm wondering where God is and thinking I shall never study theology, for I don't believe in it anymore. You know, Lutie didn't wish to be a minister's wife, and now, if I survive this war, she won't have to worry about that. I wonder if she will accept such a broken spirit as I am now. She thinks she is frivolous, but she is stronger than she knows. I saw that the first time I talked to her, and it is one of the reasons I love her. Like you, she has the strength to get through any crisis. I hope she won't throw me over, because I need her. I have not written to her about my despair, but you can show her this letter if you want to.

The fighting is starting, so I close. It is God's affair now—if He cares. Where is His mercy? Where is man's? Where is God, anyway?

The letter was unsigned. I handed it back to Mrs. Howell, then took a handkerchief from my pocketbook and wiped my eyes.

"I am so sorry to distress you," Mrs. Howell said. "But I don't know how to answer Peter. I thought that together we might find a way to help him."

"Not the God part," I told her. "I can't help with that, be-cause I don't understand why God allows terrible things to happen. Peter was the one with real faith. He says I'm strong, but I'm really not."

Mrs. Howell shook her head. "You underestimate yourself. Peter knows you better than you do yourself. He knew you were strong, and I do, too." She took a handkerchief from the sleeve of her dress and dabbed at her eyes. "I thought that together, you and I might figure out a way to lift his spirits. I believe that when he returns home, he will be able to deal with all this, but my fear is that his despondency will make him careless. I want him to come back safely."

"But what can I write?" I asked.

"I believe that if you tell him you love him no matter what, that you are waiting for him, and that together the two of you will work through this, it would help Peter a great deal. He loves you very much, you know."

"I love him very much, too," I said, and I did indeed, more than I had realized.

The sunroom door was flung open, and Dorothy rushed in. I was glad to end the conversation. I found it hard to think that something might happen to Peter. Mrs. Howell and I turned to the little girl.

"Look, Lutie," she said, twirling around the room in a white dress with white tassels and a blue satin sash. She looked very like the girl in the painting over the mantel, and she was happy.

"The dress is a little dated, but you ought to be able to alter it, Lucretia," Mrs. Howell said. "You are smartly dressed yourself and so good with your needle."

Dorothy and I looked at each other, and she whispered, "You mean it's mine to keep?"

"Of course. What will I do with a child's dress? I've been meaning to clean out the trunks and send the contents to the Presbyterian orphan's home," Mrs. Howell told her.

"Mine, Lutie?" Dorothy asked again. "I never had such a pretty dress."

"There are others," Mrs. Howell said, waving her hand as though she were giving away a trifle. "I shall sort through the trunks and have them delivered to you." She smiled at Dorothy. "Did you see the dollhouse in the attic?"

Dorothy looked up.

"It belonged to my daughters and has not been used in a very long time. I thought perhaps if you would come and see me, you could play with it. I would be glad to see you alone but would like it even better if you would bring Lucretia, so that I may visit with her."

Dorothy looked at me for approval, and I said, "That would be lovely. Would you like that, Dorothy?"

She nodded.

"I have a doll," she said, and I knew she meant the rag doll I had made for her in the summer, after I discovered she had no playthings. "But it's too big to fit inside the house."

"That doesn't matter. There are dolls who live there already. But they are dirty. They need to have their clothes washed after all these years. And the dollhouse itself needs a good scrubbing. Would you do that for me? Perhaps if Lucretia is busy, you would agree to spend a few days with me. I would find it very like having my own daughter again."

Dorothy nodded, then grinned at me, and I knew the visit had taken her out of the bad place that often engulfed her. I stood, and Dorothy and I thanked Mrs. Howell for the tea. She said we had brightened her day. "Please come again. Come often. When I am with you, I do not miss Peter as much."

I told her we would, and I told her I would write to Peter that night.

Helen was waiting for us when the chauffeur stopped in front of our house. It was later than I'd thought, and the street was gloomy. An automobile I didn't recognize was parked down the block, and I saw the tip of a lighted cigarette, but when I looked at it again the light was gone, and I wasn't sure that I'd really seen anyone in the auto. I was still on edge. I wondered how long that would last.

"I thought you'd never get home," Helen told me. "Gil telephoned." She caught herself as she glanced at Dorothy. "Well, don't you look like a princess! Wherever did you get such a fine dress?"

Dorothy had removed her coat and was twirling around in the new dress. "From Mr. Howell's mother." I knew that Helen wanted to tell me something, so I suggested to Dorothy that she change her dress so the white one wouldn't get dirty.

"This came off it," Dorothy said, showing Helen a white tassel.

"I'll sew it back on for you," I said.

"No. I'll put it in my treasure box."

Dorothy went into her bedroom and closed the door. She always closed doors. Perhaps she felt safer in a closed-up room.

"I don't know how, with the sordid life she's led, she can be such an unspoiled child," I said. "She was a delight at the Howells."

"And then sometimes she is almost in a trance," Helen said.

"Like that night in the kitchen."

Helen nodded. "You heard her crying last night. I was going to go to her, but then I heard you get up."

"How long will that last?"

"I don't know. Maybe forever."

"You used to have nightmares. Do you still?"

Helen didn't answer. Instead, she asked, "Should we fix her supper?"

"I doubt that she's hungry. She filled up on sweets at the Howells.'"

"Let's leave her alone then. She can play with the things in her treasure box. That seems to make her happy."

Helen was right. Dorothy liked to sit on the cot in her room and examine the items. She'd become secretive about the box, however, and would shut the lid whenever I went into her room.

The house was warm, and Helen said she wanted fresh air. So we went outside and sat on the porch swing. The automobile down the block was gone, and I told myself I had been silly to notice it.

"Gil telephoned. He has to be careful about what he says in case the operator is listening in. He said he was at the morgue but didn't recognize any influenza victims."

"Still, the body's gone. Maybe he's already been interred."

I pushed us back and forth on the swing. Although the weather was chill, I loved sitting there. A leaf fell onto the porch, a crimson leaf from the vine growing on the house. I picked it up and pressed it between my fingers. It was perfect, with veins like fine embroidery. "I'll send it to Peter."

Helen didn't reply, and I turned to her. "There's something else, isn't there?"

"Yes." Helen was silent a moment. "A man was here looking for Mr. Streeter. It was not long before you got home. He came around to the back and I heard him rattle the doorknob. Fortunately, the door was locked."

"Did you open it?"

Helen shook her head. "I don't know why I didn't. It could have been the knife grinder or the ragman or even one of the neighbors, but after Mr. Streeter, I've become cautious." She looked down at her hands. "He came around to the front door. I saw him walk up the steps to the porch, and he spotted me through the window, so I couldn't pretend no one was home. I opened the door and he asked for Mr. Streeter."

"What did you tell him?"

"That he had moved out weeks ago, and I didn't know where he'd gone."

I smiled. "Oh, Helen, that could have been a bill collector. Or somebody selling the *Saturday Evening Post.*"

"But he wasn't. He asked about Dorothy. He asked if she was here. He had a look about him . . ." Helen's voice trailed off. Then she asked, "Do you have a cigarette, Lute?"

My pocketbook was still in my hands, and I took out the ebony case and handed Helen a cigarette. Then I took one for myself and struck a match and lighted both. "He must have been a family friend."

Helen didn't smoke much, and she held the cigarette between

her lips the way Mrs. Howell had. "There's something you should know, Lutie. I didn't tell you before because it's so awful and there wasn't any reason for you to know."

"Something about Dorothy?"

"And Mr. Streeter."

I dug my heels into the porch to stop the swing and stared at Helen, who wouldn't look at me. A newspaper page blew across the yard, startling me, but Helen didn't notice it. Finally she said, "Mr. Streeter might not have been the only one."

I didn't understand. "Only one what?"

"Who used her." Helen took a pull on her cigarette, then coughed.

At first I was confused, and then suddenly I understood. "You mean there was another man who . . . ?" I couldn't put it into words.

"I don't know, but I can't help wondering. If I'm right, maybe the man who came here was one of them."

I put my head in my hands and felt tears in my eyes. "Oh, Helen, how horrible. I thought what Mr. Streeter did to her was the most awful thing I'd ever heard, but this is ever so much worse. It explains what happened at Baur's. Remember? I told you about it. How did she stand it?"

"I think she has a special place where she hides. In her mind, I mean."

I stood and went to the porch railing. For a minute I feared I might vomit as Dorothy had that day we went to Baur's.

"Mr. Streeter even offered Dorothy to Gil."

"What!"

Helen wrapped her arms about herself as if she were cold.

"Mr. Streeter might have been joking. You know he made outrageous remarks. Still, Gil was shocked. In fact, he slugged Mr. Streeter. That was when we told him to get out."

"Too bad he didn't kill him." When I realized what I'd said, I added, "I mean . . ."

Helen sighed. "You're right, of course."

"Well, thank God *you* did," I said hotly. "What did the man who came here tonight say?"

"He only asked about Dorothy. I told him that she was gone, and I didn't know where she was."

"There was a man in an automobile down the street when we came home. It must have been the same man, and he would have seen her. We ought to go to the police."

"No!" Helen said. She sat up and looked at me. "We can't go to the police. We can't tell them anything. It's too late. Besides, they'd question Dorothy."

Helen's fierceness moved me. I wasn't sure she was right. We should have called the police the night Mr. Streeter was killed. And it wasn't too late now to explain what had happened. But Helen was adamant. Dorothy should never talk to the police. Helen began to shake.

"Oh, Lutie, the world is so evil. I didn't want you to know. I wanted to protect you."

I put my arms around her as we rocked back and forth in the swing. When it grew too cold to sit there, we went inside, and I wrote the letter to Peter.

A few nights later, after turning the jump rope for Dorothy, Helen and I sat on the front steps. Dorothy was in her room, sitting with her treasure box, and since the night was nice, with the smell of burning leaves, we decided to stay outside. We watched the boy down the street speed past in his auto, and I suppose we were both looking for the one that had parked in the street the night Helen told me about Mr. Streeter offering Dorothy to other men. We hadn't seen it since.

The streetlamps came on and then people began turning on their porch lights, sending yellow circles onto the pavement. A mother came out and called her son home for supper. From far away came the sound of a whistle—another mother calling a child home. There was the scratchy sound of "Red Wing" on a Victrola again. The record ended, and I heard the needle going round and round on the record until somebody lifted the arm, and the night was still.

We didn't feel the need to talk. Helen was worn-out, and I knew we should go into the house and fix supper. But I stayed on the wooden steps, and after a time Helen reached for my hand and held it.

I watched a big touring car glide down the street, thinking it looked like the Howells' auto. Then it stopped in front of our house and the chauffeur got out. Perhaps he'd brought the trunk of clothes Mrs. Howell had mentioned. I stood and started walking toward it but stopped when I saw the chauffeur open the back door and Judge Howell step out. Helen had risen, and I grabbed her arm. I should have gone to greet him, but I couldn't move. There was only one reason the judge would come calling unannounced, and I prayed, *please let him be only injured, please, God, don't let Peter be dead.*

My knees felt weak and I could barely stand, but finally I forced myself to walk toward him. "Judge Howell . . . ," I said.

He removed his hat and stopped, his shoulders stooped. "Mrs. Howell sent me. She said you should know right away, that I should tell you in person."

Helen came up behind me and put her arms around me in support.

"Peter?" she asked.

"I wrote to him Sunday night," I said, as if that would mean something.

The judge opened his mouth to speak, but for a time no words came out. Then he said in a strangled voice, "Lucretia . . ."

"Dead?" I whispered.

He nodded. He began to cry, huge convulsing sobs, and at that the chauffeur came and led him away. Helen held on to me as the auto pulled out, and I stared at it until it turned the corner when I began to wail.

Eleven

Dorothy must have heard me crying, or maybe she'd heard the car, and she came out onto the porch. She didn't ask what was wrong but only looked at me with sad eyes, as if she already knew.

Helen and I moved to the ends of the swing to let Dorothy sit between us. Then both of us put an arm around her.

"That was Judge Howell," Helen said softly. "Mr. Howell—Peter—was killed in the war."

"Killed dead?" Dorothy asked.

Helen nodded. "He's in heaven—with your mother."

Dorothy thought that over. "She'll like that. She doesn't know anybody up there." She put her little hand into mine. "I'm sorry, Lutie."

The Victrola started up again, this time playing "There's a Long, Long Trail." My eyes were sore from crying.

"We should go inside," Helen said.

She put Dorothy to bed while I sat on the davenport in the living room, not listening to their conversation. Eventually Helen came and sat beside me. "Dorothy didn't want supper. Can I fix you something? I could heat up some soup. It would be good for you."

"No. You go to bed, too."

"I could sit with you for a bit. Maybe you'd like to talk about him. I liked him awfully well. I didn't at first, but I did later."

"I just want to be by myself," I said. And I did.

I knew I would not sleep that night, and I did not. I sat in the living room for a long time, staring at a fire I had built in the grate. It was not cold in the house, but I couldn't stop shivering. I rocked back and forth in the old rocker we had brought with us from Cedar Rapids. It was large and ugly, but it had been in the family for many years. Mother had sat there when she nursed us as infants. Whenever Helen or I was hurt or unhappy, we'd sit on her lap as she rocked. As an adult, I sat in the rocker whenever I was tired or distressed, finding the movement comforting. But of course, it didn't help that night. Eventually I went to bed, pulling the covers up to my shoulders because I was still chilled.

After a time, when sleep didn't come, I rose and turned on the light, and I sat with Peter's picture in my hands. As I stared at his face, I was struck by how young he was. Peter was three years older than I, and I had never thought about his being a *young* man. But he was only twenty-seven. I wondered how he had been killed. I might never know; the Howells would probably receive a letter saying he had died quickly and hadn't suffered, and I would not tell them it was a lie. Perhaps they already knew that and would not tell me. I cried for the death of someone I loved, for the life we would not have together, for the joys and sorrows unlived and the children unborn.

Helen awoke early. She lighted the stove and heated water for coffee, and we sat at the kitchen table. She asked what I was going to do, and I said I didn't know. Everything seemed

so strange, as if I had entered another world and was looking back at my old self. It was Sunday, and I wondered if the
Howells would go to church. But most churches were closed
because of the influenza, so they probably would be at home.
I wanted to see them.

"I would like to call on Mr. and Mrs. Howell," I said. "Do you
think that's a good idea, or would they think I'm intruding?"

Helen thought for a moment. "I believe you should. It's better to err on the side of good intentions. If the Howells aren't
accepting callers, you could just leave your card." The women
who shopped at Neusteter's had calling cards, and in a moment of extravagance, Florence and I had gone to Kendrick-
Bellamy, which was Denver's finest stationery store, to order
them for ourselves. I had rarely had a chance to use one. "I'll
go with you," Helen added. "We'll take Dorothy."

That was a generous offer, because Helen was tired. Her
face was pale, and there were dark circles under her eyes. Most
nights now she came home exhausted, too tired even to eat.
She'd sit on the porch, her white mask in her hands, staring
out at the street. She deserved a day's rest. "You don't have to,"
I told her.

"You're my sister. I want to."

I reached up and took Helen's hand. Her presence would
make it easier, since the Howell house would be filled with relatives and friends I didn't know. I did not want them staring at
me and whispering that I was Peter's fiancée, a career girl, and
wasn't it lucky for the Howells that we had not gotten married
before Peter went overseas. I told Helen that, and she asked
where in the world I had gotten such an idea. She told me that

I was every bit as good as Peter and that the Howells had never been anything but kind to me.

We waited to call on the Howells until the afternoon, when the sky was overcast and the streets were wet with rain. We dressed in black—even Dorothy had on black under her new coat—and we took the streetcar to Grant Street and walked past the old mansions, which were gloomy in the gray light. Their stones looked as cold as death. I'd wanted to take the Howells something. In Cedar Rapids when a person died, Mother had brought food—a cake or a batch of cookies or even a full meal. But the Howells had a cook, so food didn't seem like the right gift. Then I remembered the quilt I had made of flags and streamers that I had hung on the wall. Peter had helped me collect the red-white-and-blue fabric the day he proposed, and Mrs. Howell had given me a flag that Peter had had as a boy. I'd included it in the quilt, along with the small French flag Peter had sent me from the Front.

George, the butler, had a mourning band around his arm, and when he opened the door to us, he said, "I'm sorry, miss. He was a fine lad. He treated me all right. It's a loss for us all." I wasn't sure it was proper, but I grasped his hand and squeezed it.

We waited in the hall while George went into the library and said, "Miss Hite is here with her sisters, Madam."

I was prepared for Mrs. Howell to say she couldn't see anyone just then and would we sign the mourning book that lay open on the hall table. Instead, the butler ushered us into the library, which was so small that the few people who were there made it crowded and close. I went to Mrs. Howell, who hugged me. Then Judge Howell took my hand and patted it. They greeted Helen, and Mrs. Howell smiled when she saw Dorothy.

Helen and Dorothy and I stood awkwardly until the minister, whom I had met when Peter had taken me to church, took my elbow and said, "You do not know the rest of Peter's family, Lucretia. Peter's sisters arrived a short time ago." I turned and saw two women with drawn faces. One looked like Peter, with dark hair and blue eyes, and the other was small and blond. They stared at me as if I had intruded. They murmured something polite, but neither made me feel welcome.

I felt silly standing there with the flag quilt and wished I had left it at home. What would Mrs. Howell do with such a cheap little thing, made of tawdry fabrics, in that elegant old house? I tucked it under my arm, hoping it was inconspicuous, but then Helen said, "Lutie brought you something, Mrs. Howell."

I had no choice but to hand her the quilt. She had seen it once, when I'd taken it to dinner there. Now she held out her arms and I put the quilt into them, wondering if Peter's sisters would be offended by it, would consider it frivolous and inappropriate. "I wanted you to have it," I said. Mrs. Howell unfolded the quilt and then buried her face in it, and said, "My dear Lucretia, nothing could possibly ease my grief as much as this." She touched the tiny flag she had given me and said, "Look, girls, this was your brother's when he was a boy. Why, he even helped Lucretia collect the flags and bunting she used to make the quilt."

The two women took a step forward to peer at the quilt but said nothing.

"We will put it over Peter's coffin," Mrs. Howell said.

"But, Mother, there won't be a coffin. Peter will be buried in France," one of the sisters said. She was the one who looked like Peter, and I supposed she was Evelyn. The smaller one would be Louise.

Mrs. Howell looked stunned, then turned to her husband, who nodded.

"I did not know." Her eyes grew wide. "If there is no grave, where will I go to grieve?" she asked.

Judge Howell squeezed her shoulder. "There are too many bodies of American boys, too many for the army to send home. We will grieve in our hearts."

"Oh, just so," Mrs. Howell said, sounding lost. "Then we shall display Lucretia's quilt at the service, and later I will hang it in Peter's room with all his mementos. Looking at it will bring us solace." She took my hand as tears ran down both of our faces.

Evelyn softened then, and she said, "That was very thoughtful of you, Lucretia—Lutie, is it? Peter said you did not use your given name much."

I nodded, too tired to speak.

"We haven't set a date for the service yet. We shall let you know. You and your sisters will sit with the family, of course," Evelyn said.

"Thank you," I managed to utter, and I thought I had been wrong. Evelyn and I might not have been sisters, but we would have been friends. Maybe we still would be.

George came in then with a tray of some liqueur. He handed me a glass that was small and delicate and as cold as a shard of ice. I all but gulped it down, and I felt disoriented, as if I were standing outside my body watching myself.

Evelyn seemed to understand that I did not feel well and took my hand. She led me to a chair and said, "Won't you sit down? This has been altogether too hard on you. On all of us."

The chairs in the library were large and comfortable, and I sank into one, while Evelyn seated herself on the arm. "Peter had written me about you, and of course, I was thrilled that he had found someone. I was so looking forward to meeting you, but not . . ." Evelyn's voice trailed off, and she reached up and wiped tears from her eyes.

"Not like this," I finished for her.

Louise came over and put her arm around her sister's shoulders. "Evie, why don't you lie down? You were on the train all night from Kansas City, and you still aren't well. You must be half-dead." She grimaced at her choice of words and added, "That was clumsy of me."

"You've had a long journey yourself, Lou." Evelyn patted her sister's hand. They had the same sort of bond that Helen and I did. I looked up at Helen, who seemed uncomfortable standing alone in the room with Dorothy. I set my glass on the table, then rose and said we must be going.

"We will have a little supper in a while. Will you stay?" Louise asked. "I would like to know your sisters. I admire a girl who can carry off an orange coat." She smiled at Dorothy, who did not look up, but instead glanced at Helen and mouthed, "Can we go home now?"

There was a blaze in the fireplace, and the room was hot. The shutters were closed. The heavy, sweet smell from a bouquet of lilies on the library table overwhelmed me, and the liqueur made me sleepy. "I think we ought to get home before it rains again," I said.

"But it's raining already," Evelyn told me. "I'll ask the butler to bring an umbrella and walk you to your auto."

"We took the streetcar," I said.

Evelyn looked embarrassed. "Of course. So patriotic to observe gasless Sundays."

"We don't own an auto," I told her.

Evelyn reddened. "That's sensible. They can be such a nuisance, and you must find the trolley altogether more reliable. I agree entirely. Melvin, Mother's chauffeur, will take you home. I'd drive you myself but I can't leave Mother." Evelyn went out into the hall, and I heard her talking to the butler. After a time, he came to the doorway and nodded at Evelyn.

Mrs. Howell kissed my cheek, then shook Helen's hand and hugged Dorothy, thanking us for calling. Judge Howell patted my hand again. He started to say something to Dorothy but turned away and told his wife, "Peter might have had a child like this." Then Evelyn walked us to a side door.

"You were a comfort to Mother today. I'm so glad you came. It was kind of you," she said. "There is so much grief . . . such a loss . . . He was a wonderful brother, but I'm sure you know that." And then she said again, "I'm glad he found you, that he had a chance to think about a life with you." She began to cry and put her arms around herself until she was still. Then she clasped my hands and said she would ring me the following day to let me know the arrangements for the memorial service. I told her it would have to wait until evening, because I worked during the day and wasn't allowed to receive telephone calls. Evelyn bit her lip and said, "Of course. I forgot you were a career girl."

It struck me then that I had lost not only Peter but his family. For a time, I would encounter them at church. They might invite me for Sunday dinner. But after a while, seeing me would be painful for them and we would draw apart.

When we reached home, Helen and I lit a fire in the grate, then she went into the kitchen and fixed us cocoa. "You look very tired," she said. "You ought to get some rest. Won't you lie down, Lute?"

I nodded. My feet felt leaden, and I could barely stand. And I had a terrible headache.

Twelve

I had the headache all that night, and toward morning it grew worse. The pain was lodged behind my right eye, and I felt as if a spike had been driven into my forehead. When I moved my head, I feared it would split open. I had never had such a headache, and I reached for the glass of water and the bottle of Aspirin on the bedside table and shook several into my hand. Helen would be horrified that I had taken so many, but I had to stop the hurting. My throat felt swollen. I tried to return the glass to the table but I missed, and the glass crashed to the floor, splintering. I did not have the strength to sweep up the shards, and I told myself to remember the broken glass in the morning and get out on the other side of the bed. I lay back against the pillow, exhausted, although it was unlikely that, with the pain, I would sleep.

The light went on in the hall, and in a minute, Helen opened my door a little and whispered, "Lutie, are you awake? I heard something break."

"I dropped my water glass," I said in a voice that sounded as if it were coming from somewhere outside my head. "Be careful where you step."

"What's wrong?"

"I've an awful headache. I've had it since last night, and it's gotten a hundred times worse. It feels as if I've been hit in the face with a hammer." My mouth hurt, and it was hard to get out the words.

Helen reached inside my door and turned on the overhead light. The light made the pain worse, and I pulled the quilt over my head.

"I'd better check you out," Helen said.

"I'll be all right. It must be my sinuses. I think I'm coming down with a cold. I was coughing last night," I mumbled, as I lowered the quilt below my left eye.

Helen came to the bed and touched my head. Her hand was as cold as the rain outside. I could hear the drops pinging against my window. It had been raining all night, and it was coming down in sheets now. It might even turn into snow. My mood was as dreary as the night. "You have a fever," Helen said. She took my pulse and frowned. "I'll get a thermometer." She went into the bathroom, and I heard her open the door of the medicine cabinet.

"I'm starting to ache. I'm sure it's a cold," I said when she returned with the thermometer. She shook it, then put it under my tongue. When she removed it, she read it and sighed. "Your temperature is over a hundred."

"A bad cold," I said. "A lulu of a cold."

"Not a cold," Helen told me. "The influenza."

My brain was foggy, and it took a minute for her words to register. "The influenza," I said in a voice that was more slurred than ever. "A regular influenza, you mean—the influenza like I got a couple of years ago?" That had been during finals week at the university, and I'd been afraid that if I missed the tests, I wouldn't graduate. I'd dragged myself to the campus and gone to classes. Helen was furious. She said I could have come down with pneumonia, and even if I hadn't, I'd probably infected everybody I'd come into contact with. But at least I'd passed, and I'd graduated, and I was all right in a couple of days.

Helen shook her head. "You have the influenza."

"The influenza?" My voice sounded as if came from someone else now. "Are you sure?"

"I've seen it before, you know. I'm a nurse."

Of course I knew Helen was a nurse, and what she'd said was so funny that I tried to laugh. Instead I coughed, and when I looked down at my pillow I saw that it was spotted with blood. I touched my face, and when I pulled my hand away there was blood on my fingers. Despite the pain in my head and the listlessness in my limbs, I clutched the quilt, horrified, as if the blood were contagious. "Blood," I whispered. "There's blood there, Helen."

She reached over and stroked my forehead, and her cool hand felt good because I was burning up. "That's one of the symptoms. You have a nosebleed," she said.

"I . . . ?" My tongue felt as if it were made of cement.

"Hush," Helen said. "I'm here. I'll take care of you. You'll be all right." She went into the bathroom again and returned with a wet washcloth and held it against my nose. "This will stop the bleeding in a few minutes. I'll take off the quilt—you wouldn't want to spoil it—and change the pillowcase." Her voice was comforting, just as it had been when I was small and sick in bed. There was no trace of panic, although Helen knew better than I how serious the influenza was.

She started for the other side of the bed, but I flung out my hand. "The glass," I managed to say. "Be careful."

Helen glanced at the floor. "First things first. I'll clean it up." She went to the broom closet and took out a broom and a dustpan and carefully swept up the pieces of glass. The sound was harsh and louder than it should have been, and it hurt my ears. When Helen returned, she was wearing slippers and had put on a bathrobe. She asked me if I wanted anything to eat. "Broth would be good. We have some bouillon powder. I could feed it to you, if you think you can keep it down."

The idea of food made me gag, and I shook my head, which made the headache pound.

"I'll bring another glass of water. I don't want you to get dehydrated."

"No," I muttered, but Helen didn't pay attention.

She went into the kitchen and turned on the tap, then returned with a glass in her hand, a metal one that would not break if I knocked it over. She held a basin in the other.

"This is in case you feel like throwing up. It would be nice if you could manage to use it, but don't worry if you can't. We've got plenty of sheets and pillowcases." She folded the quilt and set it on a chair, then removed the bloodied pillowcase and replaced it with one Mother had made. She had embroidered it with a design in red cross-stitches and edged it with crochet. "It's always nice to have something pretty to sleep on when you're sick, although I doubt you'll notice it," she said, fluffing the pillow.

My neck hurt when she raised my head to put the pillow under it. "I might bleed on it," I whispered.

"Oh, don't worry. It will match the red embroidery." My sister had never cared about needlework.

Then Helen dragged the rocker from the living room into my bedroom and sat down, placing a knitted throw over her legs. "I'll just rest here," she said. "I wish I had your flag quilt to wrap up in. It's such a gay thing. You were very kind to give it to the Howells. Mrs. Howell seemed to appreciate it."

At least that's what I thought she said. My mind had begun to whirl, and Helen's words slipped in and out of my consciousness.

"I'm right here if you need me." Helen touched my forehead again, and for a moment it seemed as if she were my mother. In some ways she was.

"Dream about clowns," Helen whispered.

She reached up and turned off the light, and I lay there, trying to think about clowns. But other thoughts kept intruding, strange thoughts that didn't make sense, and I was not sure whether I was awake or asleep.

The bulb in the hall was still on, and I stared at the sticky yellow flypaper that hung from the ceiling. There weren't many flies now. We should take down the flypaper, I said to myself. I stared at it for a long time, watching as the paper slowly began to glow and turn red, a red as bright and as evil as hell. And then it burst into flame. The flames ran up the wall and across the ceiling, like long red veils in a wind. The fire consumed the hallway and kept on toward the bedroom. Helen should have seen the brightness, felt the heat, but she sat there rocking back and forth as if nothing were wrong. She was reading a book in the light from the hall and not paying attention to the fire.

The flames grew closer. They engulfed the door, and suddenly there was a clown's head in the center of the flames—an evil clown, not a jolly one like we'd seen at the circus. He leered at me, and when he opened his mouth his tongue was a long flame, a glowing crimson flame that touched the top of Helen's head and set her hair on fire. I tried to warn her as her hair burst into flame, to tell her to open the window so that the rain would come in and put out the fire. I could hear the raindrops lash the window, as if offering to help, but Helen didn't hear them.

And then the flames turned into an ice pick, a long one, as long as a broom, and the clown morphed into Mr. Streeter. I opened my mouth again to call to Helen, to warn her that Mr. Streeter had come back. He wasn't dead. But no words came out. I thrashed around on the bed, trying to get up, to drag Helen away from Mr. Streeter and the inferno. She came over to me and laid a cool washcloth on my head. She hadn't seen the fire, hadn't felt it. I pointed to the hallway and gave a muffled cry, but she didn't understand. "Fire!" I croaked at last, and fell onto the pillow, exhausted.

"You're burning up. Try a little water. It will cool you," Helen said, holding the glass to my lips.

With a mighty effort, I grabbed the glass and flung the contents toward the hall, but the water only soaked the bed. Still, it must have done something, because when I looked again, Mr. Streeter had disappeared, and the fire had gone out. The hallway was back to normal. There was no burned wood. Not even soot. Someone had cleaned it up and painted the walls.

I sighed with relief at having missed the conflagration. Helen told me to go back to sleep. She wiped my face again, and the headache was there, but it wasn't as bad. Instead, my chest hurt. My skin was hot, and I wondered if the fire had burned it. I was about to tell Helen this, but I heard a ringing. It must be the fire wagon. She would have to tell the firemen we were all right.

Then I heard Helen on the telephone. The bell hadn't been the firemen after all but our telephone ring, two longs and a short. The telephone was in the hall and must have made it through the fire all right, because Helen was talking to someone. Perhaps she was telling the police about Mr. Streeter.

"I know it's disappointing to ask them to send another nurse to tend him, Gil. He was my case, and I cared about him. But I can't leave her. She's still delirious. She's been thrashing around and muttering . . . No, I don't know what it was, something about a fire. I suppose it's because she's burning up." She laughed a little. "Hold on, let me get a match. All that talk about a fire makes me want a cigarette." My hearing was very acute then, as if Helen were shouting, and I heard her set the receiver on top of the telephone box and step into the kitchen.

"There, that's better," she said when she returned to the telephone. "Exhausted," she said, in reply to something he asked. I could picture her leaning against the wall with the receiver in her hand. "There was a nosebleed, but only for a moment, not the gush of blood I've seen in other cases. And none since. No cyanosis either, thank God. She hasn't turned that ghastly blue color. I can hope for the best." She paused. "No, I don't know anybody who could sit with her. Besides, I won't leave her alone even for a minute."

Helen must have finished her cigarette, because she said, "Hold on again." Then "No. That was the first one I've had all week. Two won't hurt." She set down the receiver, and I heard the sound of a match striking. "Here I am blabbing on about Lutie. Have you . . ." She must have stopped to choose her words carefully in case someone was listening in. "Are they finding more bodies?" She paused, then asked, "Mr. Streeter? Are you sure? Well, it serves him right." Helen gave a hoarse laugh that wasn't a laugh at all.

My mind couldn't focus on Helen's words for long, and I drifted off, hearing only snatches of her conversation. "Yes, bring the pills . . ." and "You know I had the influenza once . . . No, not the *Spanish* influenza, but still, I think I must be immune." And, "No I won't send her there. They're nothing but death houses. She's my *sister!*"

Helen hung up the receiver and came back to my room and said, "Poor dear, you've thrown up all over yourself." She was wrong. If I'd vomited, I'd have known it. Still, I let Helen raise me to a sitting position and wiggle my nightgown over my head. "Don't worry. I'll clean you up. Thank God we can sponge the sheets a little and not have to change them again. It's the last pair, and there's no one except me to do the laundry."

She sat down on the edge of the bed and leaned toward me, her voice low. "Mr. Streeter is dead," she said. She spoke each word as if it were a sentence. "He died of the influenza. Gil said they found his body. He saw the name written down someplace." She repeated, "He died of the influenza."

I tried to nod. "He died of the influenza." Then I asked, "Dorothy?"

"She's with the Howells. I telephoned Mrs. Howell. Evelyn sent the chauffeur to pick her up. I thought it was awfully forward of me to ask, but I didn't know where else to send her, and Evelyn told me having Dorothy there would make things less gloomy. Both she and Louise have had the influenza—mild cases, as these things go—and Judge and Mrs. Howell are too old to catch it. Mostly people our age are affected. The Howells are first-rate, aren't they? Evelyn promised that if Dorothy comes down with the influenza, she'll hire a nurse to care for her. I didn't tell her there wasn't one to be had."

"You would take care of her."

"Of course, but right now, I've got my hands full with another patient."

I drifted off to sleep again. I woke when I heard a knocking. I didn't want to wake up and had to force myself to do so, but then I was glad I had because Peter was standing in the hall with his hat in his hand! He wore white trousers and a shirt made out of my flag quilt. Peter! No, it couldn't be him. Peter was dead. But there he was, smiling at me.

We must let his mother know that the news of his death had been a horrible mistake. Then I had a wonderful idea. Instead of a funeral, we would have a wedding. Peter and I could be married. Wouldn't it be the funniest thing? People would gather to mourn Peter, but instead they would find they were attending a wedding.

I didn't have a wedding gown. I'd planned to use my employee discount at Neusteter's to buy one, something simple to go with the antique lace veil I had picked up at a secondhand store. Of course, there wouldn't be time to buy white flowers to pin to it, because someone had already started playing the wedding march. Maybe I could use the lilies at the Howells' home. Perhaps one of his sisters had a white dress she could lend me.

Oh, it was a terrible mistake about Peter, but what a lovely ending. I was walking down the aisle on Mr. Streeter's arm. Why had I chosen him to give me away? And why had he insisted that I wear a red dress? It was the ugliest dress I'd ever seen. I had drawn it for an ad, and Florence and I had wondered who would wear such a hideous creation. And my veil had a huge tear in it. Why hadn't I repaired it? I reached for a needle I'd put into the sleeve of the red dress. I'd fix the tear when I reached the altar.

What would Peter think of the red dress and the torn veil? He was standing in front of the altar, waiting for me. The altar was covered with the flag quilt, and on top of it were black flowers. I'd never seen black flowers before. And Peter looked so strange. He was dressed in a uniform, but it wasn't his uniform, because he was wearing a German helmet. He reached out to me and I saw he had no hands, just bloody stumps. What would I do with his wedding ring? I turned to ask Mr. Streeter, but he had an ice pick in his hand and said, "You won't get away from me now." He was holding Dorothy by the hand, and she was wearing my red dress. Then they, too, disappeared. Everybody was gone except for Peter and me. Even the Howells had vanished. They were in a side chapel waiting for Peter to be buried.

Then Peter beckoned me. He gave me a hideous smile as the flesh disappeared from his bones and his face became a skull. He reached for me, and I screamed.

He put his arms around me and said, "It's all right, Lutie. It's only a dream." I woke then. It was Helen who had her arms around me.

She left, and I heard the water running in the bathroom sink, but instead of Helen, Gil came into the room, carrying a glass of water. "You gave us quite a start," he said. "But I think you'll be all right. The dreams can be pretty bad." He put his arm around my shoulders and lifted me. Then he slid a pill into my mouth and held up the glass. "This will help the fever."

I managed to utter "Thank you," and slid back down into the bed.

Gil took out a stethoscope and listened to my heart, then glanced up at Helen, who was leaning over me and nodding. He took my temperature and wrote down something. When he felt my pulse, he said, "It's not as thready." Then he checked my nose and eyes and told Helen, "I think she'll be all right. It's not as bad a case as it might have been. She's lucky you were here when the attack came. . . ."

He stopped when he saw I was listening. "Your sister's a pretty good nurse," he told me. "In fact, the best there is."

I glanced at Helen, whose face was drawn. I thought I saw tears in her eyes, but I wasn't sure, because my eyes hurt.

"Dorothy?" I asked.

"Still safe at the Howells'. Her only danger is too much cake."

"Are you in pain?" Gil asked.

"Sort of." It wasn't the sharp pain I'd felt earlier, but I ached all over and was weak. I turned my head toward the wall and stared at a water stain on the wallpaper. The wallpaper had been there when we bought the house, and I disliked its design of thin vertical stripes with vines twining through them. It was the sort of pattern spinsters picked.

"You're not out of the woods yet. You should stay in bed until Helen tells you it's all right to get up," Gil said.

"But I have to work tomorrow. Mr. Neil will be furious that I took off both yesterday and today. If I don't show up tomorrow, he'll fire me."

Helen came into my bedroom then with a bowl of soup, chicken with carrots and celery and noodles. "Evelyn brought it. She came with the chauffeur when he picked up Dorothy. She told me they were having a service at home for Peter with just family. Mrs. Howell wanted to wait until you were well so that you could attend. But Louise had to go home. The service was Thursday."

Helen sat down on the edge of the bed, dipped the spoon into the soup, and held it to my mouth.

I swallowed the soup, then said, "Thursday?"

"Today is Saturday. You've been ill the better part of a week."

"A week?"

Helen nodded. She leaned over to straighten the bedcovers.

"I dreamed about Peter," I told Helen and Gil. "It was awful. I dreamed he didn't die. I dreamed he was right in this room, and we were going to get married." I buried my face in my hands. "And I dreamed about Mr. Streeter, too. That was the worst part. I dreamed he got away."

Gil gave a small laugh. "No, he didn't get away. He's dead. They picked up his body less than a day after we left it. You remember that, don't you?"

I nodded. "Is it over, then?"

Gil and Helen exchanged glances. "You'd better tell her," he said.

"Two policemen came to the house. They asked about Mr. Streeter. I told them I would invite them in except the house was quarantined. I guess they hadn't seen the sign. They said they'd come back."

Thirteen

—·—

I no longer had the influenza, but I was too weak to return to work and didn't know whether I even still had a job after taking off so much time. Florence telephoned and told me that Mr. Neil himself was out with the influenza, and with so few women shopping now, Neusteter's had reduced its advertising. So maybe I was all right.

From time to time, people came to the house because they knew Helen was a nurse, and they were desperate. Mostly I felt awful telling them that Helen couldn't take on any more patients. But there were a few I didn't mind turning down. One woman believed her cat had the influenza and wanted Helen to make a house call, since it was too cold to take the poor thing to our house. Another said her maid had the influenza and that she needed someone to do her laundry and thought that since Helen was a nurse, she would do a good job. I closed the door in their faces.

So when the doorbell rang, I considered not answering it. I didn't want to refuse people who needed a nurse. Nor did I care to talk to the two policemen who had called when I was sick. But I knew I was putting off the inevitable. I opened the door. When I saw the well-dressed woman in black standing on the porch, I smiled at her, thinking I could at least be kind when I told her that Helen had all the patients she could handle. She looked familiar, but her black cloche hat was pulled down to her eyes, so I wasn't quite sure who she was. When I glanced past her to the street, however, I recognized Peter's roadster. "Evelyn?" I said.

"Yes, I've come to see how you are. I'm so sorry you've been ill. I brought you a custard."

"That's kind of you. Helen said your mother has sent meals."

"Oh, don't thank me. I didn't make it. Mother's cook did." When I opened the screen, Evelyn handed me the bowl and stepped inside. "Have you a moment? Am I interrupting?"

"No, I'm glad for the company." Dorothy had moved back home, and I did not want her to hear us talking about Peter's death, so I suggested we sit on the porch. "Peter and I used to sit there," I told Evelyn, leading the way to the swing.

"I can see why. It must be lovely in the summer. Peter said you had beautiful flowers, hollyhocks, mostly. He loved hollyhocks. I wish we had them at the house, but people sent those dreadful lilies."

"The man in the basement did our yard work sometimes. He's gone now," I said.

"The father of the little girl? Isn't she darling? I suppose you know she was staying with us when you were ill. Peter wrote to us about her. He said she was a scared little thing, but he thought he'd made friends with her."

"Your brother made friends with everybody."

"Yes."

The air was clean and clear, the way it often is in the fall in

Denver, and I was glad to be out of the house. We sat on the swing and swayed back and forth a little, and a sadness came over me as I realized that Peter and I would never sit there again. It was an odd thing about death. You'd forget somebody had died. You'd think, Oh, I must remember this to tell him, and then it hit you that you never could tell him anything ever again. After my father died, I'd found a putty knife on the street, a good one, the blade strong and the wooden handle polished by years of use. Whoever had lost it would be sorry. I'd picked it up and thought I'd give it to Father and we would smile at each other over our good fortune. But then I remembered he was gone. Now every time I used the knife, I thought of his death.

It would be like that with Peter. It already was. So many things had happened in the days since he died that I'd wanted to tell him, had thought for just an instant that I would write to him about them. A columbine had bloomed late in the year, which was strange because they were spring flowers, and I'd wanted to press it and put it into a letter. I'd wanted to tell Peter how much his mother loved the flag quilt. Each thought was followed by the pain of remembrance, a pain as sharp as when I'd seen Judge Howell getting out of the automobile and realized why he'd come. With Mother and Father, the hurt had faded into a kind of acceptance. After all, I had expected them to die sometime. They were older. But with Peter, the sadness was for something that would never happen, for a life not fully lived.

"Mother would have come to see you, but the doctor has ordered bed rest for her. And of course, we're worried that even though older people don't get it, she might catch the influenza.

She's so run-down." Evelyn added quickly, "I don't mean catch it from you." She shook her head. "Oh, what am I saying? I have made a mess of this, haven't I?"

"Of course not," I told her. "Who knows where you could pick up the influenza? Who knows how I got it? I wonder that you don't stay home yourself."

"I'm as strong as a horse." She was quiet a moment. "This is a nice place to sit. So quiet."

"How is Mrs. Howell?"

"As well as could be expected, I suppose. But you can imagine how she feels losing her son."

At least she had had one. Peter would never have a son. We would never have a child together.

"Your throw with all the flags on it, it comforts her. It was lovely of you to give it to her. I want to thank you for that."

"Did she put it in Peter's room?"

"She intended to. But now she sits in her room with it wrapped around her shoulders. She touches the flag she gave you, the one that belonged to Peter when he was a boy, and then she tells me about when he got it. She's done it a dozen times. Sometimes the story changes."

"I'd like to call on her when I'm better."

"Mother would be pleased."

"Are you sorry there wasn't a public service?"

Evelyn waved her hand. "I'm very glad there wasn't. They've had ever so many influenza deaths in Denver that it's dangerous to gather. Myself, I think funerals are beastly, with the candles and that sickly lily smell and all the talk about God's purpose. I'd have screamed that there wasn't any purpose in letting Peter die. I wouldn't want you to remember him like that."

"No. Peter didn't like funerals either." We swung silently and watched yellow leaves blow across the porch. Evelyn picked one up and crumbled it in her hand, letting the brittle pieces fall to the floor. "Do you want to hear something funny?"

I nodded.

"Not really funny, I suppose. Just odd." She gave a sort of laugh. "Louise and I thought you were a fortune seeker. We believed you were after Peter for his money."

I turned and stared at her, stopping the swing as I did so. "I wondered if you did."

Evelyn looked uncomfortable. "We probably would have thought that about anybody Peter was interested in. Mother said you were grand. She greatly likes you. Still, Peter was naïve in some ways, and we knew you worked in a store, so we figured you were after a rich catch. I was going to have a talk with Peter after he came home from France." Evelyn squeezed my hand. "Oh, we were wrong entirely, weren't we? You did truly love Peter. I wouldn't have told you this if I still believed it was the money."

"I didn't think much about his money," I said. That was true, and it surprised me. "I just worried that living on a minister's salary would mean we'd have to live like church mice." I remembered the conversation he and I had once had. "He suggested I start a hat shop or something, and I wondered if that was because he thought I might have to help support us."

"You shouldn't have worried about that. Peter would have

inherited plenty from our parents, and he had a little of his own. Now it's yours."

I pushed the swing a little as I stared out at Peter's automobile, not really listening to Evelyn. Peter had been proud of that roadster. He would drive us out West Colfax to where the Jews lived, and we'd go into their grocery stores, with their odd smells, and he'd talk about the Old Testament, with the men in long beards. On winter nights, we'd go to North Denver to the Italian restaurants, where despite Colorado's Prohibition, you could buy homemade wine that was as strong as gin. Sometimes we'd motor to the country and stop at vegetable stands to buy corn and snap beans and eggplants. I loved exploring with him. Once we drove all the way to Golden to see the big mesa, and just as we reached it we got a puncture, and I helped Peter change the tire. Then we drove home very slowly and carefully, because there was no other spare tire, and Peter had forgotten his patching kit.

Evelyn was still a moment, then asked, "Did you hear what I said?"

"I'm sorry," I told her. "I let my mind wander. I can't seem to concentrate."

"I said Peter left you some money. It's not so much, only five thousand dollars and some change, but he wanted you to have it."

"What?" I asked sharply.

"I'm sorry it's not more."

"Not more? Five thousand dollars is a fortune." Our house had cost little more than a thousand. "He left it to me? Why?"

"That's what Louise asked. Not that she's against it," Evelyn said quickly. "Peter made a will before he went away. It was only prudent. He didn't expect to die, of course, but he was realistic. He wanted everything to be in order so that if he did pass, he wouldn't burden Father and Mother more than necessary. In the will he said that with the money, you wouldn't have to work in a clothing store, illustrating advertisements all your life, when you had the talent to make more of yourself. He wanted you to have enough to set up your own business or become a full-time artist, or whatever suited you. He believed you were awfully damned good. He said if something happened to him, he'd at least make your life a little better. He said you'd be a great success. That's what he told the lawyer.

"You have to know that we think it's swell that he left the money to you," Evelyn added. "My sister and I don't need it, because Mother and Father are generous. And like I said, we'll inherit one day. It's terribly fine that Peter believed in you so much. It's quite a compliment. Most boys don't feel that way, I can tell you."

I stared at Evelyn. "I don't know what to say."

She gave a little laugh and patted my arm. "You'll accept it, of course. So just say yes."

I nodded. "He cared about me that much?"

"You know he did." She paused. "There aren't any strings attached to it, but I have an enormous favor to ask of you."

"What is it?"

"That you'll continue to call on Mother. Louise has gone home, and I'm leaving tomorrow, and Mother needs you to be a daughter to her—and little Dorothy to be a granddaughter.

She loves you that much, you know. You have to understand, you can move on with your life, maybe find someone else to love. In time you might even forget about Peter. But Mother will never have another son. He was her favorite. His death is such a loss to her. But if you keep in touch, you will be a connection to Peter that she will cherish. Please do that for her. For Peter."

"Of course I will." Then I added, "Evelyn, *I'll* never forget Peter."

I remained on the porch after Evelyn left. Dark had come on, and there was the smell of burning leaves again. Bats darted overhead. An auto came down the street and stopped, and the driver revved the motor before he shut it off. A door slammed, and then it was quiet. Not like summer, when you heard the sounds of children playing and mothers calling them in for supper, yelling, "Jimmy! Frances!," and then when the kids didn't come, louder and harsher, "Jimmy and Frances, come get your supper before I throw it out." But not that night. There weren't any sounds at all because it was too dark for playing outdoors, and the streetlamps were lit. Or maybe it was the influenza. People were hiding indoors. After a time, Dorothy came outside in her orange coat and sat on the swing and took my hand. We smiled at each other but didn't talk.

Far down at the end of the next block, the streetcar came to a stop, sending out a metallic sound. After a few minutes Helen trudged up the street, tired, her shoulders slumped, and while Dorothy ran to meet her, I went inside to make supper.

The streetcar was always crowded this time of day, and I hoped Helen had found a seat.

The two of them came inside and sat down at the kitchen table, Helen too exhausted to take off her cape. I had made coffee and handed her a cup and saucer.

"Something happened, something grand, although I'd rather it hadn't happened," I said.

Helen looked at me as if she couldn't imagine that anything good could have occurred.

"Peter left me five thousand dollars. Evelyn came by to tell me."

Helen stared at me and set down her coffee cup. "Are you quite certain? Is there a will?"

I was about to answer when the doorbell rang, a harsh, rasping sound. I went to the door, Helen following behind, her cape in her hands.

A young man stood on the other side of the screen, and for a moment I wondered if he was the man from the automobile that parked across the street from time to time. But he was young, about Helen's age, I thought, and nice-looking.

He took off his hat and smiled and asked if Ronald Streeter lived here.

Helen gasped, and I put my hand on her arm to calm her. "He did," I said in a steady voice. "He left some time ago, and I don't know where he is."

"Oh, I know where he is," the man said. "May I come in?"

"Certainly not," I told him and glanced at the screen to see that it was hooked. Then I saw a second man, short, older, with a lumpy face, exactly as I pictured the man in the automobile.

"Sorry. I didn't introduce myself. I'm a detective, Detective Doyle McCauley. This is Detective Thrasher." He reached into his pocket and took out a badge and held it up to the screen.

I studied it a moment, then unlatched the door and held it open. "What's this about?" I asked, not daring to look at Helen.

"Mr. Streeter is dead," he said, stepping inside.

"The influenza?" Helen and I said together, a little too hopefully.

"Looked like it at first, but there's something off about it," Detective Thrasher said. He looked at me, not blinking.

"Dorothy?" Helen whispered to me.

"In her bedroom," I answered. "You look awful, Helen. Why don't you go sit with her?" Helen was so tired that I did not want her in the room, where she might slip and say something that would make the detectives suspect her.

Helen was as pale as cream, and her hand trembled. She went into Dorothy's room and closed the door.

"My sister is a nurse. She's been taking care of influenza victims. She's exhausted," I explained. "She is a wonderful person who wouldn't hurt a fly." I shouldn't have said that, and I made it worse by trying to turn the remark into a joke. "She doesn't even like to put up flypaper."

Neither man laughed. The older detective stared after Helen, but the younger one paid no attention.

"Dorothy is Mr. Streeter's daughter?" Detective McCauley asked.

"Yes. My sister and I hope to adopt her."

Detective Thrasher frowned. "Then you already knew her father was dead?"

"No, of course not," I said quickly. Too quickly. "It's a long story. You see, Mr. Streeter disappeared weeks ago, deserted his wife and daughter. Then Dorothy's mother died. She died of the influenza, too."

The detective didn't react.

"They lived in our basement, and there wasn't anybody to take in Dorothy. She's an orphan. At least she is now. She has no family." .

"Maybe not."

I looked at him, startled. "What do you mean?"

"She has an uncle, but that's not why we're here. That sort of thing is up to the courts. We came because Mr. Streeter didn't die of the influenza." He paused, narrowing his eyes. "It appears he was murdered."

The horror of that night came back to me. Mr. Streeter's body on the floor, Helen with the ice pick, Dorothy crouched beside her. "How dreadful." I wrapped my arms around myself and tried to sound surprised but did not know if I carried it off. I began to shiver and said, "You must forgive me. I'm just getting over the influenza." The detectives ignored that.

"We found his body. It was lying in a vacant lot—not far from here, by the way," Detective Thrasher said. He was dressed in a rumpled suit and had not taken off his hat. "It *looked* like he died of the influenza, but there was a puncture wound. That's what killed him. He almost got buried as an influenza case—there was an influenza note pinned to him—but a doctor spotted the wound. Lucky thing."

"Yes, lucky," I mumbled. "He was stabbed?"

Detective Thrasher said, "We probably wouldn't have paid

too much attention. You know, an unidentified man, and all those influenza deaths. But his brother-in-law came round looking for him. He identified the body. He said Mr. Streeter lived here." The detective looked around the room.

"In the basement. He lived in the basement."

The detective nodded. "Any idea who'd want him dead?"

I didn't answer. Instead I said, "I never heard he had a brother-in-law. Are you sure of it?"

Detective McCauley twirled his hat in his hands, then asked, "Mind if we take a seat?"

I pointed to the davenport, and the two men sat down. Detective McCauley set his hat beside him, but the other detective left his on.

"Do you know for sure he's Dorothy's uncle? She's never mentioned one. Is there proof?"

"Why would he claim he was if he wasn't?" Detective McCauley asked. "He said he and his wife would take in the little girl. Don't you think he's her uncle? I guess we could ask the kid."

"No," I said, too quickly, and the detectives looked at me, waiting me out. "Mr. Streeter was . . . he wasn't a very nice man," I said.

"Oh?"

"He was cruel."

"Whipped her, did he? There's nothing in the law says you can't whip your kid." Detective Thrasher narrowed his eyes again. "Some kids need it."

"It was more than that." I turned away. I couldn't tell them what had happened to Dorothy, not to two men.

"And you was going to adopt her?" Detective Thrasher asked.

"Maybe her father came back and didn't like that idea. Maybe he tried to take her away." He stood and wandered around the room, picking up knickknacks and then the turquoise vase Peter had bought for me on a day we'd driven to Colorado Springs. I wanted to tell him to put it down, that he might break it, but I didn't. "What do you say to that?" the detective asked.

"I say he didn't want her. After all, he ran out on Dorothy and her mother."

"Maybe he changed his mind."

"He was a horrible father."

"You already said that." The detective picked up the leather pillow and stared at it, then dropped it onto the couch. "You didn't answer the question. You know anybody who'd want this Streeter dead?" He paused, then added, "Other than you."

I regarded him coolly. At least I thought I did. "It was our belief that Mr. Streeter was involved with bootlegging. He had connections with men in North Denver."

"How do you know they were from North Denver?"

"They were Italian."

"How do you know?"

I had been too quick to cast blame. I shrugged. "Well, I assume they were. I was just trying to be helpful. You asked." Then I added, "They were swarthy, like you."

"I'm English," he said. "It's hot in here. You think I could have a glass of water?"

"Yes." He followed me into the kitchen, and so did Detective McCauley, who looked confused. I took two glasses from the cupboard and turned on the tap.

"Ice. You got ice?" Detective Hammond asked.

I opened the icebox, then felt chilled, but not from the cold air. I knew what he was after. The ice pick. I had intended to get rid of it, but I'd forgotten. Helen must have thrown it away. We had not yet bought another. We'd been using a hammer to chip at the ice. I did not know what to say, but behind me Helen said, "Here's the hammer, Lutie." She explained to the detectives, "We had an ice pick, but it broke weeks ago, and we haven't gotten another. We should have. It's a bother to use a hammer." I hadn't heard her come into the room.

The two detectives studied Helen, but she didn't flinch. "Where's the girl?" Detective McCauley asked at last.

"She's in her room. I told her that her father was dead. We are raising her."

"They say she has an uncle," I told Helen.

"Uncle?" Her hand went to her mouth. "There's no uncle."

The two detectives forgot about the water then and went back into the living room. "Guess we better talk to her," the younger man said.

Helen told them Dorothy was distraught, that she was a frail child who'd lost her mother and now her father, that she was in no condition to be questioned by two strange men.

"Maybe we ought to turn her over to a matron," Detective Thrasher said.

"No!" Helen told him. "You will not put her in an asylum. I know about such places." She stared at the detectives, then turned and went into Dorothy's room. In a moment, the two came out. I could not read what was in our little sister's eyes.

"These men are police officers. They're here to tell us your father died, dear," I explained.

"You didn't know that, did you?" Detective Thrasher asked.

Dorothy shook her head.

"Don't seem too upset, do you?"

"Like I told you—" I began.

He interrupted. "I know. He was a lousy father. Well, what about your uncle? He says he wants to take you in."

Dorothy slowly raised her eyes to look at the man.

"Do you have an uncle, Dorothy?" I asked. Fear gripped me.

Dorothy shook her head.

"Mr. Vincent," Detective McCauley said. "Your uncle Gus Vincent."

Dorothy stared at him a moment, then slowly her face distorted and she screamed, "No!" She clutched me and began sobbing. "Don't let him take me, Lutie. Don't let him."

The detectives looked uncomfortable. "Mr. Vincent claims he came here about the time Mr. Streeter died," the older man said. "He says he waited in the car for Mr. Streeter, but he never came out of your house."

I looked the detective in the eye and without blinking said, "He's a liar. We haven't seen Mr. Streeter since before Maud died." Detective Thrasher stared at me for a long time, but I wouldn't look away.

As soon as the two detectives left, Helen collapsed on the davenport with Dorothy in her arms. "Oh, Lute, what do we do?" She was crying.

"We won't let them take Dorothy, Helen. We'll move back to Iowa if we have to." I went into the kitchen to put away the glasses, and I heard something in the backyard. I pushed aside the window curtain in the door and looked out. Detective Mc-Cauley was climbing out of our ash pit with something long and shiny in his hand—something that looked like an ice pick. Helen should have put it in the garbage, because the metal pick hadn't burned. I dropped the curtain, but not before Detective Thrasher saw me watching. No, I'd never let them take Dorothy, and I wouldn't let them take Helen either.

Fourteen

In the morning, I called Mrs. Howell and asked her to recommend a lawyer. "I am so sorry to bother you when you are grieving over Peter's death. And you have done so much for us already, caring for Dorothy when I was sick. But the police were here yesterday. It seems there is a relative who wants to take in Dorothy. We're frantic to keep him from getting her."

"Of course you should bother me. Peter is gone. There is nothing we can do for him. But we must save Dorothy. I would have been distressed had you not turned to me. I have already consulted the judge, and he recommends a dear friend to be your attorney. The man may seem decrepit to you, but he is the best there is."

I telephoned the lawyer, Ted Coombs, and when I told him that Mrs. Howell had said the matter was urgent, he agreed to see me that afternoon. I called Neusteter's and said I was still too ill to return to work.

Mr. Coombs was elderly, with a craggy face and a shock of hair like old snow, and I wondered about his mental state and how he would react when I explained what Mr. Streeter had done. It wasn't easy discussing such things with anyone, let alone an old man. But Mrs. Howell was right; age had not dimmed his mind or his zealousness, and while he was incensed when I told him about Dorothy's father, he was not shocked. He said he had once worked on a case in the mountains in which a wealthy man was accused of fathering his own daughter's child.

While Dorothy stayed in a reception room with Mr. Coombs's assistant, a man nearly as old as his employer, I told the lawyer about Gus Vincent.

"Poor kid," he said. "No mother, a devil of a father, and now a depraved uncle. I know the name. He's a bootlegger. Those fellows are as vicious as they come. Likely he'll make Dorothy help with the business, send her out alone, and who knows what could happen to her. Beat her if she refuses. Maybe he already has. As you said, you thought Gus Vincent and Dorothy's father were in business together. The police have been after Vincent, but he's tricky. They haven't got anything on him yet."

"Maybe he wants Dorothy because he's afraid she'll tell the police about him."

"That could be. Do you think he's abused her, too?"

"Maybe." The idea repulsed me. "She's never said, of course. She's never told us about her father either. She'd have to testify, wouldn't she?"

"Yes, and I can't tell you how hard that would be for a little girl, especially in a courtroom. There's a good chance she wouldn't admit it, and even if she did, having to talk about it could destroy her. That girl I told you about in the mountains, I saw her years later. She had married a good man, but there was a sadness about her. She couldn't hold up her head. She never got over it." He paused. "Dorothy's testimony might even work against her, because it would be easy for Mr. Vincent's attorney to challenge her, and she might recant or fall to pieces. And of course he would deny it, deny he was a bootlegger, too."

"You mean Mr. Vincent could claim her even though the police think he's a criminal?"

"Yes, and he might succeed." Mr. Coombs leaned back in his chair, a swivel chair that was as old and creaky as he was. His office looked as if it had been set up when he started practicing law half a century earlier and never changed. There were law books stacked on shelves and dusty file cabinets, their drawers half-open and overflowing with papers. His desk was piled with legal documents and correspondence and notes. It was one of those desks with a rolltop that could be pulled down to cover the mess, but I doubted that it ever was. I would not have been surprised, however, if Mr. Coombs could have instantly put his hands on anything he wanted in that morass.

"What can we do? Should I take Dorothy and move back to Cedar Rapids, where her uncle couldn't find us?" I asked.

Mr. Coombs put his elbows on the arms of his chair and made a tent out of his fingers. "No, I wouldn't advise you do that. You might be charged with kidnapping, and that's a serious matter." He suddenly sat up very straight. "What we do is file adoption papers, file them today, before Dorothy's uncle knows what we've done. Perhaps a judge would rule before the uncle applies to adopt her. If we're too late and he protests and the case goes to court, we can't officially charge him with anything, because, as I say, we have no proof, and it would be his word against Dorothy's. But we might bring up his profession in some way." He paused and stared at his fingers. "Right now, we must proceed with the papers, on the assumption that there is no one else interested in taking in the girl."

"Will that work?"

Mr. Coombs nodded. "It should if the uncle doesn't show up before the adoption is final. I doubt a judge would throw a child into an orphanage when there is someone willing to raise her, particularly now, with all the orphans being created by the influenza. The judge would be glad to dispose of one more child. I suppose someone could object to two women adopting Dorothy, but as you say, your sister is to be married, and we can assume that she and her husband will take the child."

"We haven't talked about that."

"We will make that assumption at the hearing."

I said I understood.

Mr. Coombs rose, and so did I. He held out his hand and said he would prepare the papers immediately and would file them right away. And then he would have his clerk check the records to make sure Gus Vincent's wife was indeed Dorothy's aunt. "I've never forgotten that young woman in the mountains. I believe that men such as her father are pure evil." He shook his head at the thought. Then he added, "It would be a good idea if Mrs. Howell were to attend the hearing. She is well known for her work with orphans. I do not believe many judges would have the fortitude to stand up to her."

He walked me to the door, then said, "You will not be taking

on an easy task, Miss Hite. Children who've been raped—
women, too—they learn to live with it, but they never get over it."

When Helen got home that night, I told her about my visit to
Mr. Coombs. The fatigue on her face seemed to lessen, and she
smiled. "That's splendid, Lutie, just splendid."

"He said Dorothy might never get over what her father did
to her, but I know she will."

Helen shook her head. "He's right."

"I don't know. She hasn't had a nightmare the last few
nights."

"A week! Oh, Lutie, don't be naïve."

"I think if we give her enough love, she'll be fine." I sounded
defensive.

"I wish you were right. But you're not."

"You don't know everything, Helen."

"I know about this," she snapped.

I stared at my sister. I couldn't remember the last time we
had had words.

She stared back at me a moment. "I'm sorry, Lutie. I'm just
tired." We were in the kitchen, where I was preparing supper.
I had put ham in the oven and was removing the lettuce and
the salad cream from the icebox. Dorothy was at the dining
room table, drawing a picture and not paying attention to us.
Helen, sitting on one of the wooden chairs that I had painted
orange, ran her finger along the edge of the table, along the
white line where the oilcloth had been folded over and was
worn. Suddenly, she put her face down on the orange flowers
of the oilcloth and began to cry.

"It's all right, dear," I said. "You've been under such an awful strain." I sat down beside her and stroked her hair.

"She'll never get over it, Lutie. Never. Her life is ruined. You have to understand that."

"We'll do everything we can for her."

"It won't be enough. I know. It isn't enough for me."

I continued stroking Helen's hair, removing the hairpins and combing it with my fingers, as the words slowly sank in. "What do you mean?" I asked.

"Dorothy just won't. That's all."

"I mean, you said it wasn't enough for you."

"Did I say that? I didn't mean anything."

"But you did say it. What is it Helen? Tell me."

Helen had stopped crying. She sat up and brushed the tears from her face with her fingertips. "It's nothing."

I waited.

Suddenly, she threw her arms around me. "Oh, Lute, I never wanted you to know. What would you think of me if I told you? It's bad enough that Mother blamed me."

"For what?"

Finally, she said, "I was raped."

"You?" I was astonished. I let go of Helen and sat back in my chair, trying to understand. Who could have done such a monstrous thing?

"You see, you're ashamed of me."

"Helen, I'm not ashamed. I'm horrified. I'm ashamed you felt you couldn't confide in me."

"It happened in nursing school."

"A doctor?"

"The husband of a patient." Helen sighed deeply, then spread her fingers on the oilcloth.

"Do I know him?"

"Of course. Dr. Harwood."

I thought back. "Dr. Harwood. You mean our minister?" I put my hand to my mouth.

"You don't believe me. Mother didn't either."

"Of course I believe you. I'm just shocked is all. I thought he was a good man. He used to pat us on the head when we were little. People admired him."

"Any man can be a rapist—rich, poor, ne'er-do-wells, respected men." She had curled her lip when she said "respected." Then she said, "It was when Mrs. Harwood was ill. You remember, she had cancer, and she died."

I remembered the thin, mousy lady. In fact, when I'd first considered marrying Peter and being a minister's wife, I'd thought of her, wondering if I'd become just like her. Dr. Harwood, on the other hand, was a handsome man with a booming voice and a friendly manner. After Mrs. Harwood died, people at church gossiped about the widows who suddenly took an interest in religion.

"I was in my first year of nursing school. Dr. Harwood needed someone to sit with his wife at night. I thought I was very lucky when he asked for me. She was dying, and she was in terrible pain. I wanted to give her something, but Dr. Harwood said pain was God's punishment."

"For what?" I asked. "She was a sweet lady."

"Maybe for marrying him," Helen replied, acid in her voice. "I used to hear him tell her she was a sinner. She slept only about half the night, and while she was asleep, I studied or napped. There was a daybed in an alcove off the bedroom. Dr. Harwood slept in another room."

Helen took a deep breath and forced herself to go on. "She was really quite dear. She asked me to read Scripture to her. She apologized for being a burden to me. Dr. Harwood never knew that I gave her Aspirin, but it didn't help the pain much. She bore it well. She didn't bear him very well, though. She would get tense when he came into the room. I think she was afraid of him. Sometimes when she slept, she would curl up into a ball and cry out, 'Don't, oh, please, don't.' It wouldn't have surprised me if he hurt her—on purpose."

"What a horrid man. I guess you never know," I said.

Helen was silent for a moment. She kept running her finger back and forth along the edge of the table. "Like I said, sometimes I napped when Mrs. Harwood slept. I woke up one night when Dr. Harwood touched my arm. At first I thought his wife needed me, that she had cried out and I hadn't heard her, and I was embarrassed. I tried to sit up, but Dr. Harwood's hands were on my shoulders, pushing me back down. There was a light on near the bed, and I could see he wasn't wearing his pants. I told him to stop, but he said, 'Be still. You don't want to wake her, do you?'"

Helen looked up then, but not at me. Instead, she stared at the kitchen clock, her head slowly making a circle with the second hand. "I told him to get off me. He said, 'Shut up. I know what you want. You women who won't stay home and be wives, you're unnatural, an affront to God.' He called me a temptress and a whore and accused me of working in a hospital so that I could see naked men. He pushed me back down on the bed and tried to kiss me, and I could feel his drool on my cheek."

She rubbed her cheek, as if the wetness were still there. "He said God had given me to him to meet his needs, since his wife couldn't. I told him I wasn't the Virgin Mary."

I laughed, I couldn't help myself, and Helen looked at me for the first time since she'd started her story and smiled a little. "What did he say to that?" I asked.

"He called me a blasphemer and was so angry he slapped me. Then he put his hands on me. They were chapped. I can still feel them sometimes. He ripped my uniform, and when I tried to kick him he cursed me. I said I'd tell, but he asked who would believe me." Helen paused, remembering, and her eyes filled with tears. "Oh, Lute, I couldn't stop him. He forced himself into me. It hurt, and when he was finished, I was sticky and bloody. I grabbed my cape and ran all the way home in the rain. It was the middle of the night, and I filled the bathtub with water so hot it nearly scalded me, and I scrubbed and scrubbed, but sometimes even now I feel his seed on me."

I shut my eyes against the horror of what Helen had gone through. "Did you tell on him?"

"I hadn't planned to, but my supervisor called me in and said the minister had complained he'd had to dismiss me because I'd left his wife in the middle of the night. So I told her what happened."

"What did she say?"

"That he was a man of the cloth—those were her words, 'man of the cloth'—and that he had merely been trying to wake me up. I asked, 'With his pants off?' She was embarrassed and told me I was mistaken. And even if something had happened, it was my fault for encouraging him. I said, 'By sleeping?' She told me that was beside the point."

"So nothing happened?" I asked, incredulous.

"Of course not. He was right. Nobody believed me. People think ministers don't do such things. They sent another girl to replace me. A week later, she dropped out of school. I went to her and said it wasn't her fault, but she claimed she didn't know what I was talking about."

I realized I had left the ham in the oven and got up and turned off the gas. The meat was burned, but that wasn't important. I sat down beside Helen. "Did you tell Mother and Father?"

"Mother. She was embarrassed, too, and said I was young and confused and must have misinterpreted things. She told me not to tell anyone, especially you."

"I would have believed you."

Helen turned and looked at me. "I knew you would. That's why I didn't tell you. You were so innocent. I didn't want you to know about such things."

"Oh, Helen, you've had to deal with this all by yourself." I took her hands. "I would hate ministers, too."

She squeezed my hands. "I thought I could handle it, and I did. Only sometimes . . ."

"Does Gil know?"

Helen jerked up her head to look at me. "No, of course not. I wouldn't dare tell him."

"Why not?"

"What would he think of me?"

I shook my head. "He loves you. He'd know it wasn't your fault. Gil's a wonderful man. He'd never hold it against you." Then I had a sudden thought. "Is that why you keep putting off getting married, because of . . . um . . . going to bed with him? Do you think you'll hate it?" Maybe Dr. Harwood was the reason Helen and I had never spoken about sex.

She let go of my hands and stood and stared out the window in the back door. "Every time I think of being with Gil like that, I just cringe. I couldn't bear to have him touch me the way Dr. Harwood did. I can barely stand to kiss him."

I got up and stood by Helen. She reached over and turned on the back-door light.

"That's why you sleep with the light on, isn't it? You and Dorothy."

Helen didn't answer. She didn't have to.

"You haven't coped with it after all."

Helen stared out into the night. "That's what I tried to tell you. Dorothy won't either. It takes more than love." She turned around suddenly. "But you know what, Lutie, I feel better now that I've told you."

"And Dorothy knows we know what happened to her and love her anyway. That's why we can't let go of her," I said.

We held each other for a long time, until Dorothy came into the kitchen. I had forgotten she was in the dining room and now realized she might have heard us. But maybe it didn't matter that she knew Helen, too, had been abused. She might not feel so alone. She held up her picture. It showed the backs of two women, one tall and blonde, the other dark and short, holding hands.

Fifteen

Helen was so distraught she couldn't eat her dinner, and I wouldn't have been surprised if she had come down with a case of nerves. I led her into the bedroom, where she sat on the bed, took off her shoes, then lay down, too sleepy to remove her uniform. "I'm glad you told me," I said.

She smiled but didn't reply.

Near morning, I heard her go into the hall. She woke me because she had stumbled, and when I turned on the light I saw her leaning against the bathroom door.

"Are you all right?" I called softly.

"I'm . . . I'm . . . ," Helen whispered.

I pushed back the covers and put on my dressing gown and went to her.

She was still wearing her uniform, and she seemed disoriented. "Can I help?" I asked.

"No . . . no." She waved me away and stumbled into the bathroom and closed the door.

I went down the hall to her bedroom and took her nightgown off the hook on the closet door. Then I straightened her sheets and fluffed her pillow, and as I did so I saw the bloodstains. I went to the bathroom door and listened, and I heard

Helen vomiting. I tapped on the door. "Do you need me?" I asked.

"I'm all right," Helen said in a muffled voice.

But she wasn't. I remembered my own illness, and I knew then that my sister had the influenza. I was sure of it. I sank down onto the floor beside the bathroom door and put my arms around myself, because I had begun to shake as the awfulness of Helen's situation hit me.

What could I do? As a nurse, Helen understood the influenza better than I. She was aware of the steps to take. What did I know about caring for a patient? As I sat there, I tried to remember what she had done for me when I was sick, but I had been delirious. I didn't remember much about eating or taking medication, only the terrible dreams and Helen by my side, stroking my hair, wiping my face with a cool washcloth, changing my sheets and nightgowns.

As I rubbed away the tears, I thought I should stop feeling sorry for myself. It was Helen, not I, who was threatened. I stood up and tapped on the door, then opened it a little. Helen was sitting on the floor. "I can't get up," she whispered. "Something's happened to my legs."

I went to her and lifted her, feeling how little flesh was on her bones, and she held on to me as I led her into her bedroom. She sat on the bed while I took off her uniform and her underwear, then slid her nightgown over her head. "What do I do, Helen? How do I take care of you?"

"Get Dorothy out of here," she said slowly. That was just like Helen, to think of someone else before herself.

I helped her lie down, then went into the kitchen and got

out the enamel pan she had given me when I was ill and set it on the bed next to her in case she had to vomit and could not make it to the bathroom. I filled a pitcher with water and put it and a glass on the bedside table. "Are you cold?" I asked. "Hot?" She closed her eyes and lay back in the bed and did not answer.

I went to the telephone and gave the operator the Howells' number. George answered, and when I told him what was wrong he woke Mrs. Howell, who said she would send Melvin right away. Dorothy could stay with her—stay with her again—until Helen was well.

Then I telephoned Gil's rooming house. It was a shame to wake all the tenants, but Gil had told us he always answered the telephone when he was there because most of the calls were for him, from hospitals or patients. If he wasn't at home, I'd try every hospital in Denver. But he answered, sounding tired.

"I'm so sorry to wake you. She has the influenza, Gil."

"Dorothy?" He sounded almost hopeful. I knew he was thinking, Not Helen.

"It's Helen."

"Oh God!" And then after a pause, "I'm coming over."

"Can't you just give me some instructions?" He needed sleep as much as Helen did.

"No, I'll be there."

"But you've got patients."

"Do you think I care more about them than Helen?"

The remark made me shiver. Gil loved Helen as much as I had loved Peter—still loved Peter. Of course he would be here. Thank goodness!

Helen was sleeping now. The basin I'd set beside her was empty, so she hadn't thrown up again, and I hoped that was a good sign. Her breathing was labored, and she was perspiring. I dipped a cloth into cool water and washed her.

Gil arrived just after the Howells' chauffeur picked up Dorothy. Gil was breathless. He hadn't shaved, and he looked wild. There were fewer streetcars that early in the morning, so he'd run the distance to our house.

"How is she?" he asked, leaning over to catch his breath.

"She's not that blue color, like Maud was," I said.

"That could come later." Gil went into the bedroom and stared a minute at Helen. Then he touched her forehead and wiped her face with the washcloth I'd left on the table. He took out a stethoscope and unbuttoned the front of Helen's nightgown so that he could hear her heart. For a moment I felt embarrassed for Helen, that her breast was exposed like that. She would hate it. But he was a doctor. He was a professional, and when he was finished, he covered her up. Then he turned to me.

"Her heart's racing a little, but it's not bad. Has she eaten anything?"

"Not much, and she vomited it early this morning. She hasn't thrown up since, but then, there's nothing left in her stomach."

Gil nodded. "I'll sit with her."

"Don't you have other patients?"

"To hell with them," he said fiercely. He turned and put his arms around me, and I could see how shaken he was.

"She'll be all right, won't she, Gil? You won't let her die?"

"No, she won't die. We won't let her." The words were false, but still, they made me feel better. "I'll sit with her," he said again, and I realized how tired I was. I went into my room and lay down. I wasn't sure I would sleep, but I did, and it was late morning when I awoke. I went into Helen's room and found Gil sitting on a dining room chair he had set next to the bed. "She hasn't wakened since you left."

"That's a good sign, isn't it?"

He gave me a stiff smile. "Yes, although she could be unconscious."

"You don't know? You just let her lie there?"

"What difference does it make?" he snapped. "Either way, she's resting."

I put my hand on his shoulder.

"I'm sorry, Lute. After all the deaths . . . well, I couldn't bear it if something happened to Helen."

"Me either."

"She's been delirious," he said.

I waited, fearful of what he might tell me.

"I can't make it out. She's talking about Dorothy, I think. Once she said something like 'I won't tell.' I wonder what that means."

"I'm sure it had something to do with Dorothy. Did you talk to her yesterday? Did she tell you we've started adoption proceedings?"

Gil shook his head. I pulled another chair into the room, and then I told him about Gus Vincent.

"Do they know that Helen . . . ?" Gil couldn't finish.

"That she killed Mr. Streeter? No, of course not. But they

know something isn't right. They went through our ash pit, and I think they found the ice pick. I was going to throw it out, but Helen beat me to it."

"It's not a crime to throw out an ice pick."

"Can they tell if it's the one that killed him?"

"I don't think so. An ice pick's an ice pick. You washed it, didn't you? And you've burned trash since Helen threw it in there. I doubt they'll find blood on it."

"But there's still Mr. Vincent. He told the police he saw Mr. Streeter go into our house and not come out."

"If he really is Dorothy's uncle, they might be inclined to listen to him. But because they suspect he's a criminal . . ." Gil shrugged.

I felt a little relieved, but not much. I stood and glanced out Helen's window at the ash pit, but no one was there. I told Gil I would fix coffee. "There's ham, and I can fry you an egg," I said. "If you're like Helen, you probably haven't eaten much lately."

"I'm not hungry," he said.

I wasn't either. I left the room and went into the kitchen, where I filled the percolator and turned on the gas. Helen moaned and I rushed back into the bedroom.

Gil was sitting on the bed next to my sister, wiping her face with a washcloth. When he took it away he folded it over, but not before I saw the blood.

"What?" I asked.

"It's a blood-tinged froth that comes from the patient's nose and mouth. Quite common."

"That sounds terrible."

"It's all terrible."

Helen had sunk into a deep sleep. I remembered the coffee and went back to the kitchen.

As I waited for the coffee to perk, I listened to the familiar sounds of a new day. Next door, the chickens clucked as our neighbor threw out breakfast scraps. The milkman stopped his horse in the alley and came up the back walk, taking the empty bottle from the milk chute in the kitchen wall and replacing it with a bottle of fresh milk. I set it in the icebox, hoping the iceman would come that day.

The boys down the block called to each other. Before long, the girl two houses down would come looking for Dorothy. She would see the quarantine sign I had put on the door that morning and go away.

The milk chute was open. I stooped and shut it, and then I sat down with my head in my hands. The cold floor felt good on my legs, and I rested my head against the kitchen wall and closed my eyes, listening to the faint sounds of Gil moving around in the bedroom. He was talking to Helen. I put my hands over my face and cried, the tears seeping through my fingers, until Gil came into the room.

"Here now," he said with fake cheeriness. "That won't do Helen any good. Most influenza patients come through just fine—ninety percent of them. You know that. You did. Helen will, too."

"I feel so useless. Helen is the one who knows how to heal people. Even as a girl, she could read a thermometer. She'd feel my forehead to see if I had a fever, and she'd tell Mother when

I needed ice or a custard. When I ate too much at the circus, she stayed up part of the night to care for me, and she wasn't any more than eleven or twelve. That's when she came up with that silly expression 'Dream about clowns.'"

"I never heard that."

"It was just for us." I wiped the tears from my face with my fingers. "She's a good person, Gil."

"I know that. And you're a lot like her. Don't sell yourself short, Lute."

I loved Gil for saying that and scrambled to my feet. "I think the coffee's ready." I poured it into two cups and leaned against the drainboard next to the sink while I sipped mine. "Is she any better?"

"The truth?"

"Yes."

"No. The influenza will have to run its course, which it will if we're lucky."

"That's all we can do, hope for luck?"

"You can pray."

I snorted. "I've tried that. It doesn't do much. It didn't do anything for Peter."

Gil shrugged. We'd never talked about religion, so I didn't know if he believed in God.

"I gave her Aspirin. That will help a little with the fever and the pain."

"Nothing else?" I asked.

"The patients who survive seem to be those who go to bed as soon as the symptoms show and stay in bed long after the influenza is gone. We'll both insist she stay in bed after she's herself again."

"After she's herself again," I repeated.

We took turns sitting beside Helen. When it was my turn, Gil was restless, walking around the house.

After a time, Helen began to moan and cry out. She tossed her head back and forth and muttered, "No! No!" Once, she said, "Get . . . off . . . me."

"She's delirious," Gil said.

I knew what she was dreaming about, and I held Helen's hand and said over and over, "He's not here, dear. He's gone. You're safe." I don't know if she heard me, but after a while she stopped moaning.

"What was that about?" Gil asked.

"Something that happened a long time ago."

"What?"

I shrugged. It wasn't my story to tell.

"Tell me," Gil insisted. I shook my head, but he kept at me. "I've always thought something happened to her before I met her. I heard a lecture in medical school about, well, women who've been . . ." He sounded embarrassed and didn't finish.

"Raped?" I'd rarely said the word out loud, and it sounded harsh and ugly.

"Oh my God. Did that happen to her?"

"I can't tell you."

Gil was persistent. "Is that why she doesn't like to be . . .

touched? I can barely kiss her good-night, you know. She freezes up. I've imagined all kinds of things. Is that why she puts off the wedding?"

"You should talk to Helen," I said.

Gil reached down and took Helen's hand.

Then I said, "It wasn't her fault. She's ashamed. I think she believes you'd hate her if you knew."

"Hate her? Oh my God, Lute. How could she think that? I'd want to protect her." He sat down on the bed beside Helen and took my unconscious sister in his arms. The scene was too intimate, and I left the room and stood in the hall, remembering what it was like to have Peter's arms around me and hoping for Gil's sake, as well as Helen's, that he would not know what it meant to never again hold the person you loved.

I said I would sit with Helen and made Gil go into the living room and lie down. Helen was quiet for a time, and then she began to moan and thrash around. Once she called out, "It's all right." I touched her arm to soothe her, but she brushed it off as if it were a hot poker. She turned her head back and forth on the pillow, and I used the washcloth to wipe the blood from her nose. She pushed my hand away, and suddenly she sat up, her eyes open but unfocused, and said in a clear voice, "It's all right, Dorothy. I'll say I did it. Give me the ice pick."

"Helen!" I said. "What is it?"

She stared straight ahead, not looking at me.

"Didn't you stab Mr. Streeter?" I whispered.

Helen didn't answer. Instead, she slumped over and began to moan again.

"Did Dorothy kill him?" I asked again. But Helen didn't respond.

I sat back in the chair and clutched the washcloth, now dirty, in my hands, realizing then what had happened. Dorothy had stabbed her father, and Helen had taken the blame for it. She'd lied to the police, and even to me.

"Helen?" I whispered, but she didn't respond. "You protected Dorothy, just like you always protected me," I told her. "That's what sisters do."

Sixteen

The rain started that afternoon and made me feel itchy and restless. When Helen quieted, I tried to sit beside her, but every few minutes I'd get up and walk around. Over and over in my mind, I pictured Helen walking into the kitchen and discovering Dorothy with Mr. Streeter's body. She'd kept the truth from me because she'd known I'd have tried to save *her*. I wondered if I would have been as selfless.

Gil and I had eaten little all day. So that evening, when Helen seemed to be sleeping, I heated soup that Mrs. Howell had sent to us. I set the bowls on the kitchen table, then went to get Gil, but he had fallen asleep on the davenport. He needed rest more than food, so I left him there.

Perhaps if I had sewing to work on I would not be so restless, I thought. I took out my boxes and bags of lace and trims and old fabric and found a crazy quilt that was almost finished. I had forgotten about it. Mother had tried to teach Helen and me how to quilt when I was ten or eleven. We had dutifully fitted the shapes together, and the three of us had stitched the top to the back. Helen did not care for sewing, and back then I had considered all quilts dumpy and old-fashioned, so we had never finished it. I had almost tossed it out when we moved from Iowa, but the three of us had worked on it together and I couldn't bear to leave it behind. Now I took the quilt into Helen's room and sat down beside her to work on it.

It wasn't a quilt, really, just a throw. We had done everything except for the binding, which was a long gold ribbon, faded now to a dull color. It was strange that I had forgotten about the quilt, because now I loved piecing together bits of old silk and velvet and lace.

I ran my hand over the patches, which were odd pieces— some scraps, others cut into shapes to fit the quilt. We had included ribbons with lettering on them. There was one that Father had worn at an Elks convention and another that Helen had gotten for achievement in science. She told us how her teacher had been upset that a girl had won first place. There was leftover lace from a dress Mother had made for me when I was in first grade as well as a plaid hair ribbon, a piece of velvet with a duck Helen had drawn on it, a fan made from silk ribbons, and two patches with the outline of a small hand—one Helen's, one mine.

I put my hand over the outline of Helen's hand. My hand was much larger than that tiny shape. Now Helen's hand was curled up, birdlike, on the coverlet, and I thought of her touching my forehead when I was hot with fever. How odd that her hands, which were so precise at her nursing chores, were clumsy with a sewing needle.

I, on the other hand, had been fascinated with the way we stitched the pieces to the paper backing, which we tore off later, and I loved seeing how the quilt came alive when we embroidered over the seams with gold floss. I had learned to embroider on that quilt, experimenting with different stitches.

Helen had learned to embroider on that quilt, too, but she had never liked it, and her stitches were lumpy and knotted compared with mine. "I think embroidery was the only thing I was better at than you," I said as I sat beside Helen now. Gil had told me to talk to her because she might hear me, and indeed, Helen's voice had come through my own delirium. "Look at how you knotted this up. Why, you didn't even fasten the thread before you cut it, and now it's pulled out." I laughed a little. "No wonder you became a nurse instead of a seamstress."

I had felt foolish talking to Helen when Gil was there, but now that he was in the living room asleep, it seemed natural. "Of course, I wouldn't make a throw like this now. It's too much of a hodgepodge and the colors are gaudy." I thought a minute. "I remember that you actually thought this quilt was pretty. It was stitching on it that you didn't like. You wanted me to complete it, but you wouldn't work it, and I was too stubborn to finish it by myself. Silly, isn't it? Well, I'll finish it now, and you can keep it in your bedroom."

I cut a length of thread and inserted it through the eye of the needle, knotted one end, and pulled it through the binding. As I did so, I spotted Helen's initials, HH—three upright lines and one cross-line that ran from end to end. I touched them, feeling the roughness of the embroidery. Helen Hite. It was such a pretty name. I smiled. "I used to wish I'd been named Helen, you know. I always thought you were the lucky one," I told her. "But really, *I'm* the lucky one because I have *you* for a sister."

I stitched for a long time, then set down the quilt and stood and stretched. Because I was stiff from sitting, I wandered around Helen's room, looking at her things in the dim light that came from the lamp on the table beside the bed. I picked up the formal photographs of our parents and grandparents and the aunt Helen was named for, all taken in studios. Faded now, the pictures were displayed in silver frames on a white dresser scarf. As I looked at the portrait of our grandmother, I saw that Helen favored her. I'd never noticed that before. There was also a picture of the two of us, little girls in starched party dresses, Helen with her bright golden hair and me small and dark.

In front of the portraits was a snapshot of Helen and Gil, the two of them sitting on a rock in the mountains. Peter had snapped the picture the day the four of us took the train to Georgetown for a Sunday outing. We had gone there to gather columbine, and the boys had picked bunches for us to take home. Of course, most of the flowers died on the train, but Helen had kept one and dried it, and it lay on her bureau next to the picture.

That trip was one of the best times we four had had together. We'd wandered around the town looking at the quaint houses, one of them a mansion with a tennis court that had gone to seed. The house was seedy, too. A woman sat on the porch with a book, and Helen and I speculated about her. Peter knew who she was, a spinster whose father had lost all his money.

I opened Helen's jewelry box, a glass casket with pink silk lining, moving her few pieces with my finger—some nursing pins, plain gold earrings, Mother's wedding ring, and another ring that had belonged to our grandmother, gold with rubies in it. Mother and Grandmother were partial to rubies, and Helen liked them, too, although she rarely wore jewelry. And there was the small gold cross that she had received when she was confirmed.

Helen's bedroom was plain. Mine was filled with pillows and throws and scarves hanging on the walls, with pictures and paintings and a collection of pretty rocks and bits of driftwood and objects I had picked up in junk shops. But Helen's room had only the things on her dresser—the jewelry box, the photographs, an old California Fig Syrup bottle turned purple from the sun that Gil had found on that same trip to Georgetown. The only picture on the wall was one I had painted, a bench beside a pond with weeping willows around it. I had not liked the picture much, had thought it too sentimental and was going to paint over it, but Helen wanted it. I offered to paint a figure on the bench because the scene was lonely, but Helen said no. What had she seen in it that I hadn't?

Toward morning, Helen woke me when she cried out, "No! Dorothy! . . . Oh God!"

I sat up, disoriented, not remembering at first where I was. When I did, I touched Helen's forehead, which was hot. Her eyelids were inflamed. Helen had beautiful eyes, like pale blue silk, and I wanted her to open them; I wanted her to look at me and know I was there. But she didn't. I went to the bathroom and ran cold water over a washcloth, then returned to Helen and wiped her face and neck and chest. She had spots on her cheeks the color of mahogany. She coughed again, and suddenly she coughed so hard that she threw up. I held her while she vomited into the basin. There wasn't anything solid in her stomach, because she'd taken only a little water with the Aspirin Gil had given her. But there was blood in the bowl.

"Gil!" I called, but he was already at the bedroom door. Helen's spasms had awakened him.

"I fell asleep," he said, as if chastising himself.

"She's only now started coughing. But there's blood."

Gil pushed me aside, sitting on the bed with his arms around Helen. "She's chilled," he said. Helen was shaking now.

"But she was hot only a few minutes ago."

"It's that way." He thrust a thermometer into her mouth, and when he withdrew it, he said, "A hundred and three."

Helen began gasping for breath and crying, and Gil pounded her on the back. "She's congested, and she's in pain."

"What do we do?"

"I don't know." His voice was raspy. "I'd give her morphine, but I don't have any. We can try more Aspirin, but I don't think it will help much."

Helen moaned then, and I shook four Aspirin into my hand and put them in her mouth, then forced her to drink some water. I sat down on the other side of the bed. "Tell me what to do. Please, Gil, isn't there something?"

"Rub her back. Sometimes they have back pain."

I placed my hand on the small of Helen's back and began to knead the muscles, but Helen only cried more. "Shouldn't we call someone? Another doctor?"

"If we could get one. But what could he do? Nobody knows how to cure this, Lute."

Blood began to spurt from Helen's nose, and Gil washed it

away with the cloth. Then he stopped, his finger on one of the spots I had seen earlier. He touched each one.

"What is it?" I asked. "I meant to point them out to you."

"Cyanosis." He laid Helen against her pillow and put his hands to his face to catch the tears.

"What is cyanosis?" The word was familiar, but I couldn't remember its meaning.

"She's begun to turn color."

I gasped. "That obscene blue? That horrid color you told me about? Oh my God." I touched my sister's face. "Does that mean . . . ?" I couldn't finish the sentence.

Gil nodded.

"No!" I covered my face with my hands, and now I really was crying. "Isn't there anything we can do?"

"Pray." Then he added, "We can make her comfortable."

All of Helen's nightgowns were soiled, so I got one from my room. Gil and I removed the old one and washed Helen gently. We dressed her in the clean gown, and I brushed her hair and tied it with a ribbon, then put a dab of scent behind her ears and on her wrists. Gil had given her the perfume, a lily of the valley scent, and Helen wore it on special occasions. I put on fresh pillowcases, but we left the sheets because we would have had to move Helen to change them, and we thought that might hurt her.

Gil told me I should sleep. He would call me if there was any change. Perhaps he wanted to be alone with Helen, so I went into my room and lay down, and I did not wake until it was morning.

I got up and washed my face and went into Helen's room.

Gil was stretched out on the bed beside her, just as I had been. He was not sleeping, however. He was brushing a strand of Helen's hair out of her eyes. The ribbon had come undone, and Helen's hair was around her face like long grasses that had been blown about by the wind.

"She didn't like her hair color, you know," Gil said, which surprised me, because Helen had beautiful hair that shone gold, only now it was dull, the color of maple syrup. "She wished it was dark, like yours." Gil must have sensed my surprise. "She told me you had always been the most beautiful creature in the world. From the time you were a little girl, she thought of you as a china doll, with dark hair and eyes and white skin. But she loved you too much to be jealous."

"Jealous? What could she be jealous of?"

"Your talent. Your spirit. Your way with people. She was very protective of you, and she worried about you all the time. Worried about the way you were treated at work. Worried at first that you would fall for Peter, then worried that he wouldn't come home. One of the reasons she put off marrying me was she didn't want to leave you alone." He thought that over. "At least I think that was a reason." He looked unsure of himself. "Maybe she just didn't want to marry me."

"Of course she did," I said quickly.

Helen coughed, and Gil, who was still lying next to her, sat up.

"She hasn't coughed much, has she? Isn't that a good sign?"

"No, Lute, don't."

"But she could get better. It would be a miracle, but she could."

"You don't believe in miracles. I don't either. Besides, look at her color."

I studied my sister and saw that her skin, especially on her lips, was darker now. "Will it keep on turning blue like that?"

Gil nodded. "Sometimes a patient's skin actually turns black. It stops when . . ." He didn't have to add "the person dies."

"Why don't we try those methods that were in the newspaper? Maybe they're not really quack remedies. One of them might work. Dover's powder or Epsom salt."

"Lute," Gil said. "Let her die in peace."

"If it were done, when 'tis done, then 'twere well it were done quickly," I said. "Peter said that about the war."

"*Macbeth*." Gil and Helen had attended the play with Peter and me.

There was blood on the pillow and on the sheets, and the bowl of water beside the bed was red with it. I told Gil to go into the living room and lie down on the couch while I sat with Helen, but he wouldn't leave. "It won't be long," he salt, standing up.

While he went into the bathroom to get fresh water, I straightened the bed and fluffed the pillow. I combed her hair and tied it again. Then Gil sat down on the bed beside Helen while I took the chair. We were there for a long time, not talking. Our telephone rang, but I didn't answer it. Someone knocked on the door, but I didn't answer that either, only heard the door open and the Howells' chauffeur call that he had left a basket for us.

The sky was light outside now, although there was no sun. The room was stuffy and smelled of sickness, and I went to the window and opened it. The rain had stopped. Water dripped off the trees onto the dead hollyhocks. Rainy days made Helen nervous, and now I knew why. It had rained the night the minister attacked her. She had liked Colorado because of the sunshine. The rain gushed out of the downspout, pooling on the sidewalk. In winter that spot was always slippery. The wind came up and blew drops of water onto the curtains and the floor, and the cold air felt good in the hot room.

Behind me, Helen gasped. "Dorothy!" she cried. "Lutie!"

I rushed to the bed and took my sister's hand, holding the bluish fingers in mine. "She's gone," Gil said after a minute, but I already knew that. And then he said, "Oh God! She's gone," and began to cry—sobs that shook his body.

I didn't cry, however. Not then. I only felt a great weight pressing down on me. "Why?" I asked. "Why Helen and not me? Why Peter and Maud and not me?" I reached out my hand to Gil and he clutched it, then stopped crying and apologized for breaking down. Doctors weren't supposed to do that, he said. But he was not a doctor then. He was a man who had lost the girl he loved. I was sorry Helen had not said his name at the end.

We sat like that for a long time. The telephone rang again, but I stayed beside Helen. At last, Gil stood and said, "There are things we have to do. There are papers to be signed. And we'll have to dispose of the body. I'll take care of it, Lute."

"Don't leave her on the street," I said suddenly, recalling the bodies of influenza victims that had been left outside for the death wagons. I thought of Mr. Streeter's body abandoned in a vacant lot. I couldn't let that happen to Helen. "Promise me you won't." I was a little hysterical.

"Of course I won't."

"Call Fairmount Cemetery. That's where the Howells are buried. Maybe we can get a plot near theirs. Maybe if you mention their name, they'll find us a space." Then I added suddenly, "A plot for two graves." I would not let Helen sleep through eternity alone. Death would not separate me from my sister.

Gil made the calls, and late that morning, two men wearing masks came for Helen's body. Gil and I had dressed Helen in a clean uniform. She was proud of being a nurse and would have wanted to be buried in it. Gil reminded me there wouldn't be a service, because they were still forbidden. I had forgotten.

The men carried Helen's body to a wagon. They were about to leave when I remembered the throw I had been stitching, and I told them to wait while I ran back inside to fetch it. "This should go into her coffin," I said. She should sleep with it forever.

"They might lose it," Gil told me. What he meant was that the quilt was likely to be tossed aside. Perhaps there weren't even coffins now. For all I knew, people were being buried in shrouds. But I wanted Helen to have something we had made together wrapped around her.

"That's real pretty, lady," one of the men said. "We'll keep it with her. We got orders she's somebody," and I knew mentioning Mrs. Howell had helped. The man had taken off his cap when he saw Helen's body, and now he put the cap back on. I was grateful that all the death he had seen had not deadened his compassion.

The two men climbed into the wagon and one picked up the reins, but I told them again to wait. I went to the back of the wagon and lifted Helen's hand and held it until the driver turned around to show he was impatient. "Good-bye, my sweet Helen," I said. Then I whispered, "Dream about clowns."

Seventeen

After the wagon pulled away, Gil left, his shoulders slumped as he walked down the street. I knew he wanted to be alone, and I did, too.

I went back into the house and stripped the bed and carried the bedding to the ash pit, along with Helen's nightgowns and underwear and the uniform she had worn the day she got sick. I struck a match and dropped it on top of the clothing, but I could not bear to see her things consumed by the flames, so I went back into the house. I washed Helen's room with soap and water and vinegar, wiping down the bed and the other furniture. Then I scrubbed the floor. The boiling water scalded my hands, and my back and knees hurt from kneeling on the wood with the scrub brush, but I was glad; I wanted pain in my body instead of my heart.

When the room was clean, I changed my dress and put on my coat and hat, and impulsively I fastened Helen's gold cross around my neck. Then I walked to the trolley stop, because I would have to tell Dorothy that Helen was dead. I could have called a taxicab. I could even have called the Howells and asked them to send Melvin. But I was in no hurry. There was nothing I could do for Helen, and Dorothy would have a few more minutes to play with the dollhouse before she heard the news.

I did not know how to tell her about Helen or how she would react. It might be too much for her, losing her mother and her "sister" so close together. And coping with having killed her father. I knew that now. Helen must have taken the ice pick from Dorothy's hand when she heard me come into the house.

The streetcar rumbled in the distance, the metal wheels screaming against the metal rails. I wasn't far from the stop, but I didn't hurry. I would let the streetcar go past, and there would be another one. Perhaps I would not take the streetcar at that stop but would walk to the next one. The cold air was cleansing. Drops of water fell onto my neck as I continued to walk. It had begun to drizzle, and I had not brought an umbrella. I went on past the second streetcar stop and the third one as rain splashed onto the black streets, drops falling on me and falling on the cast-iron fences that surrounded the old houses. The cold numbed me. I walked too near a curb, and a driver sprayed water on me and yelled, "Watch it, dearie," but I barely heard him and did not even look up.

I held out my hand and caught the raindrops and rubbed the moisture onto my face, and I remembered how Helen and I once had been out in the rain when we were girls and had walked through the mud, watching it squeeze up between our toes. Helen and I would never do anything silly again. We would never do anything together again at all. I had never felt so abandoned. I remembered what Peter had written in his letter: "Where is God?" And for the first time since Helen died, I cried, tears running down my face and mixing with the rain.

I walked along weeping, not caring if people turned to stare at me. Or maybe they didn't. Maybe with the war and the influenza, death was so ordinary now that no one paid attention. I walked all the way to Grant Street, to the Howells' home, and stood on the sidewalk in front of it to get control of myself. I went to the door but could not raise the knocker. I walked around to the side of the house and sat down on the stone bench in the rose garden. The roses were Mrs. Howell's pride, but they were gone, of course. The bushes had been cut back so that the sharp stems were thrust into the air. The little gravel path between the bushes was muddy. I sat on the bench in the rain until the side door of the house opened, and I heard footsteps. Mrs. Howell hurried toward me, with George behind her holding an umbrella over her head.

"Oh, my dear," she said, sitting down beside me, even though the bench was wet and she was wearing a silk dress. "She is gone, then?" She took the umbrella from George and nodded at him to leave.

"Yes," I replied.

Mrs. Howell put her free arm around me. "I am so sorry. It is quite a trial for you, coming so soon after Peter."

"I can't remember a time when she wasn't with me. I knew Mother and Father would die one day, but Helen . . ."

"I know. You feel as if you have lost your heart."

"Yes," I said, forcing myself to remember that I was not the only one who had suffered a great loss.

"Come inside. George has gone to prepare tea for us. He is the one who saw you from the window, and I knew. Dorothy is out with Cook. They have gone to market." She helped me rise, and we went inside. George took my damp hat and coat, saying he would dry them in the kitchen. Then we went into the library, where there was a fire. We had sat there after Peter died, and I wondered if the room would always mean death to me.

"She died at home?" Mrs. Howell asked.

I nodded.

"Yes, I would want to die in my own bed surrounded by those I love. You have made arrangements for the body?"

"Gil called the cemetery. I asked for a plot near yours."

"Of course. I shall telephone them myself to make sure of it."

George brought tea, and we drank it without talking. Suddenly I was very sleepy from the warm drink and the hot fire. George came to say that Mrs. Howell was wanted on the telephone, and after she left, I fell asleep. When I awoke the room was very dark, and someone had covered me with a blanket. The fire had gone out. My clothes were dry, but when I took out my hairpins and shook out my hair, it was still damp. I knotted my hair again, then stood and tried to brush the wrinkles out of my skirt. I stirred the fire.

George must have been listening for me, because he knocked at the door, then entered.

"It must be late," I said.

"Only four. The rain makes it dark outside. Mrs. Howell is upstairs with Dorothy. She said to let her know when you woke."

He left me and fetched Mrs. Howell, who said that Dorothy was in Louise's room with the dolls.

"You haven't told her?" I asked.

"No. I thought it was your place. Would you like to tell her alone, or do you want me to go with you?"

"Please, Mrs. Howell," I said.

"Anne," she said. "I would like you to call me Anne."

She reached out her hand, and together she and I went to tell Dorothy that our sister was dead.

"Helen is with your mother. And Peter," I said.

"But I want her here," Dorothy whispered. She broke into sobs, and her little body shook. I took her in my arms.

"What if you leave me, too, Lutie?" she asked through her tears.

"I won't."

"But Helen wasn't going to leave, either."

She was right, and I didn't know what to say to that. I held her for a long time. Judge Howell came in and took my hands and said he was sorry. "So much death," he said. Then Mrs. Howell asked us to stay for supper, but I could not sit in that formal dining room and make conversation. And I did not think they could, either. They had suffered enough with Peter's death. I said we must get home.

Cook gave us a container of soup, and Mrs. Howell took us to the side door, where Melvin was waiting with the touring car. "I hope you can accept that the Lord is with you in your sorrow," she said.

But I couldn't.

On the way home, Melvin told me, "I am sorry, miss. It is so hard."

And because I remembered that Mrs. Howell had told me his son had died in the war, I reached up and patted his back and asked, "How do you cope with it?"

"You don't. You just go on."

"Does God help?"

He didn't answer, but instead said, "You have the little girl."

When we got home I lit a fire in the fireplace. Dorothy and I ate the soup Mrs. Howell's cook had given us, and then Dorothy put on her nightgown. She had not let me out of her sight since I had told her of Helen's death. We knelt beside her bed, because it seemed the right thing to do. I did not say a prayer, and I did not know if Dorothy did, either. She took her treasure box, which she had brought home from the Howells', and set it on the table beside her bed. When I saw how carefully she lifted her mother's beads and ran her hands over them, I took off Helen's cross and put it around Dorothy's neck. That pleased her, and she gripped it until she fell asleep.

As tired as I was, I did not want to sleep. I went into Helen's room and sat on her bed. The room was sterile now, antiseptic, the bed stripped, Helen's robe and nightgown and uniform burned. Nevertheless, Helen's presence was so strong that I couldn't stay there. I wandered through the house, picking up the cup Helen used for coffee and setting it down at her place at the kitchen table. In the living room, I touched the leather pillow with the Indian in his feather headdress. We'd thought it was tacky, but it had made us laugh so we'd bought it. I lit a cigarette from the silver box. The cigarette was stale, but I smoked it anyway as I went out onto the porch and sat on the swing, where Helen and I had spent so many summer evenings—with each other and with Gil and Peter. The night was very cold after all the rain. I threw the cigarette butt into the yard and shivered, but I did not go inside. We had loved this house, the two of us. No matter how long I lived here, I would always think of it as *our* house.

There was so much to do. I'd never been good at planning. Helen had always been in charge, and I had been happy just to let things happen. I couldn't do that any longer. I was the big sister now.

I wanted another cigarette, but I was too tired to go back into the house, so I stayed in the swing, putting my arms around myself to keep out the chill. I had not seen Gil since that morning, and I thought he might come around.

I was about to go inside when I saw a figure far away, and I knew it was Gil. I watched as he came onto the porch and tapped on the door—softly, in case I was asleep.

"I'm here," I told him, and he sat down beside me on the swing.

Gil was beat, and I put my arm around him. "A bad day," I said.

"They'll all be bad days."

"I know."

"At least you have Dorothy to keep you going."

"*We* do," I said. "She's yours, too. She loves you."

Gil turned to look at me.

I said, "I thought you and Helen would probably take

her when you married. She'd have been better off with two parents."

"I thought she'd stay with you. Helen never talked about children. I don't know if she wanted them."

"She'd have been a wonderful mother. She helped raise me."

"You might have been enough."

Eighteen

During the worst of the influenza, Denver had been all but shut down. Schools and churches, pool halls and theaters were closed. Public and private meetings were banned. Streetcars kept their windows open, and passengers were told not to spit on the floor. Neusteter's and other stores asked their customers to wear masks. Police stopped raiding brothels and arresting vagrants for fear of bringing the virus into the jails. I read in the paper that the madam in Salida, a mountain town, shut her brothel so that her girls could work as nurses.

People were discouraged from kissing and shaking hands. Doctors advised patients to wear loose shoes and clothing and breathe deeply. Denverites were encouraged to remember the three Cs: clean mouth, clean heart, and clean clothes. The makers of Vicks VapoRub and Kolynos Dental Cream advertised their products as preventatives, and some people turned to folk remedies, such as carrying an acorn in their pocket.

By mid-November the influenza, which had begun in the summer and peaked by mid-fall, was easing up just a little. The schools opened again. I walked Dorothy to school on Monday morning. Then I went back to work. I had been out for weeks. So much had happened during that time that I was surprised I hadn't been away longer—surprised, too, that I still had a job. But Mr. Neil had been sick most of that time, and Florence told me his nephew had been wounded in France. "He's different. In fact, he's almost human," she said after she welcomed me back.

I was glad for the familiar routine, grateful for the kindness of the people I worked with. But still, I found the work disquieting. Had I really cared that much about fashions? It all seemed so frivolous now. I listened to two buyers squabble over whether a dress should be shown in an advertisement with or without gloves and wondered what difference it made. In the past, I would have jumped in with my opinion—gloves, of course—but now I thought, My fiancé is dead, my sister is dead, who cares about gloves?

Still, I was grateful I had a job to go back to. The Howells' attorney had sent me a check for the money Peter had left me, and I knew I could forgo working for months and maybe years if I were careful. But I did not want to spend the money. It should be saved in case I ever did go into business for myself, or maybe for Dorothy. Besides, I wanted my life to be normal, if indeed it could be normal without Helen. It was difficult enough coping without Peter, but I had met him less than a year before. I had seen Helen every single day of my life. The smallest things upset me—not hearing her tuneless hum, glancing into her bedroom and finding it empty, not being able to show her how I'd trimmed a hat. Just the night before, I had clipped a recipe from the newspaper that had spinach in it, because Helen loved spinach. When I realized what I had done, I crumpled the recipe and threw it into the fireplace.

The glove contretemps continued, and I brought myself back to the present. "What do you think, Miss Lucretia?" one of the buyers asked.

I wanted to say they could throw the gloves into the lake for all I cared. But instead I suggested, "Perhaps the figure could hold the gloves in her hand." The two agreed, and I turned to my drawing board.

At noon, Florence and I went next door to the Denver Dry Goods tearoom for lunch. Whether it was because of the influenza or the deaths, I didn't feel like eating, so I ordered a lemonade and chewed on the ice while Florence ate. She made gay conversation, telling me all the store gossip, but after a while she stopped. "No wonder you're not listening to my jazz. You've got the blue devils. Well, I don't blame you with what you've been through. Honestly, sweetie, I don't know how you even came back to work."

"I don't have a choice," I said.

"Is that dear little girl still with you?" she asked.

I smiled. "Dorothy."

"It must be hard for you."

Suddenly the Armistice came! I was so trapped in my grief that I hadn't paid much attention to the news that the war was ending until I heard the whistles and shouts and automobile horns. Church bells rang. There were firecrackers and even gunshots. Only a month before I would have been thrilled, knowing it meant that Peter would be coming home. Of course I was glad that the fighting was done with, glad that no more American boys would die, but it was too late for Peter and for me. I went outside with Florence and Mr. Neil into a street thronged with people celebrating victory, waving flags and cheering. They poured out of office buildings and department stores, screaming and crying. A man grabbed Florence and kissed her. Mr. Neil shoved him away and said, "None of that, young man."

Florence and I looked at each other and giggled. A woman handed us flags, and even Mr. Neil waved one. After a time, he said, "Tomorrow we shall run the advertisement we prepared in anticipation of the Armistice. After you are finished, ladies, you have my permission to leave." He had never before dismissed us early, and we hurried back inside to complete the ad. Neusteter's had known the war would be over one day, and while I was away the advertising department had designed the ad. There was only a little work remaining to complete it. We left the store mid-afternoon.

I walked home because the streets were clogged with people, blocking the trolley tracks. School had been dismissed, and Dorothy was waiting on the front steps, jumping up and down with excitement. When she saw me halfway down the block, she ran to meet me. "Did you hear? Did you hear?" she yelled.

"We'll celebrate," I said, glad that there was something to make her happy. I'd change into sensible shoes and we'd go back downtown and join the excitement.

Just as we were leaving, Gil came to the door, and Dorothy cried out, "Dr. Gil, do you know the war is over?"

"Is it really? That's wonderful news," he said.

"Lutie's taking me downtown. Come with us," she said.

"I can't think of a better way to celebrate than with two pretty girls," he replied.

At the corner of Broadway and Seventeenth Avenue, the crowd was even larger than when I'd left work. Flags were everywhere. They flew from buildings, and people waved them above their heads. The streets were crowded with men and women, families, soldiers yelling and cheering, some of them crying. One band played "Over There" and another "The Star-Spangled Banner," the music clashing until all we could hear was a din. A group of women outside Trinity Methodist Church sang the doxology.

We stopped in front of the Savoy Hotel, where someone handed Dorothy a noisemaker, a stick that held a box filled with pebbles that rattled when you shook it. We clapped and sang and yelled "Victory!" with everyone else. We wandered down Seventeenth Street, where people were singing "There are smiles that make us happy," and "It's a Long Way to Tipperary," and "There'll Be a Hot Time in the Old Town Tonight." Dorothy shook her noisemaker and a flag she'd picked up off the street. She had not been this happy in a long time, maybe ever.

I did not hear from the two policemen, and I thought they had gone away. But one evening I opened the door to find them standing there. "We're here to talk to your sister. She around?" Detective Thrasher asked.

I stared at them. "My sister had the influenza."

"I don't see no quarantine sign."

"No."

"She here?"

"My sister is dead."

Detective McCauley blanched, but his partner only nodded. "Yeah, there's plenty's died." He turned to his partner. "Kind of spoils our theory, don't it?" The younger man had the decency to blush.

"We need to talk to the little girl, then. You mind if we come in?"

"Yes, I do," I said. "We are grieving. Dorothy's lost her mother, and now our sister is gone."

Detective Thrasher caught my wording. "What do you mean, 'our sister'?"

"Dorothy will be my sister when the adoption goes through."

"Well, yeah, maybe there won't be that adoption."

I looked at him for a long time and then opened the door, and the two men came into the living room, although they didn't sit down. Dorothy was in the kitchen washing dishes. She came to the doorway but wouldn't go any farther.

"Hey there, kid," Detective McCauley said in a friendly way, but Dorothy didn't reply. She backed up and gripped the doorjamb. He took a few steps toward her, and Dorothy seemed to shrink.

"Why don't you sit down," I said, to keep Detective Thrasher from approaching her, too.

He ignored me. Instead, he asked Dorothy, "Do you know what happened to your father?"

"He's dead," she whispered.

"Yeah. You know how he died?"

I opened my mouth to answer, but the detective held out his hand. "I asked the girl."

"The influenza," she said.

"You know he got stabbed, don't you?" Detective McCauley asked.

Dorothy didn't answer. Finally, she shook her head.

"Did he come here to see you?" the older detective asked.

"He went away. He left Mama and me."

Detective McCauley frowned. "You coach her?" he asked me.

"No," I said sharply. "She's telling the truth."

"Funny thing. We found a real sharp spike in your ash pit. It was burned pretty bad, but it might have been an ice pick."

"Was it an ice pick?" I asked.

"Could be. Is there something you want to tell us?"

"My sister told you ours broke, and she threw it out. Maybe she threw it into the ash pit. I didn't ask her. It wasn't important."

I wanted the detectives to leave, but my knees began to wobble and I sat down, reaching for the leather pillow. Dorothy came and squeezed into the chair next to me, and I held the pillow in front of both of us.

"You see, we think maybe you or your sister stabbed Mr. Streeter with the ice pick so's he wouldn't take Sis here, and then you dragged his body to the vacant lot where we found it," Detective Thrasher said.

"Two women?" I hoped he caught the disdain in my voice.

"You could have borrowed a car. Or you might have had help."

"And what proof do you have?" Suddenly I realized they had nothing on us. "You have a piece of metal that might not even be an ice pick, and you have the word of that evil man Mr. Vincent. You're just guessing," I said.

"Might be we are," Detective Thrasher told me. "My guess is Mr. Streeter came here to claim his girl, and you or your sister stabbed him, maybe in the kitchen, where there was an ice pick handy." He thought a minute. "Probably your sister. That'd be my guess. Too bad she's dead."

My jaw dropped in astonishment, not because he believed exactly what I had thought before I knew the truth, but because he had given me a way out. But even if that were true, I would never admit Helen was a murderer. She was my sister, someone I loved more than myself. She was a good person, and I would not allow her memory to be tarnished like that, even to save Dorothy and me. I simply stared at Detective Thrasher.

"What do you say to that?" he asked.

"Nothing. My sister killed no one."

"Maybe it was her, then," Detective McCauley said, pointing at me. "You think maybe she done it?"

Detective Thrasher considered that, and I felt my hands grow cold. "My bet's on the older girl. There was something about her. You get a feel for it when you've been a copper as long as I have. I think she'd have admitted it if I pushed her hard enough. This one, she'd never admit it. I guess we'll never know," Detective Thrasher said.

"Could have been the little girl."

"Now, how do you think a kid like that could kill a man the size of her father?" Detective Thrasher turned and made his way to the door.

His partner looked confused, as if he had expected to come to our house to make an arrest and was now being told the case was dropped. That was the way it looked to me. He shook his finger at me and said, "I don't get it, Thrasher. One of them did it. You know it."

"Which one? How do we prove it? We'll put it down as the sister. The captain will be glad to write it off and not waste no more time on it. Come on, we got other cases." When Detective McCauley didn't move, the older man said, "Justice ain't perfect. It's about time you learn that."

After the door had closed, I told Dorothy, "I don't think they'll be back." I hoped I was right, but I wasn't at all sure that our troubles were done with.

And, of course, they weren't.

A few days later, Ted Coombs called me to his office. Gil went with me, and I was glad for his support.

"There's a complication," Mr. Coombs said as soon as we sat down. "A Beulah Vincent has asked for custody of Dorothy. She claims she is the girl's aunt."

"Is she truly?" Gil asked.

Mr. Coombs nodded. "Yes, I'm afraid she is. She has proof. She is married to Gus Vincent."

I shivered, and Gil put his arm around me. "I've never met her," I said. "She's not come to see Dorothy even once."

"She claims you wouldn't allow her access."

"That's a lie," I said, coming out of the chair.

Mr. Coombs held up his hand. "Of course it is. But who knows what the court will believe? She may be very credible. If she is Dorothy's aunt, and we know she is, a judge will be inclined to give her custody. The outcome is troublesome."

"But they are awful people," Gil said.

"It will be up to us to prove that." He stood and held out his hand. "I did not mean to upset you, Miss Hite, but I thought you should know where things stand."

"What about Mrs. Howell? She'll testify in Lutie's favor," Gil said.

"Yes, and she will be very persuasive. But that will not be enough."

"Dorothy's terrified of Gus Vincent."

"Has she told you why?"

I shook my head. "She hasn't volunteered anything, but I know."

"If she won't tell you, it's doubtful she'd tell a judge. And even if she did, Mrs. Vincent could claim you put that idea into her head."

"Then I might have to take Dorothy and move back to Iowa or someplace—"

Mr. Coombs held up his hand again to stop me from talking. "As your attorney, I must warn you against breaking the law. I cannot be a party to something illegal." He gave me a sly smile. "So you must not share such thoughts with me. If the judge rules in Mrs. Vincent's favor, we could ask for a few weeks to let Dorothy adjust. But, of course, I cannot advise you during that time to sell your house and put the money into an account that you could access in another city. Nor could I tell you not to transfer Dorothy's school records, which would allow someone to track her down. No, I can't tell you to do something illegal."

I understood him perfectly.

"You should give consideration to your options, but don't give up hope yet."

I had an idea. "Maybe Judge Howell will hear the case."

Mr. Coombs smiled, then shook his head. "He would have to recuse himself." He thought a moment. "Of course, who knows what judges say to each other in private."

As we left the office, Gil took my arm. "They will never get Dorothy," he said. "We will figure out something. You are not in this alone."

I felt better. I didn't have Helen at my side, but I had Gil.

Nineteen

I didn't get off work until six, and it bothered me that Dorothy came home from school to an empty house. Of course, she was nearly eleven, and girls only a little older were already on their own. Still, I worried that her going into the house by herself would bring back bad memories. Perhaps we should have moved, but I was not ready to just yet. Helen and I had loved the house, and her presence still lingered. Besides, having a nice home would be in my favor when the judge ruled on the adoption. Perhaps I would sell it later, but until then, I thought the solution would be to find a good couple to rent the basement. So I put out the "For Rent" sign.

Apartments were scarce, what with little residential construction in Denver during the war, and I had my choice of renters. I could be particular. I did not want a single man, and I turned down a couple who were grouchy. Gil helped me interview the potential renters.

I was grateful for his help. I should have encouraged him to get on with his life, but he relieved my loneliness, and I think I did his. It seemed we had more in common than our mutual loss. He stopped by when he had time off, and I was always glad to see him. He made me laugh again. Moreover, he cared about Dorothy, and being around her lifted his spirits. Hers, too. So when he could get away for an evening, he had dinner with us.

"I could sit with Dorothy if you want to go out on a date," he told me. But I wasn't interested in dating. I had had Peter, and I did not want anyone else—any more than Gil did. On Sundays when he was free, he accompanied Dorothy and me to the Howells' for dinner.

One snowy evening, Gil took Dorothy to a moving picture without me. With the influenza all but over, the theaters were open again. I was tired, and I wanted to stay home and listen to the radio and sew. It seemed like a long time since I had stitched anything, and I liked the idea of taking out my scraps of old fabric and seeing what I could create.

When the doorbell rang, I thought it was probably someone wanting to see the basement apartment.

I wouldn't show it at night. I would tell the people to come back—and I won't rent it to you anyway, I thought as I saw the woman standing under the porch light. She was large and over-dressed and brassy. Her eyebrows were penciled in, and she wore too much dark lipstick. Dorothy wouldn't want to come home from school to a face like that.

"I should have taken down the sign," I told her. "The apartment is rented. I'm sorry."

"I'll come in," the woman said, trying to push past me.

"No," I said, holding on to the door with one hand and the frame with the other.

"I don't care about your apartment," she said.

I glanced down the street, hoping to spot a neighbor, but

the night was cold and the street was covered with snow from a recent storm. The only person I could see was a man standing in front of an automobile. I had seen it before, and I shivered. "Go away," I said.

"Not without Dorothy," she said, shoving me with her large hip and sliding into the room.

"Get out or I will call the police," I said, but the woman only laughed.

"Do so. Explain how you've kept me from seeing my niece, my own flesh and blood. By rights, she's mine. You're nobody." Then she called out, "Dorothy, come see me. It's your auntie Beulah come to get you."

So this was Beulah Vincent! No wonder Dorothy was afraid of her. "She's not here," I said.

The woman turned and yelled, "Gus!"

Her husband was smoking a cigarette. I could see the lit tip as he tossed it into the snow and started across the street.

"You've no right to her. You're a criminal," I said.

"You've no proof of anything, dearie. The girl's a liar. Where've you hid her?"

Gus came up onto the porch and took off his hat, as if he were making a social call. He was well-dressed, better dressed than Mr. Streeter had ever been, and he grinned at me. My mouth felt sour, and I nearly gagged when I thought of the two of them taking Dorothy. He scared me, but his wife scared me more. Her eyes were cruel. She held my arm, pinching it until it hurt.

"She says the girl ain't here," Mrs. Vincent told her husband.

He shoved me aside and came into the house, then went to

the back. I could hear him opening doors. After a few minutes, he returned. "She's gone," he said. "But she still lives here, all right. That's her bedroom." He pointed down the hallway.

"We'll wait for her," his wife said.

"Yeah, we got nowhere to go." He unbuttoned his coat and unwrapped the scarf from around his neck. Then he cocked his head and smirked at me. "Could be there's a little something in it for you, Miss Hite."

I shivered at the use of my name.

"Could be if you turn her over to us, we might could work something out. I guess living here by yourself, you could use a few bucks."

"We ain't paying her," his wife argued.

"Now, Beulah, you know the kid's worth more to us than to her. We could make the money back in a month. Business." He tapped his head. "Sister here knows how bread's buttered. Look at them clothes she's got on. She don't make that kind of money. I'd say Dorothy's worth fifty bucks to her, maybe even a hundred. What do you say?" He gave me an oily smile.

"Get out!" I told him.

Gus shrugged. "Suit yourself. I was just being generous. You don't have any right to her, you know."

Through the open door, I saw the neighbor boy come out of his house and begin to shovel his walk. He was a big kid, and strong. "Jimmy!" I yelled. "I need your help." He looked up and started toward me, the snow shovel in his hands.

Gus looked wary and said, "We don't want no trouble. We'll get her later. Come on, Beulah." He edged toward the door.

"You could have made a little dough. Stupid broad," she said.

She turned, but before she followed her husband, she kicked my leg hard, and I'd have fallen if I hadn't grabbed the door.

Jimmy stared at the couple as he passed them on the sidewalk. "You all right, Miss Hite?" he asked. "They look like a pair of hard cases."

I thanked him for his concern. "They came to look at the apartment. They frightened me."

"Yeah, I've seen that auto before. It looks like it belongs to a bootlegger." He laughed as if he'd said something funny.

I watched the Vincents drive off, then grabbed my coat. I wouldn't wait for Gil to come home with Dorothy but would find them at the theater. By the time I'd locked the door, however, I spotted them at the end of the block. Thank God they hadn't come any earlier. I waved and started toward them, then stopped, because I did not want to upset Dorothy. When she spotted me, she scooped up snow, made a snowball, and threw it at me. Gil pelted me with a second one, and I would have retaliated but I wanted to get them inside in case the Vincents returned.

"I think we ought to have cocoa. Would you make it for us?" I asked Dorothy as we went into the house and locked the door. I put my hand on Gil's arm to stop him from following her into the kitchen.

He glanced at me and mouthed, "Trouble?"

I nodded.

When Dorothy went to the icebox for the milk, I whispered to him what had happened. "We have to get her out of here," I said.

"The Howells?"

I nodded. "They've cared for her so much already that I hate to ask, but what other choice is there?"

Gil agreed. "I'm sure they'll take her. They love her as much as we do. She's ours—I mean yours."

"Ours," I said, for he cared as much for Dorothy as I did. He patted my arm as Dorothy came into the living room carrying a tray with three cups. She had put cloth napkins on the tray and three silver spoons, the way I did.

While Gil kept her busy, I went to the telephone and gave the operator the Howells' number. When Mrs. Howell got on the line I explained the situation, and she said she would send Melvin immediately. "I hate to ask—" I said, but she cut me off. "Do not ever think Dorothy is an imposition," she said.

Early the next morning, I went to the police station. It was grimy, and there were torn newspapers and cigar butts on the steps. Inside it was stale with the smell of cigarette smoke and unwashed bodies. Three women in tawdry outfits were sitting on a bench smoking. Their hair was bleached and their lipstick smeared, and one appeared to have dressed in haste because her dress was buttoned wrong. Prostitutes, I thought, glancing at them. I had never seen such women—hookers or soiled doves, they were called—and I looked too long, because one blew smoke at me and asked, "What you staring at, dearie?"

"Thinks she's too good for the likes of us," another said.

I wanted to apologize but didn't know how, so I looked away and went to a desk and asked for Detective Thrasher.

"Thrasher in yet?" the man yelled to another officer.

"Yeah, I saw him."

"Lady wants to see him."

"Is that what you call 'em?" the officer asked, tilting his head at the prostitutes. Then he saw me and blushed. "I'll get him, ma'am."

The women heard him and twittered. "Hard to tell us apart. Just some's better dressed," one said.

That struck me as funny, and I had to smile. The woman saw it and winked at me.

In a moment the detective came into the room, surprised to see me. I didn't greet him but said abruptly, "I need to talk to you."

"About your sister? You decided to tell me what happened?"

"I don't know what happened. For all I know, Mr. Streeter stabbed himself."

"Which is why there wasn't no ice pick next to him but a sign saying 'influenza victim.'"

"I'm here about Gus Vincent."

He motioned me to a desk, and I sat down on a hard wooden chair beside it. The desk was cluttered with police forms and "Wanted" sheets with pictures of criminals on them and an ashtray filled with half-smoked cigarettes. The smell of the cigarettes made me wonder why I smoked.

Detective Thrasher didn't make small talk. Instead, he waited for me to tell him why I was there.

"You know who he is? Gus Vincent?" I asked.

"Sure."

"He's an evil man. He and his wife tried to take Dorothy away yesterday. They failed only because Dorothy wasn't home. You have to stop him, arrest him or something. I want to keep him away until I can adopt Dorothy."

The detective held up his hand. "Miss Hite, I don't get involved in adoptions. You might be a better mother, but if Mrs. Vincent is the girl's aunt, she's got a right to the child. You need to hire yourself a lawyer. This isn't police business."

"She's got no right!" I said so loudly that the three hookers looked at me.

"You better get yourself a lawyer."

"I have a lawyer. What I have to tell you *is* police business." I paused and looked away, not sure what to say. In my own home, I hadn't been able to tell the officers what Dorothy's father had done to her. It was even more difficult in that cold room with its hard furniture and others listening in.

"How's that?" Detective Thrasher asked. He didn't seem aware of my discomfort. Or maybe he didn't care.

I took a deep breath and whispered, "Mr. Streeter had carnal knowledge of his daughter. I believe Mr. Vincent is no better."

"What's that?" the detective said. "You have to speak up. I don't hear so good."

I doubted that was the case. Perhaps he wanted to embarrass me. I said a little louder, "You yourself said the world was a better place without Mr. Streeter." When he didn't respond, I cleared my throat. "Mr. Streeter had illegal contact with his daughter. I do not know Mr. Vincent's intention, but it is my belief he and his wife intend to use her in their illegal liquor business."

Detective Thrasher seemed taken aback. He ran his tongue over his lips, thinking. Then he called, "Evans, get over here."

A tall, thin man with sad eyes came to the desk, and Detective Thrasher introduced him to me as Detective Evans. "You ever hear of a Beulah Vincent?"

"You mean Beulah Vincent, like in vice? Hard as shoe nails?"

Detective Thrasher turned to me and asked, "What's she look like?"

"Large, sort of a horse face, maroon lipstick. Cruel eyes," I said.

"That's Beulah, all right," said Detective Evans.

"What do you know about her?" Detective Thrasher asked.

"We never was able to pin nothing on her, but I know her and her husband are bootleggers. They're connected to the North Denver mob."

"She wants to stop me from adopting a little girl," I said.

"Then more power to you. You better work damn hard—pardon my language, miss—to keep her from doing it. They like to use kids in their operation. Put the fear of God in 'em. Probably beat them. Send them out to make deliveries, and if they get caught, they're too scared of the Vincents to tattle."

"She claims the girl is her niece, and I'm afraid that's true."

"I wouldn't worry. No judge in the world's going to give Beulah Vincent custody of a kid. You have your lawyer come see me, and I'll give him plenty to open his eyes."

I said, "She may not wait for a judge to rule. The Vincents tried to take Dorothy from me yesterday, and they would have if she'd been home."

Detective Evans turned to Detective Thrasher. "You want me to do something?"

"Yeah, might be a good idea to have a little talk with her, if you can find her."

"A pleasure." Detective Evans dipped his head at me and said, "Good luck to you, ma'am. I wouldn't let that woman within a mile of your kid. Like I say, I'll talk to her, but who knows what she'll do."

"You should have told me about them before," Detective Thrasher said after the other officer left. "I didn't know they were such hard cases. You think he might . . . ah . . . you know, done what her father did?" He had the decency to blush.

"I wanted to, but Dorothy was sitting right there. You see, she's never actually told me what her father did. It was so disgusting, I was afraid Dorothy would deny it. My sister says . . . said . . . that women who have been . . . well, you know . . . blame themselves."

"I guess that'd be a good reason for your sister to stab this Streeter."

"But she didn't," I said. And then, for no reason, I burst into tears.

The detective looked uncomfortable and shifted in his chair. He took out a handkerchief that was wadded up in his pocket and handed it to me, but I had my own and dabbed at my eyes with it. "I am so sorry," I said, more embarrassed than he was.

He promised to tell me what Detective Evans reported and asked me to let him know if I saw Gus or Beulah Vincent again. I stood and thanked him, then turned and walked past the prostitutes.

They had watched me so intensely that I wondered if they had heard my conversation with the detective, but apparently they had not, because one said, loud enough for me to hear, "You think her man walked out on her? Maybe we know him."

The hooker who had objected to my staring at her elbowed her friend and told her to hush. Then she looked up at me and smiled a little and said, "Don't you worry, dearie. No man's worth it."

Twenty

Something seemed off, and I thought it was because Dorothy wasn't home. She was still at the Howells' and would stay there until Detective Evans had a talk with the Vincents. So far, he hadn't been able to find them.

Dorothy had called me earlier that evening to tell me about her day at school. The Howells' chauffeur had taken her there and picked her up, so I didn't have to worry about Gus waylaying her. I spoke to Mrs. Howell after I'd finished talking to Dorothy, and she told me that Melvin had looked for Gus's auto but hadn't seen it. There was nothing to worry about, she said. But still, I did worry.

I was home that evening by myself, and I took out a scarf I had been making of burgundy velvet, amber silk, and lace the color of dark tea. I thought I'd to give it to Mrs. Howell for Christmas because the colors would suit her. I turned on the radio, but the reception that night was so bad that I switched it off. The static matched my mood, and I felt twitchy. I hadn't stitched for more than five minutes when I set down the scarf and went to check the locks on the doors. I had replaced them after the Vincents' visit, thinking that it was possible Mr. Streeter had given them a copy of the key.

I'd rented to the perfect tenants—Greg and Gladys Hoover, a young couple with a baby. Gil had found Mr. Hoover, who was the assistant manager of a drugstore. His wife had been a nurse, although now she stayed home with the baby, and she would be glad for Dorothy's company after school. They would not move in for another week, however, so I was alone in the house.

I turned on the switch for the back-door light, but it didn't go on. I knew I should replace the bulb but didn't feel like going outside. I shivered. The house was chilly, and I thought about building a fire, but the wood was in the shed in the backyard and I didn't want to go outdoors to get it either. I put on one of Helen's sweaters, wrapping my arms around myself, and went back to the living room and picked up a magazine I had begun reading earlier.

An auto in the street backfired. I went to the window but the car was gone. There was no sign of Mr. Vincent's vehicle. There was no sign of anything. The night was very cold, and the yards and street were deserted. I remembered Helen, wrapped in her cape, going out on winter evenings for emergencies, then coming home late, tired and cold and out of sorts because they hadn't been emergencies after all. There was no wind, and the snow, which had begun falling early in the evening, muffled any noise, even the screech of the trolley far down the street. Helen had loved watching the snow fall because it was clean and antiseptic, and I stood there thinking that she would never see it again.

I missed her. I missed her terribly, and I began to cry. I'd tried so hard to keep my tears in check around Dorothy and

Gil, and I had done a good job of it. But now, alone, I let them fall. It felt good, and I cried until I was exhausted, resting my head against the velvet of the throw.

Then I heard footsteps and sat up, my senses alert. I tiptoed to the window and peered out, then gave a sigh of relief. Gil.

"I saw the light," he said when I opened the door. "I'm on my way home, and it just seemed natural to walk this way. I can't help myself. If you're tired, I won't stay. But I wanted to see you."

"Of course I'm not tired," I said. "Come in. It's awfully cold out. I'll fix tea."

"Coffee, if you don't mind," he said. As Gil took off his coat, I thought what a good-looking man he was, almost as handsome as Peter. And as kind. Helen had been fortunate. He had been, too, of course. In time, he would find someone else to love, but I would never have another big sister.

"You've been crying," he said as I took his coat.

Of course Gil would notice. He always knew when I had the blue devils.

"An indulgence," I replied. "I don't do it often. I cope most of the time. I just want things to return to normal, and of course they never will."

"What's normal?"

"Those days before Peter went away."

"That was a wonderful time for all of us. But not for Dorothy, of course. Normal for her was her father. You haven't heard anything from the police about her aunt and uncle?"

"Not yet."

Gil followed me into the kitchen and took out the can of

coffee. I filled the percolator with water and he inserted the basket, spooned the grounds into it, put on the cover, and set it on the stove. We sat down at the kitchen table to wait for the coffee to percolate. Gil might have been Peter, I thought, if Peter had come home. We would be sitting there making plans for our wedding. Perhaps Gil was thinking the same thing about Helen. Now it was Gil and me sitting there.

"You make it easier for me," Gil said, squeezing my arm. "It would have been awful dealing with Helen's death by myself."

"Do we help each other, or do we keep each other from moving ahead?" I asked.

The coffee was ready, and Gil got up and poured it into two cups. "Perhaps I shouldn't stop by so often."

"No," I said quickly. "I'm glad you do. Dorothy is, too."

"Staying away, I would miss her."

Gil grew more serious. "Of course, I would miss you, too. Some of the best times Helen and I had were with you."

"Peter and me," I said, and he nodded. "The four of us would have been good friends forever."

"You and I still can be."

We were silent then, and I thought it was nice that we drew comfort from each other just being together. I hoped we would always be friends.

I was at work when the secretary from Neusteter's executive office told me I had a telephone call. I froze. "Me?" I asked.

"I told the caller that our associates are not allowed to receive calls at work, but she said it was an emergency."

"Who is it?" I asked, getting up.

"Mrs. Judge Howell."

I followed the secretary into an office and held the telephone phone in one hand and the receiver in the other.

"Lucretia, is that you?" Mrs. Howell asked, then, without waiting for a reply, she continued, "Did you take Dorothy out of school?"

"No." I closed my eyes.

"I thought not. Melvin waited for her after the bell rang, and when she didn't come out of the building he went inside to look for her. The principal, Miss Ford, told me her aunt had taken her away. She said I was ill and that Dorothy was to come immediately."

"No, I never—"

"Then it was the Vincent woman. Miss Ford said she was a large, most unpleasant person, and she insisted that Dorothy go with her immediately, that it was a matter of life and death."

"But Dorothy wouldn't do that," I replied. "When that detective was here and mentioned Gus Vincent's name, Dorothy screamed and begged me not to let him have her."

"That's the odd thing. Miss Ford sent for Dorothy and said that at first, Dorothy just looked at the woman and didn't say a word. It seemed as if she had given up. Miss Ford said it was very peculiar. She asked Dorothy if this was her aunt, and Dorothy didn't even reply. I suspect she turned inward the way she does sometimes when things are unpleasant.

"Miss Ford explained that her aunt wanted her to leave immediately because I was very ill, and at that Dorothy began to moan and say no. Miss Ford thought that Dorothy was upset that I was in danger, but it is clear to me she didn't want to leave with Mrs. Vincent. And when I asked her, poor Miss Ford admitted I might be right. Unfortunately, she is not an assertive woman and was afraid of causing trouble if she did not let Dorothy leave."

I began to shake and leaned against the secretary's desk. "When did it happen?" I asked.

"An hour or more ago. Melvin telephoned me the moment he found out what had happened. He is still at the school. I will contact the police. No, I will have the judge contact them. They'll take him more seriously. Will you get in touch with your detective? Shall I send Melvin to the store to pick you up?"

"Yes, please," I said. "Oh, Mrs. Howell."

"My dear, I promise you we shall find her."

"Of course," I said, but I knew she couldn't promise that. Peter, Helen, Maud, and now Dorothy. Not Dorothy! I thought. Couldn't Peter's God at least let me keep her?

I hung up the receiver, and the secretary reached for it, a frown on her face. She did not approve of my having received a telephone call.

"I'm sorry. I have to make a call," I said.

"Really, Miss Lucretia. The telephone is not for the use of associates—" she began in a scolding tone, but I kept hold of the phone and turned away and asked the operator to connect me with the detective bureau. At least Detective Thrasher was in— I could thank God for that—and I explained what had happened. He said he would meet me at the Howells'.

I finished the phone call and set the telephone on the desk, putting my arms around myself to stop the shaking. The secretary had heard the conversation, of course, and she stared at me.

"I . . . someone kidnapped your sister? Oh, Miss Lucretia! Do you need to make another call?"

I nodded and telephoned Saint Joseph's and left a message for Gil.

That was the longest night I had ever spent, worse even than the nights I had sat up with Helen. The police chief, half a dozen policemen, and the detectives Thrasher, McCauley, and Evans were at the Howell mansion when I arrived, and I knew that Mrs. Howell had been right to let the judge report Dorothy's kidnapping.

"They would like a photo of Dorothy," Mrs. Howell said, after George escorted me into the library. "Have you one? I could send Melvin to pick it up."

I opened my purse and removed a snapshot. The picture was of Dorothy, Helen, and Peter, and I had taken it in the summer.

"It's lovely. I should like a copy of it one day," Mrs. Howell said, pausing for just a moment before she handed the picture to the police chief.

"I don't suppose you have one of Gus or Beulah Vincent," the chief said.

"No, but I'm an artist. I can show you what they look like." I went to the desk and took out a pencil and paper and drew their likenesses. "He has black hair and a mustache, dyed, I would guess, and her hair is bleached, very brassy."

"We have a mug shot of her," Detective Thrasher added. He had been talking with the other officers and hadn't heard the chief ask about the Vincents.

"We might have one of him somewhere. He uses aliases," Detective Evans said. "We've picked him up four or five times, but nothing ever sticks."

"For what?" the chief asked.

Detective Evans glanced at Mrs. Howell. "Ma'am, if you'll excuse us."

Mrs. Howell responded, "You may speak freely, detective. I know a great deal about what goes on in the world. And I believe Miss Hite would like to know exactly who our adversaries are as well."

"Yes, ma'am. This Vincent's been arrested for bootlegging, gambling, even kidnapping. He also lures little kids into helping him, picks them up off the street. Sometimes parents turn the kids over to him. You can't hardly blame them. They're so poor they can't afford to feed them, and every nickel helps. He started using them with gambling, then kept on after Prohibition started. He beats them pretty bad if they don't do what he says."

"And the woman?" Mrs. Howell asked.

Detective Evans looked at the chief, who nodded for him to continue. "She's a tough one. I think she might be the one who disciplines them. The kids are so scared of her that they won't talk."

"Her brother was another bad one," Detective McCauley said. "He's dead now, murdered." He looked at me when he said that but didn't add that Helen and I had been suspects in that case. "Good riddance, I'd say," he added.

That seemed like a long time ago.

The chief turned to me and asked, "You think they want to keep the girl, or are they after a ransom?"

I hadn't thought about that. "I have five thousand dollars," I said.

"And we have more," Mrs. Howell added. "They must know about Dorothy's connection to us."

I stared at her, dumbfounded. The Vincents were depraved enough to demand a ransom. And if we paid it, would they really give up Dorothy?

"I shall meet their demand, of course," Mrs. Howell said.

"I can't ask—" I began.

"That is not up for discussion."

"I have brought you so much trouble, Anne," I said, taking Mrs. Howell's hand. "It is too much for you, with the grief you have already, with Peter's death."

"Hush, Lucretia," she said. "We must take care of the living. The dead won't mind waiting."

The chief told me to go home and wait to see if the Vincents contacted me. He would send a policeman to stay with me for protection, but I said that was not necessary. I'd rather have the officer searching for Dorothy than sitting in my living room waiting for a telephone call. Besides, I was safe. If the Vincents were after money, they weren't likely to hurt me.

Melvin drove me home, and he insisted on going through the house to make sure no one was there. He even offered to park the auto down the street in case I needed him, but Gus Vincent would surely be suspicious if he saw it as he drove by.

After the chauffeur left, I went into the kitchen and made myself a sandwich, since I had not eaten since breakfast. But I couldn't swallow the food and ended up throwing it in the garbage. Instead, I drank the bitter coffee that had been left in the pot since that morning. The coffee tasted foul; it matched my mood.

I went into Helen's room and sat on her bed, which I'd made up with her favorite blue-and-white quilt. It was an Irish chain design, and it was very old. Helen had liked things that were white, I thought. She wore dresses as white as her uniforms, and her favorite flowers were daisies. I'd embroidered her pillow slips with white designs, and her iron bedstead had been painted white. I thought about how she must have lain there, sleepless, remembering the minister who had fouled her, thinking of how she had scrubbed his fluid off her, scrubbed it that night and maybe every night since. Helen had bathed frequently, sometimes twice a day. I had thought that was because she was a nurse, but now I wondered if she was trying to rid herself of a filth that never went away.

I wandered about the house, picking up and discarding pillows and vases, scarves and knickknacks. The phone rang and I tensed. It was three shorts, not our ring. I wanted to tell the person on the party line to hang up, that there might be a call about Dorothy. But when I picked up the receiver a minute later, no one was there.

The phone was across from Dorothy's room, and I stood for a long time looking through her door. Her room was dark, and I switched on the light. Perhaps there was something there that would give me a clue as to where she had gone. I went to her closet and searched her pockets but found nothing. Then I looked through her bureau, but there were only her clothes.

I glanced at the bed. I had bought it to replace the cot that had been in the room when it was my studio.

And then I thought of Dorothy's treasure box, the Whitman's candy box. That was where she kept anything important. I remembered how Dorothy had begun closing the lid when I was nearby and kept it under her bed, hiding it. I did not like snooping, but I had to look through it to see if it held any clues to her disappearance. As I reached under the bed, I realized she might have taken it with her to the Howells'. But I had packed her things in a hurry and had forgotten it. I got down on my knees and looked under the bed. At first, I did not see it. Then I spotted the box, which had been pushed into the far corner. I had to crawl under the bed to reach it.

I sat on the floor and stared at the picture on the lid of the girl with stars in her hair. Then I opened the box and looked at Dorothy's treasures. There were odd buttons, cards, a china doll's foot. I touched a dried rose, and its crimson petals crumbled. There was a tiny rubber ball that Peter had given her with a set of jacks, and the white tassel from the dress that Mrs. Howell had given her. And Maud's beads and wedding ring, of course. But what caught my eye and made me stare was a gleaming lethal weapon. It was our ice pick.

Twenty-One

Not long afterward, I heard a tap on the back door, and I quickly closed the lid of the candy box and slid it back under the bed, shoving it to the far corner. My heart thumping, I went to the door and asked in a shaky voice, "Who is it?"

"Detective McCauley."

I pushed back the curtain on the door and recognized the officer.

"I told the chief it was better if you had someone with you," he said as I opened the door, and I was grateful, because I really was scared. I had been foolish to turn down the chief's offer of protection. What if the Vincents did contact me about a ransom? I wouldn't know what to do.

The detective said, "We think that if this was a kidnapping for money, we'd have heard from them by now. I guess that's good news."

"Is it? Or maybe Dorothy's dead." I clasped my arms around myself.

The officer slipped into the house. He explained that he'd parked his auto two blocks away and sneaked down the alley, in case someone was in the street watching.

I asked if he wanted coffee, and he nodded. It had been

a long night for him, too. He sat down on one of the orange chairs and looked around the room. "You got it real nice here." When I turned to the sink for the water, he said, "Say, I'm sorry about that business over Mr. Streeter. I didn't really think you or your sister done it."

I knew he was lying, but I appreciated the remark just the same.

"I'd say Denver was better off without him," he added.

I offered him something to eat, and he shook his head. "Mrs. Howell fixed us a real nice dinner. That's some house. I heard that the judge bought it cheap because the lady who lived there killed someone. My uncle solved that murder, you know. He's the reason I wanted to be a copper."

And he'd wanted to get credit for solving another murder, I thought—by arresting Helen or me for Mr. Streeter's death. Now he was hoping that if Dorothy was killed, he'd find the killer. I shook my head at the idea. Then I decided I had been harsh. The detective was only doing his job.

After a time, he told me to look in the mailbox to see if someone had slipped a note into it. He wouldn't do it because he didn't want to show himself. I checked the box, but there was no note. Then he asked to use the telephone. He stood in the hall and gave the operator the Howells' number. When the chief came on the line, he told him that no one had contacted me. He asked if there'd been any progress. After he hung up, he said that the police had an address they were checking out, but so far no one had seen Dorothy. "We have a description of the car and the license number. I expect every copper out there is watching for it."

Suddenly there was a pounding on the front door, and I jumped. I peeked through the curtains on the front window and saw an auto, but I did not think it was Gus Vincent's.

"I'll stand behind the door, and you open it just a crack. Did you hook the screen?" Detective McCauley asked.

I didn't remember and shrugged. There was more pounding, and Detective McCauley positioned himself out of sight. I slowly opened the door to find two men standing there.

"Miss Hite?" one of them asked, and I nodded. My throat was too constricted to speak.

"Goddamned reporter. Get out of here," Detective McCauley said when he heard the voice.

"Hey, McCauley. How about letting us in?" the man said, pushing me aside and entering the house. "Miss Hite, I'm Walter Field from the *Denver Post*. You made the front page." He thrust a newspaper into my face, and I read the giant headline: ORPHAN CHILD KIDNAPPED. Below it was DOROTHY STREETER FRIEND OF WEALTHY JUDGE RANSOM MAY BE MOTIVE. Below the headlines was the photograph I'd given the police chief.

"How did you get this picture?" I asked.

He smiled. "I got sources."

"You're scum," Detective McCauley said. "Get out. She doesn't want to talk to you."

"Hey, we want the same thing. We want the little girl to come home safe," Field said.

"You want to sell newspapers," Detective McCauley responded.

"We got the mug shots of the Vincents right here on the

front page. And a description of the auto. Everybody in Denver's looking for them, thanks to us."

"Yeah, and you've muddied up the investigation."

Out of the corner of my eye, I saw the second man slide around the room until he stopped in front of a framed picture of Helen. He picked it up and I quickly grabbed it away and held it against my chest. "That's my sister, and don't you dare take it," I said. "There are no other photographs of Dorothy, so you can stop snooping."

"And stay where I can see you," Detective McCauley said.

The reporter took out a pad and a pencil. "Got any leads yet?"

"None to tell you about," the detective replied.

"What about you, miss? What can you tell me about the girl? Anybody ask you for money yet?"

"I have nothing to tell you. Now please leave. No one will try to contact me if you're here," I said.

"Well, get used to it." He gestured at the street, where I saw a man getting out of an auto. "That's the *Rocky Mountain News*, and there'll be others. You don't talk to us, we'll wait on the porch. Or maybe we'll talk to your neighbors, see if they know anything."

The phone rang then, our ring, and I glanced at Detective McCauley, who nodded for me to answer. "Now you fellows just be still," he said.

"Hello. This is Lucretia Hite speaking," I said. I'd never answered the phone that way before.

"Miss Hite, this is Winifred White from the *Denver Post*. I am so sorry about your troubles, and we at the *Post*—"

I slammed down the phone, then screamed at the two men, "Get out! Get out! How do you think anybody will contact me after what you've done?"

The two men backed away just as a third man shoved his way into the house. I started to tell him to leave, too, but then I recognized Gil. He rushed to my side and put his arms around me. A reporter jotted down something, but I didn't care.

Detective McCauley pushed the reporter and photographer out of the room and yelled, "Go away, boys! Nobody here is talking." Half a dozen men were now on the porch.

"Will they leave?" I asked.

"No," he admitted. "Things here are spoiled. Vincent and his wife won't contact you with that bunch around. I imagine it's the same at the judge's house." He gave Gil an inquiring look, and I introduced them.

"Dr. Rushton is—was—my sister's fiancé. He is very close to Dorothy." I turned to Gil. "I left a message for you at Saint Joe's."

Gil shook his head. "I haven't been there. I heard a newsboy scream the headlines, and I came right here."

I explained to him what had happened.

"And there's no news?"

"No."

Detective McCauley added, "We don't know if they intend to keep the girl or are holding her for ransom."

"Oh, Lute." Gil turned away from me, but not before I saw that his eyes were wet. Then he asked, "How are you holding up?"

"As well as I can. I'm so glad you're here."

"Don't give up. We aren't sure what they are planning," Detective McCauley said. "All this publicity might even do some good. They probably didn't count on it. They might just let her go."

"Of course," Gil said. He smiled at me, but I knew he didn't believe that any more than I did.

The phone rang again, and this time the detective answered it. When he came back into the room, he told us the police were regrouping at the station. Newspapermen had descended on the Howell home, just as he'd thought, and the chief said it was unlikely that the Vincents would make contact there. We could only wait to see if they mailed a ransom note. He'd leave one officer with Mrs. Howell and Detective McCauley would stay with me if I wanted him to. But I could see that he was tired from being up all night, so I told him I would be fine without him. I would let him know if anything came in the mail.

"I sure hope she's all right," he said as he left. Then he called to the newsmen, "We've wrapped up things here, boys. You might as well go on home."

I heard several autos start, although there were still men milling around the yard. But I didn't care. I realized how tired I was.

"You've been up all night. Go to sleep. I'll sit up," Gil told me. He kissed me on the cheek.

"You've been up, too," I said. "You lie down on the couch. I'll go to my room. I can hear the phone from there."

I did not know how long I slept. I was awakened by the phone and picked up the receiver just as our ring ended. "Yes, this is Miss Hite," I said. "Yes. All right. Thank you."

The call had awakened Gil, too, and he was beside me. "Dorothy?"

I shook my head. "That was Neusteter's. They know about Dorothy and said I don't have to go to work today." For the first time since Dorothy had been taken, I laughed.

Late in the afternoon, the doorbell rang. Gil came with me to answer the door. I thought it would be another newsman, but instead Melvin stood there, a basket in his hands. The few reporters left had followed him to the porch. He looked at them angrily and slid into the house and slammed the door. Then he rushed into the kitchen and opened the back door to let Detective Thrasher in. "A bit of subterfuge, Miss Hite," Melvin told me.

Detective Thrasher said, "We don't want them to know there's a copper in the house. The chief thinks there's still a chance Gus Vincent might call you." He tapped his forehead. "Crooks ain't all that smart."

"You haven't made progress, then?" I asked. Gil took my arm.

"No," he said. He didn't try to soften his reply. Perhaps he was preparing me for the worst.

"I brought your dinner," Melvin said, then, to Detective Thrasher, "You want me for anything else?"

"I'll call if I do," the detective said. He eyed the basket of food, and I told him to help himself. I wasn't hungry. He turned to Gil. "Doctor."

Did they know each other? I couldn't remember introducing them. "Dr. Rushton was my sister's fiancé," I said.

"I'll be damned," the detective said. "I didn't know it was you."

Then Gil explained, "I've helped with autopsies for the police." He turned to Detective Thrasher. "So you're the damn copper who went after Lute and Helen."

"Small world." The detective reached into the basket and took out a chicken leg. "I thought I'd go through the basement. Didn't Mr. Streeter live there? Maybe I can find an address or something else that will tell us where he might be."

"I threw everything out," I said. "And burned it—out in back, in the ash pit."

"Yeah, I know where your ash pit is." He looked a little sheepish. "Turns out that what we found there wasn't an ice pick at all, just a long nail with the head busted off." He finished the chicken and dropped the bone into the garbage, then started for the basement. I asked if he wanted me to help, but he shook his head, so I stood in the kitchen, rubbing my finger against one of the screws that held the metal strip in place at the edge of the linoleum counter. I rubbed until my finger was raw, and I put it into my mouth. Gil led me into the living room.

We heard the evening paper thud against the front door. Gil offered to get it, but I didn't care to read about Dorothy. I knew as much as the police did, and there was no reason to read the newspaper's speculation. We sat without talking, hearing occasional noises in the basement as Detective Thrasher moved things around. I picked up the leather pillow and held it in front of me and drummed my fingers on it until Gil took it away.

After a very long time, Detective Thrasher came up the stairs, his footsteps heavy. He told us he had found nothing. "You did a pretty good job of cleaning," he said, and I didn't know if he meant that as a compliment or a complaint.

"Sit down. I'll get you a plate. I'm sure you're hungry," I said.

The detective shook his head. "Not just yet. Which is the girl's room?"

He already knew, of course. Perhaps he was being polite. I pointed to the door. Then I remembered Dorothy's treasure box under the bed. "I've already gone through her things. You won't find anything there either."

"Best to have a look." He went into the room and began opening the bureau drawers. He looked into the closet, pushing aside Dorothy's dresses one by one, then felt along the shelf above them.

I stood in the doorway and watched, and I held my breath as he looked under the bed. I had pushed the candy box to the far corner and hoped he wouldn't see it, but of course he did.

Detective Thrasher was a large man, and he couldn't slide himself under the bed the way I had. So he shoved the bed aside and reached for the box. He opened the lid and used his finger to push aside Dorothy's treasures. His snooping felt like a violation to me. Then he lifted the ice pick by its metal spike and turned to me, a question on his face.

I didn't say anything.

"You recognize this?" he asked.

"It's an ice pick."

"Yours?"

I shrugged. "How should I know?"

"What's it doing here?"

"Dorothy's a very frightened little girl. Perhaps she took it for protection. It's a pity she didn't have it with her at school yesterday."

The detective laid the ice pick on the quilt, the yellow one with tulips on it that Dorothy had chosen for her bed. He set the treasure box beside it. Then he thought better of it and set them on the floor, raising the mattress to see if anything was hidden between it and the springs. "What's this?" he asked as he removed several papers. He let the mattress fall back onto the springs, then sat down on the bed. "You ever seen these?"

"No."

Gil had come into the room, and I clutched his arm.

"Looks like the kid's quite the artist," he said.

I tried to look at the paper on top, but the detective held it so I couldn't see it. Then he turned the page so it faced me, and I all but gasped. The picture was a drawing of a man and a woman lifting the body of a man. Dorothy was indeed a good artist, and it was clear the couple was Gil and me.

The detective looked from me to Gil and then back at me again, but I didn't say a word. Gil, too, was silent.

Detective Thrasher held up another picture. "This her father?" he asked.

I looked at it and glanced away, my hand over my mouth, because the picture showed a man on top of a little girl. The man had Mr. Streeter's face, but the girl had no face at all.

"Oh, that's Mr. Streeter, all right," Gil said.

There was a third picture, and Detective Thrasher studied it a long time before he showed it to us. I couldn't look, because I knew Dorothy must have drawn herself stabbing her father.

"My God!" Gil exclaimed. "Look, Lute," and I slowly raised my eyes. Dorothy had drawn her father lying on the floor, a girl without a face next to him, and a man who was clearly Gus Vincent standing over them with an ice pick in his hand.

"I thought Helen killed him. But when she was delirious, I realized she hadn't, that she thought Dorothy had. Helen was protecting her. That's Dorothy's uncle," I told the detective. "He must have stabbed Mr. Streeter."

"That's why he wanted Dorothy," Gil said. "She saw him kill Mr. Streeter. He knows she could testify against him."

"She's not safe. He'll kill her." I said what Gil couldn't. I sagged against him.

"Looks like it," Detective Thrasher said. "That is, if these pictures show what really happened." He paused. "You two take away the body, did you?"

Gil and I exchanged glances.

The detective nodded. "Taking a body away like you did, lying to the police, those are serious crimes."

"It was my idea," I said. "Gil helped because Helen had to stay with Dorothy. He wouldn't have done it if I hadn't begged him."

The detective laid the three pictures side by side on the bright tulips, smoothing them with his hands, smoothing away the outline of the springs.

"What are you going to do?" Gil asked.

"It ain't my call. I have to show all this to the chief." He waved his hands over the bed. "My guess is there's blood some-where on this pick."

I started to say I had washed it all away but caught myself in time.

"There's nothing wrong with having an ice pick," Gil said.

The detective wrapped the tip of the ice pick in his gloves and put it in his overcoat pocket. "I can't speak for the chief, of course, but my guess is if we catch Gus Vincent, we'll show him these and tell him Dorothy told us what she saw."

"But she didn't tell us," I said.

The detective held up his hand. "There's no law says we can't lie a little. I guess this is why he's so anxious to get his hands on her. With this evidence, I wouldn't be surprised if he pleads guilty, hoping he can get a better deal. Might be your girl won't have to testify. If Vincent confesses, the girl might not even have to tell the police what she saw."

"And Gil and me?" I asked, looking at the picture of the two of us with the body.

"Oh, I wouldn't worry about that." The detective tore the picture in half, then into strips, and handed them to me. "Two pictures ought to be enough."

I felt a great sense of relief when the detective turned and went into the kitchen to help himself to the basket of food. I sat down on the bed.

"Everything's all right now," Gil told me, sitting beside me.

But it wasn't all right. It was even worse. Now we knew that Gus Vincent wasn't after money. He wanted to silence Dorothy.

Twenty-Two

A few minutes later the phone rang, and while I knew now it was unlikely that the Vincents would call, I still felt my heart thump as I picked up the receiver and identified myself.

"You the lady whose kid got stole?" a voice asked.

"Yes." I glanced at Detective Thrasher, who had come into the hall.

"I know where she is."

"Where?" I held the receiver against my chest and mouthed to the detective, "He knows where Dorothy is."

"I guess you want to get her back," the voice said.

"Of course I do. Please tell me what you know. Please."

"I guess it would be worth money to you, say, a hundred dollars."

I put my hand over the phone and whispered, "He wants one hundred dollars. I can pay that." I thought of Peter's money. I could pay five thousand dollars.

The detective yanked the receiver out of my hand and pushed me aside so he could talk. "This is Detective Thrasher with the Denver Police Department. If your information pans out, we'll pay you the hundred."

"He hung up," the detective said, as Gil came to the doorway.

I was furious. "Why did you do that? He knows about Dorothy."

"Yeah, him and every other sharper in town. He ain't the first to ask about a reward. We got two calls already at the judge's house. You can thank the newspapers for that."

"You mean he lied?" I couldn't imagine someone being so cruel.

Gil led me back into the living room. "There are some bad people out there, Lute. We see them at the hospital, people who say they saw an accident and want money to testify. Or they claim to be relatives of the dead and demand their wallets or purses. They're real lowlifes."

"But maybe he does know," I protested. "It would have been worth a hundred dollars."

The detective explained, "Oh, it doesn't stop there. Once he knows you'll pay, he'll up the price, tell you he risked his life by talking, and there're others who know, and they'd have to be bought off. And if you pay, why, he'll tell his friends and you'll get dozens of calls."

Gil nodded. "If he knew anything, he'd have telephoned the police, not you."

The detective added, "Now that the newspapers have the story all over their front pages, you'll likely get a phony ransom note or two. I'm just glad the judge didn't offer a reward. His wife wanted to, but he wouldn't let her. He knows that only causes the rats to come out of their holes."

"Then how will we find her?" I asked.

"We'll find them. There isn't a cop in town that isn't hoping to spot that car," the officer said.

"But will they have Dorothy?"

Detective Thrasher shrugged. He didn't have an answer for that.

In the afternoon, Melvin brought Mrs. Howell. She had never seen the house before and glanced around the living room and remarked, "It is clear you are an artist. This is a charming home, Lucretia, warm and inviting. It is perfect for a little girl."

She had brought a silver plate of rolls, still warm and smelling of cinnamon. "When I am upset, I go into the kitchen," she said. "You will recall I told you I had worked in a bakery." She removed the napkin that covered the buns and offered the plate to the detective. "You must be very tired, Officer Thrasher. I hope this will revive you." I fetched plates and napkins and glasses of milk, then Gil and I helped ourselves. Mrs. Howell offered the plate to Melvin, who was standing by the door. "For goodness' sake, Melvin, take a cinnamon bun and sit down. No need for you to stand on ceremony. We are all Dorothy's family here."

"Yes, ma'am," he said, setting a dining room chair next to the davenport and sitting on it.

"Now, Detective, your chief just left our home," Mrs. Howell said. "I do not know if you are aware of the latest developments, so I shall tell you what he said. They found the house in North Denver that the Vincents operated out of. It seems the neighbors were well aware of what was going on there, but they were afraid of the Vincents. There is so much bootlegging in that area that they never know who might turn on them. But bootlegging is one thing, kidnapping quite another. After the newspapers ran pictures of the Vincents, the police received a number of anonymous phone calls. When the police got there, however, the house was empty. They found the remains of the liquor operation, but there was no sign of the couple."

There was a knock on the door; it was Detective McCauley. "Nothing new," he said. He turned to Mrs. Howell. "The best bet is they're holed up somewhere in the city. But we don't know where. Maybe there's a relative with a place they're using." He turned to me. "You don't know if there's any other family, do you?"

"No." Maud had told me that Mr. Streeter was an orphan, but of course, that could have been a lie. And then something odd struck me. Once, not long after the Streeters moved into the basement, before I had begun to dislike Mr. Streeter, I had ridden the streetcar to South Denver with Maud. I was going to look at a collection of old jewelry that a woman at work had told me about. I had run into Maud, not at the trolley stop on the corner but at the Loop downtown, where all the trolleys met. We had laughed about it—that we'd taken separate streetcars only to transfer to the same one—and we'd sat together. We didn't talk much because Maud was distracted and seemed a little frightened. When I'd asked if everything was all right, she'd said streetcars scared her. I'd thought that was strange—who could be afraid of a trolley?—but I'd forgotten about it.

We rode a long way, almost to the end of the line, and I suggested we stay together. I could go with her on her errand. Then she could look at the jewelry with me. Maud liked pretty things. But she gave me a horrified look and said she was in a hurry.

Maud got off first, and I saw her go into a house. My stop was only two blocks farther. The jewelry was nothing I cared about, and I didn't stay long. I'd thought of stopping at the house where Maud had gone to see if we could ride back together, but something in Maud's attitude told me not to. A few months later, when Helen and I suspected that Mr. Streeter was involved in bootlegging, I wondered if her trip had had something to do with that. Perhaps Maud had been forced to deliver a bottle of liquor. Or maybe the house had contained a still. I had forgotten all about the streetcar ride until now.

"I know of a place Maud went once," I said tentatively. The two detectives looked up as I told them about the streetcar trip. "Of course, Maud could have been there for any number of reasons." I felt a little foolish even bringing up the episode.

"Maybe, but it's worth checking out. Do you have the address?" Detective McCauley asked.

I shook my head. "I don't even know the street. But I think I could find it. I could go with you and point it out."

The two detectives looked at each other. "We wouldn't want you to get hurt," Detective McCauley said.

Detective Thrasher responded, "She'll stay in the car. Besides, like she says, it's probably a dead end."

I thought Mrs. Howell would object, but she said only "Do you want Melvin to drive you? A police vehicle would alert them to your presence."

As if a big touring car would not, I thought. Still, the Howell auto seemed less obtrusive, so the detectives agreed, and

I got into the automobile with the two officers. Mrs. Howell stayed behind with Gil, who would answer the phone in case Gus Vincent called.

We followed the streetcar tracks down Broadway to the south edge of Denver. It was the end of the workday and Broadway was crowded, and I fidgeted as Melvin drove in and out of traffic. At last he reached Englewood and slowed down so that I could spot the house. I had made the trip with Maud in daylight, but it was dark now and hard for me to see the houses. Once I told Melvin to stop in front of a corner cottage that seemed familiar, then remembered the house had been mid-block.

Finally, I pointed to an old Victorian dwelling that stood at the back of a lot. There were no lights, and the sidewalks had not been shoveled of snow. "There," I said. "That's where I went to buy the jewelry. So we must have passed the house Maud stopped at. I know it was on the west side of the block."

Melvin turned, and the big car lumbered back along the street. Suddenly I pointed to a nondescript house. It looked like every other cheap cottage on the block, the door in the center with a window on either side. I recognized the two wicker chairs on the porch and the brick edging around the flower garden. The porch light was off, but light came through the window shades. Melvin parked across the street and turned off his headlights, but he left the engine running.

"Someone's inside," Detective Thrasher said. "Let me take a look around." He opened the car door noiselessly and slipped across the street. For a big man, he moved quickly and silently. After a few minutes, he came back to the car and motioned for his partner to roll down the window. "There's an auto in a garage out back. I saw it through a window. The garage door's locked, so I didn't get a look at the plate. I listened at the back door. I think there're two people inside. You want to take the front? I'll go around back again."

Detective McCauley nodded.

"You stay here," Detective Thrasher told Melvin and me. "Anything goes wrong, we passed a drugstore a block back. Drive there and call the police."

"Why don't we call them now?" I asked.

The two detectives looked sheepish, and I realized they didn't want to look foolish to the Englewood police if they were mistaken about the Vincents being inside.

Detective Thrasher repeated, "Stay here, Miss Hite. That's an order."

I watched as Detective Thrasher hurried around the side of the house. After a moment, Detective McCauley knocked at the front door. No one answered, and the detective knocked again. I saw the shade move a little. Then a voice called, "Go away. You got the wrong house."

"Hey, Gus, it's me," Detective McCauley yelled, as if he might be a friend.

"Wait a minute," a voice called out, and then there was silence. The door stayed closed.

Suddenly, there was a commotion in the back. I couldn't make out the words, and before Melvin could stop me I jumped out of the car yelling, "Dorothy! Dorothy!"

Melvin was behind me. He grabbed my arm, but I pulled away. Detective McCauley saw us and told us to watch the front door. He was going around back. But I couldn't wait. I left Melvin and followed the detective to the backyard. When I got there, I saw Detective Thrasher pointing his gun on Gus and Beulah Vincent, who were sitting on the ground in the snow. "Tell us where she is," he demanded.

The detective glanced at me. "We got 'em. You and the chauffeur, you go call the police."

I told Melvin to telephone for more officers, but I refused to leave. They must have thought I'd gone, however, because they shoved the Vincents against the clothesline pole and handcuffed them. Then Detective Thrasher held his gun against Gus Vincent's head and threatened, "You tell us where the girl's at or I'll beat it out of you. You don't want me to do that, do you?"

"What girl?" Mr. Vincent said.

"Don't give me that. We know you took her from school."

"We took her to get ice cream. She's my niece," Beulah Vincent said in a whiny voice. "There's nothing wrong with that."

"Then where is she now?"

"We ain't got her. She run off."

Detective Thrasher studied the two as he put away his gun. Then suddenly, he reached over and hit Mr. Vincent in the face with the back of his hand.

"Hey, you can't do that," Mrs. Vincent said.

"Who's to stop me?" He paused. "Maybe you'd like to tell me. There's a matron down at the jail likes to work over women, especially them that hurts kids."

Mrs. Vincent glared at the officer, but it was her husband who spoke. "We didn't do nothing wrong."

Detective Thrasher raised his hand again and Gus winced, but before the officer could hit him a second time Detective McCauley came out the back door. "She's not anywhere I can see. But I found this." He held up a necklace with a gold cross.

I gasped, and the two officers realized I was there. "It's Dorothy's. I gave it to her," I said.

"So she's been here. Where is she?" Detective Thrasher squeezed Mrs. Vincent's arm so hard she yelped. Then he turned to me. "Best you wait in the car. You won't want to see this."

But I stayed put. He shrugged.

In the distance, I heard the whine of a police siren, and the two detectives looked at each other. "Last chance," Detective Thrasher said. Mr. Vincent smirked at him, and Detective Thrasher punched him in the stomach so hard that the man vomited.

"You can't do that," Gus whispered, wiping his mouth on his shoulder.

"I just did."

The siren grew louder, then stopped, and in a few seconds, Melvin led two officers into the backyard.

"These the two that took the little girl?" one of the police officers asked. "We know all about it."

"Damn animals. You find her?" the second one chimed in.

Detective Thrasher studied them. They were older, coarse, and looked as if they'd been cops for a long time. "You fellows mind if me and Gus here ride to the station in Denver with you? Detective McCauley can take Mrs. Vincent with him."

The officers grinned. "It'd be our pleasure," one said.

I wondered what shape Mr. Vincent would be in when they

reached the police station, but I didn't care. I didn't care if Mrs. Vincent was worked over either.

I sat in the front of the car with Melvin, and Detective McCauley closed the window between the driver's seat and the back of the car. "Be a good idea to keep your eyes on the road, miss," Melvin said. But I knew as well as he did what was in store for Mrs. Vincent.

The window didn't keep out the sound, and I heard the detective say, "Your husband, we know all about him. He's got no hope, but it might be we could help you out if you cooperate. You tell us where the girl's at, and we'll put in a good word for you."

"I don't know. Like we said, she run off."

"Why'd you take her out of school?"

Beulah Vincent sounded scornful when she replied. "She is my niece. She called and begged me to pick her up. She said that woman she was living with was cruel to her."

I was about to speak, but Melvin touched my hand on the seat in warning.

"You admit you took her, but you won't tell us where she is. Is that because she's dead?"

I closed my eyes and hugged my sides with my arms, willing myself to look straight ahead. The Vincents had killed Dorothy and hidden her body somewhere. That was the only explanation. I was sure of it.

Mrs. Vincent snorted. "I never hurt a kid in my life."

Tears rolled down my cheeks.

"You kidnapped Dorothy Streeter."

"I never done that. That's Gus. What could I do? I'm his wife. I had to do what he told me to or he'd beat me. You know how men are."

"Yes. I know about men, and about women, too—women like you. You're unnatural."

"You don't know nothing about me."

"I know plenty. You're the worst kind of human being, one who preys on children. Hell's too good for you."

I couldn't stand it anymore and turned to stare at Mrs. Vincent. She was mean-looking, her mouth without lipstick now, a crooked line like a permanent snarl. But still, she was ordinary, so ordinary that you wouldn't give her a second glance on the street, and if you did, you might think she was the wife of a railroad worker or an automobile mechanic. She glanced at me with no more expression than if she'd been looking at a chair. And then she gave me a cruel little smile, and I thought there was no good in her at all.

When we reached the station, Detective Thrasher helped Gus Vincent out of the car. Mr. Vincent was bent over, his face bloody.

Melvin and I waited in the car while the Vincents went inside. At last, Detective Thrasher came out and asked Melvin to take him back to his auto, which was parked near my house.

"Do you know where Dorothy is? Did he tell you anything?" I asked.

Detective Thrasher shook his head. "He keeps saying Dorothy ran away."

"Maybe she did," I said.

"Ma'am, I sure am sorry," Detective Thrasher said. "If she'd run away, somebody would have found her. It's more likely they killed her and hid the body. I'm afraid she's dead. I'm real sorry." His voice broke when he said that, and I knew he was indeed sorry.

Twenty-Three

It was very late at night when Melvin stopped the car in front of our house. Gil must have been watching because he came out onto the porch, Mrs. Howell behind him. She had waited all that time.

"The Vincents. They're in jail," I said as soon as I came up onto the porch.

"Dorothy?" they asked together.

I shook my head. "They said she ran away. Detective Thrasher thinks she must be . . . dead." My voice was a hoarse whisper.

"Oh!" Mrs. Howell said, while Gil put his arms around me and looked away so that I would not see he was crying. We were all crying.

"We don't know that for sure," Detective Thrasher said gruffly. "Maybe she did run away. She could be hiding."

"Oh, Lucretia," Mrs. Howell said, her voice filled with anguish. She caught herself and said, "I suppose we have to be prepared for the worst. You must be very tired, dear. Melvin will take me home now. And you, Dr. Rushton? May we deliver you to your residence?"

"The hospital," he replied. "That is, unless you need me, Lute? I'll stay if you do."

"No," I told him. I didn't want him to leave, but he had already taken too much time away from his patients. I would be all right alone. I was very tired and wanted to go to bed.

Detective Thrasher stood beside me as we watched the others leave. "There's still a small chance—" he said, but I held up my hand.

"That's not necessary, Detective. I am too familiar with death. Why should she be alive when the others I love are gone?"

"I'm sorry, miss. If it helps you, the Vincents will be put away for a long time. It might not be for the girl's murder, but we've got him on killing Streeter—he confessed to that. And to the kidnapping. I just wish we had them for murdering the girl."

"Dorothy," I said. "She's not 'the girl.' She's Dorothy." I wondered if it was easier for him not to put names to victims. Perhaps that was how he dealt with his job.

"Dorothy," he repeated. "If we don't find her, we'll find her body. There aren't many places they could have hid the body. The Englewood police are searching the house, and in the morning they'll check the yard. With the snow, it'll be obvious if there's a grave."

I thanked the detective, and when he left, I locked the door.

Mrs. Howell had left the remainder of the cinnamon buns on the kitchen table, covered with a napkin. She or Gil had washed the dishes. I sat down at the table, tracing one of the designs in the oilcloth, remembering how Helen had done the same thing. That seemed so long ago. Then I noticed the Bible at the edge of the table—my Bible, the one Helen had given me when we were both very young. Mrs. Howell must have taken it from the bookshelf and sat there reading it.

I wondered if I should go to Neusteter's in the morning. There was no reason to stay home anymore, and if I went to work, I wouldn't have to answer the telephone or shoo away reporters who came to the door. Perhaps working would take my mind off my sorrow and give my life some sense of normalcy.

I undressed, set and wound the clock, which had run down, and got into bed and dozed, but it seemed that whenever I fell asleep, I was awakened by nightmares about Dorothy. I tried to rid my mind of the images of what the Vincents would have done to her. Finally, near morning, I got up and wandered around the house

I stood in the doorway to Dorothy's room a moment. I would not clean it as I had Helen's. Helen's room had contained the remnants of a deadly disease, but Dorothy's room seemed sweet, scented with the lily of the valley perfume that had been Helen's.

I was startled by a thud outside, then realized it was the newspaper hitting the sidewalk. The paper would have the story of Gus and Beulah Vincent's arrest. Perhaps there was something more about Dorothy. Maybe the police had found her body. Detective Thrasher would have waited until morning to tell me.

Because it was very cold and I did not want to go outside in my nightdress, I grabbed my coat from the chair where I had thrown it the night before. I opened the door and looked out. One of the things I loved about winters in Denver was that after a storm, the sun came out and melted the snow. A few days later, you would never know there had been a blizzard. But it was too early for the sun now.

The paper was lying on the sidewalk, and I stepped carefully because there was a film of ice. I picked up the paper and unfolded it. A streetlamp a few houses away sent out a glow— not enough to read the paper by, although I could make out the headlines. They were big and black and screamed that the Vincents had been captured at a "hideout" in Englewood. There was no mention of Dorothy's body. She hadn't been found yet, at least not by the time the paper went to press.

The cold revived me, and I did not want to go inside just yet. The house seemed stuffy and overheated. Still, I clutched the paper and moved toward the swing. I would sit there until I grew too cold. The porch was dark, and I made my way in the dawning light. When I reached the swing I saw that there was a black lump lying on it—a dog, I thought, then realized it must be one of the reporters. I was disgusted to think that he had been waiting to waylay me the moment I stepped outside, then thought it funny that he had fallen asleep. The figure stirred, and I wondered if it might be another of the blackguards who demanded money for information about Dorothy. I backed away. I would go inside and call the police.

But I stumbled as I took a step backward, waking the sleeper. I stared, thinking I was looking at an apparition. "Dorothy?" I whispered at last.

"Lutie?"

I rushed to the swing and grabbed her and held her tight. "It's you. It's you!" I whispered. "Oh, Dorothy, are you all right?"

"I'm sorry," she whispered back.

Her face was seared with dirt, and I brushed back her hair, picking out leaves and twigs. "It's all right. Everything will be all right."

"I wouldn't have come here, but I didn't know where else to go."

"Of course you should have come here."

"Don't send me back to them. Please. I'll earn my keep, and I won't be any trouble. I'll quit school and I'll clean your house for you and do the laundry, and I'll learn to cook. Just don't send me back to Aunt Beulah."

"Of course I won't send you back. Why would you think that?"

Tears ran down Dorothy's face, and she couldn't look at me. "Aunt Beulah said you didn't want me and told them to come and get me. She told me you wanted to send me to an orphanage, but I was too old and I'd be put out on the street. They were the only ones who would take me, and if I caused any trouble or told anyone about Uncle Gus and Papa, I'd be sorry."

"They lied," I said, appalled that anyone could be so callous. "You're my sister. I love you. I want you more than anything in the world. Did you know the police have been looking all over for you so that they could bring you back to me? Your aunt and uncle are in jail, and they're going to stay there a long time, maybe forever." I held out the paper so that she could read the headlines.

Dorothy began to shiver, and I realized she had been in the cold a long time. Although she was now almost as big as

I was, I picked her up and carried her into the house. I all but collapsed onto the couch with her and sat with her in my lap, wiping the tears from her face and cooing a little.

After a time, I said we must let Gil know she was safe. And Mrs. Howell. And the police. "Everyone has been looking for you. Oh, Dorothy, I was so scared I'd never see you again."

Dorothy turned her sweet, angelic smile on me and said, "I love you, Lutie."

I told her I must make the telephone calls, but first I would give her a bath and find her some clean clothes.

She stood up, then looked down at her new orange coat. "It's spoiled. I ripped it when I crawled out the window. And I lost a shoe," she said. "But I got away."

"How?" I asked.

"They said we had to hide. They were fighting, and they took me on a long drive. I was at that house before, with Papa. They put me in a back room, but I could hear them talking. Aunt Beulah said she didn't trust me. I think she wanted to kill me. I knew I had to run away, but Uncle Gus had locked the door. He forgot to lock the window, though. I opened it and jumped out, but I broke the glass." She showed me the scratches on her hands from the glass shards. "My coat got torn. I ran. I heard them call me, but I didn't stop. I remembered that Papa took me there on the trolley, so I followed the tracks. It took a long time because it was so far away and I had to hide when a car went by. Then I recognized some buildings, and I knew how to get to your house."

"Our house," I said softly.

"I didn't want to wake you up, so I sat on the swing. Then

I was so tired I couldn't wait for you to wake up, so I went to sleep."

In the bathroom I took off Dorothy's remaining shoe and her socks and helped her out of her coat. I turned on the taps, and when the tub was full, I left Dorothy to climb in by herself. I collected her clothes and put them beside the back door. Later, I would throw them into the ash pit, her coat as well. Even if the coat was salvageable, Dorothy would not want to wear it again. I left the bathroom door ajar and went to the telephone and asked for the police station. Detective Thrasher was out, but Detective McCauley was there. "Dorothy's here. She's safe," I told him. "She ran off after all, and she came here."

"Isn't that fine! We'll call off the search." I was about to hang up when he said, "I never saw my partner so upset about a case before. You think maybe him and me could stop by and talk to the little girl sometime? I mean, we have to interview her, but we might just like to say hello now and then."

"She would like that," I said.

Next I telephoned Gil, who said he would be right over, and then Mrs. Howell.

"The two of you must have time to be together. I shall not call for a few days. But tell Dorothy I love her and that I am praying for her," she said.

I did not return to work for a week, and I was pleased that Neusteter's had not replaced me. Perhaps that was because I had become a sort of celebrity. The newspapers did not let go of Dorothy's kidnapping, and every story mentioned me. There were even likenesses of me and reports that I worked at

Neusteter's. When I walked into the store on my first day back, the other employees applauded, and Mr. Meyer Neusteter personally came into the advertising department to tell me he was glad that Dorothy was safe.

By then the tenants had moved into the basement apartment, so Dorothy did not have to come home from school to an empty house. Still, I talked with a real estate agent about selling the place and buying another one. I had been happiest in that house, with Helen and Peter, but I had been saddest, too, and Dorothy must have bad memories of it as well. It would be best if we could start over in another home. Gil and Mrs. Howell agreed. She invited Dorothy and me to live with the judge and her until we found a place, but I thought Dorothy and I should be on our own. As kind as the Howells were, I did not want us to be dependent on them. I think Mrs. Howell understood.

We began looking at houses even before the court gave us its approval. The adoption was just a formality now. It was only a matter of signing papers. I did not think there was any great hurry.

Twenty-Four

It was winter now. The snow came down in sheets of white. When it stopped, the sun shone on the ice crystals, making them sparkle like gemstones. Gil and Dorothy and I had snowball fights. We walked along snowy streets to City Park and went sledding on the big hill by the museum. When the park's big lake froze, we ice-skated. Gil and Dorothy were better than I, so I sat on a log by the fire and watched them.

"I'm hopeless at skating. I'm a terrible dancer, too," I told Gil.

"Then I'll teach you. Let's go dancing sometime," he said.

When we went home, our faces cold and red, we settled in front of the fire and drank cocoa. Once, we made our own marshmallows.

Gil visited often. The influenza was waning, and he was working fewer hours. Sometimes he came by with his books and studied at the dining room table while Dorothy did her own schoolwork and I sewed.

One evening Gil announced, "I promised to take you dancing. On Saturday, we're going to the Savoy."

I hadn't left Dorothy home alone in the evening since she had returned and didn't know if she'd feel safe by herself. Besides, I wasn't sure I wanted to go dancing with Gil.

"It's not a date," he said when I hesitated.

"I'll stay downstairs with the Hoovers," Dorothy announced, and so it was settled.

That Saturday afternoon I went through my closet, looking for something I thought would be appropriate. Dorothy watched me pull out a brown silk dress. It was understated and formal.

"Don't wear that," she told me. "You ought to put on that blue velvet dress you wore when Mr. Howell took you out one time. Remember, you came downstairs to show it to Mama and me."

It was a beautiful dress. I had gotten it for half-price at Neusteter's because the size was mismarked. Then I had cut it down to fit. I hadn't wanted to wear it, because it reminded me too much of Peter. That was foolish, I decided. Half of my wardrobe reminded me of Peter. So I put it on, and when Gil picked me up he said I looked lovely.

I thought I would feel disoriented going dancing with someone besides Peter. Despite my misgivings, however, the evening turned out fine. Gil was a good dancer, and it was easy to follow him. We talked about the influenza and Dorothy and what he would do when he graduated in just a few months. I'd thought he would set up his own practice, but he said he might go into research. I remembered then that Peter had not wanted to be a minister but had been considering teaching or running a charity. It surprised me that this was the first time I'd thought about Peter all evening.

We caught a late streetcar, then walked to the house on frozen sidewalks, Gil holding on to me to keep me from slipping.

When we reached the house I invited him in, but he said he had to get up early. He took my keys from me and unlocked the door. Then he kissed me on the cheek.

"I haven't had such a good time since . . . since before Dorothy came back," he said. He'd intended to say "since before Helen died" but caught himself.

"I know," I said. "I suppose life goes on."

"It does."

Did I want it to? I asked myself as I undressed and slipped into bed. I wasn't sure, not that I had a choice. I thought it would be disloyal if I forgot a moment of my life with Helen and Peter. I *would* forget, however. I knew that in time, the memories would start to fade.

One Saturday, Mrs. Howell invited me for luncheon at the Brown Palace Hotel. Gil offered to take Dorothy to the movies so I wouldn't have to rush home. Mrs. Howell was waiting for me in the lobby, almost hidden by potted palms. She was sitting on an overstuffed settee under the stained-glass skylight nine floors above. I loved the rotunda, with its Persian rugs and broad staircase and miles and miles of onyx.

The women around Mrs. Howell were swathed in mink coats and fur scarves of beady-eyed fox. She wore a stylish wool coat with a velvet scarf around her neck. I had made the scarf from a very old ball gown Peter and I had found in a used-clothing store. "It is much softer than fur," she said when she saw me looking at it. "Perhaps I shouldn't wear it all the time, but I do love the way it feels around my neck, and I have received ever so many compliments on it."

She led the way into the dining room, with its starched white tablecloths and polished wooden chairs. We were seated in a corner. "The judge and I had luncheon here the day Peter left. I could not eat anything. My appetite is much better today."

"I remember you were kind enough to invite me." At the time, I hadn't known if she had meant the invitation, but I knew now that she had.

"The last time any of us saw Peter." She was quiet. "It is time we did not dwell on such things. How are you getting along on Dorothy's adoption?"

I explained that it was taking longer than I had expected. The courts were backlogged because of the influenza. I was not worried, however. No judge would award Dorothy to Beulah Vincent, and no other relative had come forward. Still, I would be glad when the adoption papers were signed.

We ordered and then exchanged pleasantries. The pall of loss did not seem so heavy when I was chatting with a friend.

"I have a reason for inviting you to luncheon," Mrs. Howell said. "I thought we might both enjoy talking someplace besides the house. It is gloomy there at times."

I waited for her to continue.

"Look about you." She swept her hand around the dining room. "All these fashionable women with their money. Why, they spend a fortune on their clothes. But you work at Neusteter's. You already know that."

I remembered the conversation with Peter on our first date when he scoffed at women who wasted their money on fashion. Was Mrs. Howell going to say the same thing?

"You have no idea how many of my acquaintances have commented on my scarf."

The waiter set down our food, while I wondered if Mrs. Howell was going to ask me to make similar ones for her friends.

"I have wanted to talk to you because I believe you should go into business for yourself. You could make accessories—all kinds of scarves, hats, perhaps purses, even jewelry. You could set up a studio at home. You'd be there for Dorothy. She might even help you. She is quite talented." When I didn't reply right away, she added, "I do hope you will not think I am interfering."

"No, of course not." I picked up a roll and tore it in half, then set both halves on my plate without buttering them. "I don't know if I'm good enough. And I don't know a thing about business." Neusteter's didn't pay much, but it was steady. The idea of going into business for myself frightened me.

"I would not have brought it up, except Peter was quite certain that's what you should do. He had such faith in you. And I do, too."

"What if I failed? I wouldn't be able to go back to Neusteter's. And it would cost money. As you know, Peter left me quite a lot, but I'm saving it for Dorothy."

"Yes, you have said that. I suppose I have not made myself clear." Mrs. Howell had ordered a pastry shell filled with something in a cream sauce, and she took a bite. "I intend to underwrite you."

I had buttered one of the halves of my roll and stopped with it partway to my mouth. "You what?"

"I will put up the money."

"I couldn't accept."

"Of course you could. It is not a gift. It is an investment, and you can repay me when you are established. You see, I believe there is a ready market for what you make."

I thought about that as I stared at the fish I had ordered. It was trout, and the fish stared back at me with his dead eye. "Even if there is, how do I reach it? Neusteter's doesn't buy one-of-a-kind pieces, and it's not as if I can advertise in the newspaper. That would cost too much."

"You tap into my friends, of course. I will announce a showing at my home. We will donate some of the proceeds to the Presbyterian orphan's home. Women will feel it is their duty to buy something to support a charity." She speared a pea in the cream sauce with her fork. "Funny, isn't it. They will not donate ten dollars to a charity, but they will justify spending ten dollars on themselves if one dollar goes to a good cause."

"Then what would I do?"

"Why, that's easy. By then you will have a following. You can set up a studio in your home. Peter said you had one before."

I shook my head. "That's Dorothy's room now."

Mrs. Howell set down her fork and touched her napkin to her lips. "Perhaps it is time for Dorothy to move into Helen's room. You cannot keep it as a shrine."

"Like you do?" That was an awful thing to say and I touched Mrs. Howell's hand and said I was sorry.

"No, you are quite right. How easy to see the mote in someone else's eye and not the beam in our own. Perhaps it's time for both of us to move on from our grieving." She studied me. "I believe you have already begun to do so. Perhaps you will help me."

Of course, I told Gil about Mrs. Howell's offer.

"It's a splendid idea," he said. "Helen thought you could do so much more than draw women in advertisements. I say do it."

"Mrs. Howell suggested I keep my job until I have made enough things to sell. Besides, she says being employed is important when I go before a judge. He'll want to know how I can support Dorothy."

We were sitting in the kitchen while I cut up carrots for soup. Gil was peeling potatoes. I stopped and looked at him across the oilcloth. "Do you really think I can be successful?"

"I know you can. You have such style. Haven't you noticed how people turn to stare at you? It's enough to make a fellow jealous." He grinned.

I blushed and turned away. Did Gil really mean that? I didn't know how to reply. I said, "Dorothy and I will have to spend Saturday afternoons shopping for old clothes and buttons and such. You won't see as much of us."

"Unless I come along," he said.

I had hoped that Judge Howell would preside over Dorothy's adoption hearing, but if the case was assigned to him, he would have to recuse himself, he told us, just as Mr. Coombs had said. The judge we got would be the luck of the draw. He pointed out that most judges were humane, however, and as there was no one else who wanted to adopt Dorothy, he did not see any problem. Neither did I. In fact, I had made an appointment with our real estate agent to take a second look at a house Dorothy and I liked just after the adoption was settled.

Mrs. Howell and Mr. Coombs accompanied Dorothy, Gil, and me to the hearing. They exchanged glances when we were told to go to Judge Emil Cox's courtroom.

"Is something wrong?" I whispered.

Mrs. Howell was slow to answer. "He can be contentious," she said, then added, "He does not see eye-to-eye with Judge Howell and me. Perhaps I should not have come."

But it was too late. Judge Cox had seen her, and he gave her a disdainful look.

There were some preliminary words, and then the judge said, "State your case, Mr. Coombs."

Mr. Coombs stood up and began speaking. "Dorothy Streeter's parents are dead, and there are no known relatives who claim her. Miss Hite and her sister had hoped to adopt Dorothy, but tragically Miss Hite's sister died of the influenza. She was a nurse. A terrible loss." He paused a moment to let that sink in. "Dorothy lost not only her mother and father but a loving young woman who was to have been her sister. You undoubtedly have read in the newspapers about the attempt to kidnap Dorothy and the terrible conditions of her life. She is a frail child, and it would be unconscionable to separate her from the one remaining person she considers family—Miss Lucretia Hite."

He talked about what a good sister I would be to Dorothy, how I had cared for her since her mother died, fed and clothed her, played with her, and took her to school each day, making me sound like Edith Kermit Roosevelt. As if on cue, Dorothy leaned her head against my shoulder.

After Mr. Coombs sat down, Judge Cox turned to Mrs. Howell and asked if she had something to say.

Mrs. Howell stood, her head high, and said, "I am here as a character witness for Miss Hite. She was engaged to my son, who was killed in France. If Peter had lived, he and Miss Hite would have adopted Dorothy. Now it will be Miss Hite alone. She is the finest young woman I know. She will give love and stability to a lost little girl, a girl I consider my granddaughter." She sat down and patted Dorothy's hand.

"Thank you. Your view of orphans is well known, Mrs. Howell," Judge Cox said, and I caught sarcasm in his voice. "What your son intended to do is of no consequence, since he is dead, isn't he?"

Mrs. Howell did not answer. I thought that the judge had been cruel.

He put his palms together and stared at us, as if he enjoyed the drama. "Yes, I am aware of the circumstances of this child's life. The newspapers have been full of it. And I am aware that Miss Hite failed to protect her."

Mr. Coombs stood up to speak, but the judge held up his hand.

"Perhaps that is because Miss Hite is a very young woman, too young to be this child's mother."

I wanted to defend myself, to say that I would be a sister to Dorothy, but Mr. Coombs put his hand on my arm.

"She may get bored raising a child. She could be back here in a few months' time begging to give up the girl."

"No!" I said, and Mr. Coombs squeezed my arm.

"It appears that you do not have the maturity to control yourself," he said. "If you were married, I would grant the adoption. A husband would keep you in your place. But a single woman, and one as young as you—a bachelor girl who works as an artist." He all but curled his lip. "No, I cannot in good conscience grant this adoption. The child will be sent to an orphan's home and will stay there until suitable parents—a father and a mother—can be found for her—"

"But girls this age are rarely adopted," Mr. Coombs interrupted.

The judge held up his hand. "I am speaking, Mr. Coombs. Yes, they are rarely adopted. That means the child will go to the Denver Home for Foundlings and Orphans until she is fourteen, at which time she will be on her own."

I turned to Mrs. Howell, who was as distressed as I was. She stood and said, "Sir, I can testify that while an orphanage may be the best place for children who are not wanted, I do not believe you can justify taking Dorothy from a loving friend who is willing to be both sister and mother, and send her to an institution."

Judge Cox was annoyed. "You do not make the decisions in my courtroom, Madam. I will not put an orphan with a single woman. Miss Hite has one week to turn over the child."

"She isn't 'the child,'" I said. "She's Dorothy."

The judge glared at me.

"Could she not be sent to the Presbyterian home?" Mrs. Howell asked.

"No, she may not. I believe that if she were, you would

arrange for Miss Hite to see her. And Miss Hite . . ." He paused until I looked up at him. "Any attempt to spirit the child away will have serious consequences. I have the authority to track you down wherever you go. Make sure you do not consider it."

"Is there nothing Miss Hite can do?" Mr. Coombs asked.

The judge almost smirked. "Yes, of course. She may have the child if she finds a husband."

Dorothy had watched the proceedings without saying a word. When we left the room, she turned to me and asked, "What does he mean, the orphan's home? Can't I live with you? Can't I be your sister anymore?"

I held her close. "I won't let you go," I whispered. "I'll never let you go."

Gil had been quiet, but now he spoke. "I won't either. I promise you we will find a way."

"There is one, I believe," Mrs. Howell said. "Come to luncheon. I was afraid this would happen the moment I knew Emil Cox was the hearing officer. Judge Cox has no children and doesn't seem to like them. He doesn't much like women, either. He would as soon send a child to a workhouse as give her to a single woman." She paused. "I believe the fault is mine entirely. You see, Judge Howell once ruled against Mrs. Cox on a matter involving a servant. Judge Cox has nurtured his revenge for a long time."

Mr. Coombs told us he would try to find a way to appeal the decision, but he was not hopeful. Gil, Dorothy, and I went home with Mrs. Howell. George opened the door for us, and when he saw our faces, he said softly that he was sorry.

"Never mind, we will not give up," Mrs. Howell said as she ushered us into the dining room.

None of us felt like eating and we picked at the food. After a time, Mrs. Howell asked Gil if he would take Dorothy to the stable to see the old horse that the judge kept for sentimental reasons, because she wanted to have a private conversation with me.

"What do I do?" I asked Mrs. Howell after Gil and Dorothy left. "Do you think I should take her to Iowa?"

"No, Judge Cox is mean enough to go after you." She paused. "The answer is very simple. Judge Cox has said you could have the child if you were married. Now we must find you a husband."

I laughed, but she did not even smile.

"Do you truly understand what will happen to Dorothy if you do not adopt her?"

"I will snatch her up the moment she turns fourteen," I said.

"Of course you will, but that will be too late. In two years' time, Dorothy will be so broken, she will never mend. I know."

She must have heard stories from the orphans in the Presbyterian home, I thought. I wondered if girls had made them up to shock her.

As if she knew my thoughts, Mrs. Howell said, "I should like to tell you a story, one that only Mr. Howell knows. I never told Peter or the girls. It has been a secret all these years, but I believe that knowing it will help you understand."

I wondered if she remembered she had already told me she'd been orphaned and her brother had killed himself. "About Leadville?" I asked.

"Yes. It is not a pretty story. In fact, it is quite perverted, and I would not tell you unless I thought it was important you understood. I know you will keep it to yourself."

"You've already told me about your brother," I said to head her off.

She picked up her teacup. "I believe I need something stronger to drink," she said. Then she rose and led the way to the library. "I should not wish the servants to hear this." She closed the door, then went to a table and picked up a decanter of whiskey and poured some into a glass, then held out the bottle to me.

I shook my head.

"I lied to you. I did not work in a bakery in Leadville. Well, I did much later, but not right away. And that was not where I met Judge Howell." She sipped the whiskey. "You see, after our father left, a kind woman offered my brother and me a home. At least I thought she was kind. But, in fact, she was a procurer, and she sold both of us to a brothel that provided men with young children."

I stared at Mrs. Howell, who met my eyes and did not look away. She picked up the decanter again, and this time I nodded, and she poured a goodly amount into a crystal glass for me.

"I was thirteen, my brother younger. They gave him opium. They didn't give it to me because they were aware I would stay as long as my brother was there. We ran off once, but he went back, because he had an unquenchable craving by then. I knew he would die without me, so I returned, too." Mrs. Howell stared into her glass.

I glanced around the library and thought how I would always associate it with sorrow. I sipped my drink.

"You see, I know what would be ahead for Dorothy."

"But how did you escape?"

"I met Judge Howell."

My jaw dropped.

"No, you must not think ill of him. You see, in those days it was not unusual for a young man to visit a prostitute. An associate took him to the house where I worked, and when he found that it was filled with children, he was sickened. He had come into the parlor, and after his associate left with another little girl, he sat beside me and asked me to tell him my story. When I was finished, he said I must leave, that he would help me. I explained about my brother, and he said there were asylums that would treat his addiction.

"I thought at first that he meant to have me to himself. It was what all the girls wanted, to have a man set you up in a little house as his mistress. But that wasn't it at all. He merely wanted to rescue a young girl. He told me he felt responsible because I was one of those little souls. I'd never heard the expression, of course." She stared at the amber liquid in her glass. "Not long after that, my brother killed himself. When Mr. Howell heard about his death, he removed me from the brothel and placed me with the baker's family. And over time, he and I fell in love. So you see, not all of what I told you before was a lie."

"Why are you telling me this?" I asked.

"So that you understand Dorothy and what her future will be like without someone who loves her. There wasn't a day I did not think about ending my life, and I would have if it had not been for my brother. Even after I was rescued from that place I could not rid myself of the guilt, the degradation, the humiliation . . . I was so sick of it. I believed I was evil, filled with rot. I feel it yet sometimes. If it had not been for Judge Howell . . . For a long time, I did not believe he could love someone as wicked as I was. When I finally accepted his love, that was when I began to heal. Still, there are times . . ." She finished her whiskey. "If you truly love Dorothy and want to save her, then you must marry, Lucretia."

"But Peter is dead. Perhaps I will find someone in time, but who is there for me to marry now?"

"Who indeed," she replied. She rose then, because we heard Dorothy laughing in the hall with Gil.

"We're in here," I said, opening the library door.

Mrs. Howell invited Dorothy to go into the kitchen with her to make cookies. "You may not know it, dear, but I am very good at baking." She took Dorothy's hand, leaving Gil and me alone.

Gil glanced at the glasses of whiskey. "This must have been a serious conversation."

"Yes," I said. "Mrs. Howell believes that without me, Dorothy will never heal."

"Do you agree?"

"I think so." I turned to Gil and took his hand. "What can I do? I can't give her up. I love her so." My eyes filled with tears.

"I have been thinking about it since we left the courthouse. There is one thing you could do." Gil tightened his hand on mine, and I looked up. He started to say something, then stopped and swallowed. He stared at me a long time. "You could marry me."

I stared at him, stunned. "What?"

"We both love Dorothy."

"Yes, but do we love each other?"

"Don't we?"

"It's preposterous, isn't it? You love Helen."

"And you love Peter. And we always will love them. We are like two broken halves, Lutie."

"Yes, but are we halves of the same whole?"

"We have mended together. We started out connected by grief. I believe it has turned into love, first for Dorothy, then for each other."

I gripped the side of the chair and stared at the polished table next to me with its clutter of photographs in silver frames. Mine would have been there if Peter and I had married. "It's too soon. There are so many reasons why it wouldn't work."

"And one very good reason why it would."

"I suppose we could marry . . ." I stumbled over the word. "And after the adoption is final, we could end it."

"No. We should marry because we expect it to work. Judge Cox is right. Dorothy needs both a father and a mother. We should marry with the idea that it's for ever and ever. I love you. I think maybe you love me, too."

Did I? I went to the window and opened the shutters, looking out at the garden, which was covered in snow. It was dark in the shadows, but the snow sparkled where the sun hit it. I wondered what Peter would have thought about my marrying Gil. I loved Peter, perhaps even more after his death than I had before. He would always be in my heart. He had been dead just a few months. Even so, I wondered if it was the idea of Peter

I loved now. Did I feel about Gil as I had Peter? Maybe not in the same way. Peter had been my first love. Gil was mature. He was steady. Still, I thought how my heart leaped when I heard his footstep on the porch, how I had wanted his approval for my venture with Mrs. Howell, how I smiled to remember the touch of his lips on my cheek. Most of all, I thought how much he loved Dorothy and how the three of us had become a family. I loved him for that.

Gil touched my arm. I had not realized he was standing so close to me, and I jumped. "What are you thinking?" he asked.

I looked out at the garden again, at the skeletons of rosebushes. Peter had said that things happened for a reason, especially bad things, and that God challenged us to rise above them. He'd also told me that God made choices, but sometimes the choices were up to us. Perhaps that meant that God had chosen to take Helen and Peter but that it was our choice to raise Dorothy. Suddenly, I felt comforted—comforted to know in my heart now that there was a God up there, and that He would help us.

I said to Gil, "Peter told me that 'love seeketh not her own.' He said that means love is what you give, not what you receive."

"He was right." Gil laughed a little. I liked his laugh. "I guess I'm game if you are."

"Do we love Dorothy enough to make it work?"

"I do. What about you?"

I nodded. "Yes."

"And each other?"

"Yes to that, too."

"Well, then," Gil said, and he took my hand. He laughed

again and said, "Lute . . . Lucretia . . . Will you . . ." He paused, his face red.

I would not make him go on. After all, this was not his decision or my decision but *our* decision. I held up my hand to stop him from saying more. "Yes," I told him.

Epilogue

St. Louis, Missouri
March 2, 1929

Dear Lutie,

Little Helen is asleep in the Howell family cradle. Anne sent it months ago, long before the baby was born, saying I should have it because I am the first "grandchild" to have a baby. She offered me Peter's christening dress, but I want my darling "little soul" to wear the one you made for Dwight and John, if you will let me borrow it. She will wear it with Helen's gold cross. The baby is four weeks old today and growing so much that it won't be long before she'll be accompanying me as I scour secondhand stores in search of old fabrics.

I can't bear to be away from her for a minute, although I should be studying. Jack insists I finish college and get my fine arts degree, and I quite agree. How many girls have a husband who believes they should be educated, and a friend from long ago who provides the money to pay for the education? I am indeed lucky.

In fact, I have been thinking these past weeks just how fortunate I am, how extraordinary my life has been because of you and Gil. I was so lost back then, and so fearful of what would happen to me. Then you took me in.

I did not understand until Jack and I married, and we experienced the challenges of wedded life, what a momentous decision it was for the two of you to marry just so that you could adopt me. At the time, it seemed right that the three of us, grieving as we were, should be united. But now I know the chance that you and Gil took for my sake. You could have ruined your lives and your chance for happiness. Instead, you developed a loving bond, one that inspires Jack and me. I remember when you were in labor the first time, and Gil and I were in the waiting room. He told me he would not be able to bear it if anything happened to you. When the doctor came to tell us the baby had been born, Gil didn't ask if it was a boy or a girl. Instead, he asked if you were all right. When the doctor announced you'd had a boy, Gil turned to me and said, "You have a brother, Dorothy." Never had I felt so much a part of a family. I want little Helen to know that she, too, has parents who love each other every bit as much as they do her.

I've wondered if, without me, the two of you would have married. So perhaps I can take the credit for bringing you together. Well, if that is true, you have repaid me manyfold. You gave me the best life I could have had, filled with love and comfort, and a future that includes a wonderful husband, college, a career—and, of course, Baby Helen. I am so pleased that you and Gil approve of the name. I only wish that Helen could have met her namesake. I think of her often. Yesterday I came across my old treasure box and looked inside to find dried flowers from a May basket you and Helen gave me.

The designs you sent for the summer couture show are exquisite. Anne suggested I consider designing dresses for little girls to add to the winter line. What do you think of that? I could start as soon as school is over. I know you are busy putting the finishing touches on next season's collection and don't want to leave the final details in the hands of your employees. Still, I hope you and Gil and the boys can find the time to visit us in St. Louis soon. Helen would like to meet her grandparents and uncles. And I miss my beloved sister.

All my love,
Dorothy

Acknowledgments

The Spanish influenza may have been history's deadliest pandemic. Worldwide estimates of death range from a low of 17 million to as many as 100 million, but the number was probably between 20 million and 50 million. A quarter of the United States population was infected, and more than 500,000 Americans died. Colorado, with a population of less than 1 million, had 50,000 incidents of infection and nearly 8,000 deaths, 1,500 of them in Denver. The city closed churches and restaurants and forbade public gatherings, including church services and funerals. Residents were told to stop shaking hands and kissing. Remedies ranged from a variety of purgatives and powders to carrying an acorn in the left-side vest pocket. The *Rocky Mountain News* advised people to cut out meat and vote Republican. Policemen stopped arresting undesirables for fear of spreading the flu in the jails, and in Salida, a well-known madam shuttered her brothel so the prostitutes could nurse the sick.

Although it was called the Spanish influenza because of its deadly effect in Spain, it may actually have started in Fort Riley, Kansas, and been spread by soldiers during World War I. Unlike the COVID-19 virus, where the greatest number of victims were among the elderly, the Spanish influenza attacked young people in the prime of life.

I wrote the first draft of *Little Souls* several years ago, then put it aside because there was little interest then in the Spanish influenza. But with the onset of COVID-19, the book became timely. The randomness of that hundred-year-old pandemic, the grief, the disruption of lives, became all too familiar in 2020 as Americans faced a terrifying new infection. We began to relate to the century-old scourge.

In researching the Spanish influenza, I consulted many sources. The most helpful were John M. Barry's *The Great Influenza* and Stephen J. Leonard's "The 1918 Influenza Epidemic in Denver and Colorado" in the Colorado Historical Society's *Essays and Monographs in Colorado History*. The Denver Public Library's superb Western History Collection provided information about Denver during the 1918 scourge.

Thanks go to my agent, Danielle Egan-Miller, who never gave up on this book; to Elisabeth Dyssegaard, my editor at St. Martin's Press, for her thoughtful editing; to production editor Jennifer Fernandez; and to publisher Jennifer Enderlin. Thanks especially to my supportive family—Bob, Kendal, Lloyd, Forrest, and especially Dana, who tramped all through Rome's Castel Sant'Angelo with me to find the plaque with the "little souls" quote.